R

"Compton writes i … vel-
ists like Louis L'Am … thrilling sto-
ries of Western legend." —*The Huntsville Times* (AL)

"Compton may very well turn out to be the greatest Western writer of them all. . . . Very seldom in literature have the legends of the Old West been so vividly painted."
—*The Tombstone Epitaph*

"If you like Louis L'Amour, you'll love Ralph Compton."
—*Quanah Tribune-Chief* (TX)

continued . . .

BAD BUSINESS

"Perhaps you did pick some good folks as a family."

"I sure did."

And as quickly as Scotty's relaxed demeanor had come, it was gone. "The matter still stands that this here woman knew more than she should have and now so does the boy."

Kyle gritted his teeth and said, "If that's anyone's fault, it's yours! Everything was fine before now."

"Maybe it was my fault to put you on the spot," Scotty admitted. "But we're in something of a bind here. It's got to be set straight. You want to do it or should I?"

Shaking his head, Kyle said, "You're mistaken. Nothing needs to be set straight."

Luke's pulse sped up and he suddenly regained control of his legs. When he tried to get his mother moving with a gentle tug on her arm, he found she was now the one frozen in fear. He tugged a bit harder, which was enough to snap her out of the spell that had come over her.

"This ain't the first time you've put us all at risk," Scotty said. "But I can tell you it'll be the last."

"Don't do this!" Kyle yelled.

"Too late," the stranger said. "It's already done."

When Scotty drew a pistol from his holster, it was in a motion so fast that Luke barely saw it. The thunder that followed would follow him for the rest of his life.

Ralph Compton

HARD RIDE TO WICHITA

A Ralph Compton Novel
by Marcus Galloway

SIGNET
Published by the Penguin Group
Penguin Group (USA) LLC, 375 Hudson Street,
New York, New York 10014

USA | Canada | UK | Ireland | Australia | New Zealand | India | South Africa | China
penguin.com
A Penguin Random House Company

First published by Signet, an imprint of New American Library,
a division of Penguin Group (USA) LLC

First Printing, November 2013

ISBN 978-0-451-24021-7

Printed in the United States of America
10 9 8 7 6 5 4 3 2 1

The Immortal Cowboy

This is respectfully dedicated to the "American Cowboy." His was the saga sparked by the turmoil that followed the Civil War, and the passing of more than a century has by no means diminished the flame.

True, the old days and the old ways are but treasured memories, and the old trails have grown dim with the ravages of time, but the spirit of the cowboy lives on.

In my travels—to Texas, Oklahoma, Kansas, Nebraska, Colorado, Wyoming, New Mexico, and Arizona—I always find something that reminds me of the Old West. While I am walking these plains and mountains for the first time, there is this feeling that a part of me is eternal, that I have known these old trails before. I believe it is the undying spirit of the frontier calling me, through the mind's eye, to step back into time. What is the appeal of the Old West of the American frontier?

It has been epitomized by some as the dark and bloody period in American history. Its heroes—Crockett, Bowie, Hickok, Earp—have been reviled and criticized. Yet the Old West lives on, larger than life.

It has become a symbol of freedom, when there was always another mountain to climb and another river to cross; when a dispute between two men was settled not with expensive lawyers, but with fists, knives, or guns. Barbaric? Maybe. But some things never change. When the cowboy rode into the pages of American history, he left behind a legacy that lives within the hearts of us all.

—Ralph Compton

Chapter 1

Maconville, Kansas
1855

Luke Croft wasn't born to be a gunman. But, then again, such a plan seemed unlikely for any of God's creatures. It was something acquired after years of hard choices, bad company, and a few exceptionally bad mistakes. During the spring of 1855, the company Luke kept was set on an irrevocable course that would steer him into the arms of that very unlikely plan.

One of seventeen children seated in a schoolhouse near the edge of town, he enjoyed school and fancied his teacher, although neither of those things was apparent on his tight little features. His eyes, pinched at the corners and severe, would have been better suited on the face of someone decades older than Luke's seven years. At the moment, those eyes were doing their best not to turn in the direction of the boy to his left.

There weren't many children in school that were close to Luke's age and even fewer with last names lingering so close to the beginning of the alphabet. For those reasons alone, Luke was always forced to sit next to the Connover boy. Luke didn't know the nine-year-old's real first name. Everyone, teacher included, called him Red on account of the bright orange-red crop of hair sprouting in tufts from his scalp. Red never stopped fidgeting. He was loud and brash when the children were given time to play and often spoke out of turn during lessons. Not only did those things make Luke nervous, but they annoyed him to no end. As much as he wished he could be stuck with someone else, Luke would have settled for some peace and quiet.

All things considered, Luke wasn't a squirrelly kid. When he wasn't annoyed, he was good-natured and well mannered. He enjoyed reading, and since this was the time of day when his favorite subject was being taught by the prettiest lady in town, Luke was very happy indeed.

"Today we're going to do something a little different," Mrs. DeLoach said. She was a tall, slender woman with long brown hair that formed soft, curly waves flowing over her shoulders. Her skin had a slight olive complexion, and after all the bright days that had been coming along lately, it was even darker and accented with a dusting of freckles. She smiled widely, clasping slender hands in front of her. "We're going to write our own stories."

Some of the class let out exhausted moans. Red grumbled and dug a fingernail even deeper into the crack at the edge of his desk. Luke, on the other hand, couldn't have been happier.

"Won't that be nice?" Mrs. DeLoach asked.

"Yes," Luke said before he could stop himself. Almost immediately, he felt his cheeks flush. While he was never one who strived to be in the other kids' good graces, Luke wasn't ignorant in the workings of the schoolhouse pecking order. Although saying the wrong thing at the wrong time could affect his already shaky standing therein, nobody seemed to have taken notice of him this time.

"Well," the teacher continued, "like it or not, we'll be

working on our stories when we get back from lunch. It's a beautiful day outside, so get some food and fresh air and I'll see you back here after the bell rings. Are there any questions?"

All of the children, young and old alike, knew better than to break the silence that descended on that spacious single room.

Nodding resolutely, Mrs. DeLoach said, "Excellent. Have a good lunch."

With that, all of the seats were vacated and a stampede of excited feet knocked a path to the door.

Luke's house, like most everything else in Maconville, was a short walk from the school. He went there, ate a few quick bites of lunch, and returned to the long building beside the church so he could plan what to write for his assignment. With hands stuffed into the pockets of his battered short pants and light blue eyes focused squarely on the ground directly in front of him, he thought about all the possibilities for his story. Books had been a passion of his since before he could read them. His mother owned several and had collected a few with wonderful pictures, which were read together after supper dishes were cleaned and put away. Those were some of the first plots to jump into Luke's young mind, but he knew better than to pass them off as his own. There were plenty of other stories to be told and he didn't need to take anyone else's.

Most of the other children had returned from their homes by now and were playing in the yard behind the schoolhouse, where swings hung from a wooden frame and ropes dangled from the branches of an old oak that bore the initials of countless young lovers in its sides. Gnarled roots rose from the ground every so often, like weathered old snakes slithering in and out of a dusty sea.

Luke's mind wandered in that direction for a few steps when he heard some familiar voices drifting in from nearby.

"I got you!"

"No! I got *you*!"

"You're it!"

"No, I'm not!"

The screams filled the air along with so many others, threatening to intrude on Luke's train of thought. He would not be distracted, however, and furrowed his brow in concentration as he pondered a tale involving a giant serpent burrowing through the ground.

"You're still it!"

More footsteps.

"*Now* you're it!" That voice was followed by a string of laughter and clumsy footsteps that drew closer.

A few steps pounded so close to Luke that they shook the ground upon which he stood. When he looked up, Luke was just in time to see the wheezing, sweaty face of Red Connover. The other boy had a stocky build and his hair was an even bigger mess than usual as his face twisted into a surprised grimace. Their collision might not have been enough to shake the weakest of foundations, but the little boys felt it all the way down to the soles of their shoes.

Luke didn't have Red's bulk, but he'd inherited his father's wide shoulders and was just a bit taller than other boys his age. When Red slammed into him, he staggered back a few steps and gulped at the unexpected collision. Red teetered on one foot, flapped his arms like a wounded bird, and fell onto his backside. As soon as he realized he was on the ground, Red snapped his head up to glare at what had tripped him up.

Walking over to him, Luke offered Red a hand. "Sorry. I—"

Red slapped away the boy's hand and scrambled to his feet. "Why don't you watch where you're goin'?"

"You ran into me and fell down," Luke explained. "I didn't do anything."

Red looked back and forth. Whatever he saw convinced him to pull back his arm, ball up his fist, and take a swing at the boy in front of him. Since Luke hadn't taken his eyes off him the entire time, he saw every movement that led to Red's fist sailing in his direction. Acting on nothing but instinct, Luke hunkered down to let the punch sail over his head. While he wasn't quick to anger, Luke didn't like being attacked for no good reason. Since Red was still off-balance, Luke took advantage of his low position by sending a quick poke into the boy's stomach.

The punch didn't have much behind it, but what it lacked in brute strength, it made up for in surprise since it landed fairly well. Red's eyes widened at his having been thumped at all, and he straightened up. Both of his fists were clenched tight but remained at his sides. Before he or Luke could move another muscle, they each felt a hand firmly take hold of them by the back of their collars.

"That is quite enough!" Mrs. DeLoach said. "You know I don't allow fighting."

"We weren't fighting," Red whined.

She was already moving them toward the schoolhouse, and both boys had to scurry to keep from being dragged. "Is that true, Luke?"

Luke's stomach was tied into a knot and his mind raced. The only thing he could think of that would land him in more hot water than being singled out this way was being caught in a lie afterward. More afraid of answering to his ma, Luke found himself unable to say much of anything at all.

"That's what I thought," his teacher said. "You two will have plenty of time to think about what you've done after . . ."

She continued speaking sternly to them both, but Luke stopped listening after a while. He was going to spend the rest of the day at the back of the class and would have to stay after all the other students left while Mrs. DeLoach went to have words with his and Red's families. The rest of the details simply didn't matter.

"You fight pretty good."

Once again, Luke was lost in his own world. The rest of the day had been taxing for the little boy's racing mind, and he was now doing his best to get through the part he'd been dreading. Red, on the other hand, seemed more at ease now than he ever did when class was being taught.

"What did you say?" Luke asked.

"I said you fight pretty good."

"I didn't think we were fighting."

Red thought it over for a moment. His round face was slightly burned by the sun and his thick mane of hair looked as if it had been dragged through a sandbar before being stuck onto his head. His clothes were a rumpled mess, much like the pieces worn by Luke or any of the other farmers' children attending Maconville's school. Although the kids with shopkeepers for parents were slightly better kept, the difference wasn't large enough to create another social class within the group of children.

After contemplating for a bit, Red shrugged. "I suppose it wasn't really a fight, but you did pretty good."

"Um . . . thanks."

The schoolhouse was empty, so their words echoed within the building as if it were a cathedral. Mrs. De-

Loach had given explicit instructions for both of them to sit at the front of the room on either side of her desk until she returned from breaking the news to their parents. Any troublesome spark in the boys had been snuffed after all of the day's excitement because neither one of them was much inclined to disobey her command.

"Sorry I knocked you over," Red said.

"You didn't knock me over."

"I could have if I'd wanted to."

Luke reluctantly nodded.

Satisfied with that small concession, Red stood up and marched in front of the teacher's desk. Luke watched him as if he were witnessing a bank robbery and glanced nervously toward the front door.

"We should be friends," Red told him.

"A-all right."

Red stuck out the same hand he'd previously used to try to crack Luke in the face and kept it there until Luke shook it. Half a crooked smile appeared on Red's face and he nodded while his eyes took the younger boy's stock. After that, he walked right back around Mrs. DeLoach's desk, sat down, and rested his chin upon folded arms.

Luke watched him for several minutes, wondering what changes the new arrangement might bring. As far as he could tell, being officially friends with the older boy had bought him nothing more than a temporary cease-fire. That was enough for him. He had a story to write that needed to be handed in by the end of the week.

A few months later, the arrangement still held up. Not only did Luke and Red get along, but they shared many common interests. Both liked talking about men in their families that had served in the army or fought Indians.

Both liked running through town until the sun went down and then meeting up to explore a creek bed or drafty barn early the next morning. Luke never thought he'd enjoy fishing until Red invited him to come along with his father and brother one Sunday afternoon that summer. Even though he'd never put a single worm on a hook until that day, Luke wasn't made to feel foolish by Red or any of his kin. They walked him through step-by-step until Luke pulled a hissing old turtle from the water that made Red fall back onto his rump in panicky surprise.

While Red never made a secret about his lack of enthusiasm where book learning was concerned, he showed a true passion for the stories in Luke's books about adventures in faraway lands or battles between heroes and villains. Their conversations would often drift toward wild speculations about monsters or warriors of their own devising as the boys walked along and dragged crooked sticks against picket fences. Mostly, Luke was the one spinning those yarns and Red would contribute his own colorful embellishments to the imagined wars.

As the year wore on, the boys rarely left each other's sight. Every so often, one would cross the other and a scuffle would break out, but it was short-lived and no punches were thrown in earnest. Winter winds eventually tore across the Kansas plains, rattling shutters against windows and pushing frozen air through the smallest cracks between the planks of every house's walls. Soon a chorus of rowdy voices and wild gunshots pointed at the sky would mark the beginning of a new year.

Luke and Red's friendship had sunk its roots, and the punches that had gotten the whole thing rolling were as forgotten as the first leaf that had fallen that October.

Chapter 2

1862

Plenty in the country had changed in the seven years that had passed, but in Maconville, things moved at a slower pace. War had been raging for a few of those years, which meant several of the young and old men alike had picked their side and donned a uniform to fight in unfamiliar fields and spill their blood onto dirt hundreds of miles from home. Red and Luke were choosing their own paths, which, for the time being, still ran side by side.

A group of six boys ranging from the ages of eleven to seventeen were gathered in a stable belonging to one of their fathers. A conversation had started a day or two ago about the sport of wrestling, and the boys had escalated it to the point of boasting which of them would best the other in a proper tournament. Like a spark that had been tossed too close to a pile of dry leaves, that boasting had grown into a tournament itself, although it was anything but proper.

Marty and Joseph Paulsen had squared off and were locked in a grueling struggle. Without anything more than a lot of hot air behind them, none of the boys would have known a correct wrestling stance if it was drawn on one of the dirty walls surrounding them. The Paulsen brothers were the first to fight since they were about the same size and always at each other's throats anyway. They growled like a couple of pups as they bared their teeth and did their best to make the other look foolish in front of the others. So far, all of their efforts had only amounted to a bunch of scraping, cursing, and tugging at each other's shirts in an attempt to knock somebody over.

"You'd . . . best give up," Joseph warned as he shifted to loop an arm around his brother's neck.

"Why?" Marty grunted. "Or you'll hug me to death?"

The rest of the boys got a good laugh out of that.

Locking his hands in what looked like an effective grip, Joseph twisted his upper body and somehow managed to gain some leverage. He lifted his brother off one foot and then shoved him into a bale of hay. Marty tripped over the bale and landed in a heap on the other side amid raucous cheers from the paltry crowd.

"That's how you wrestle!" Joseph said while rubbing his hands together. "Who's next?"

"I think it should be Red and Luke!" one of the smaller boys said. He'd already had his turn, so his clothes were rumpled and his face was scratched up after he'd been tossed onto some exposed floorboards.

Those two stood at the other end of the crowd, looking on with big smiles. Red shrugged and stepped forward while Luke's smile faded noticeably. In the years that had passed, both boys had grown. Luke had sprouted up while Red had filled in through the shoulders and chest. Luke's arms and legs were on the gangly side, giving him a lean appearance. Red, on the other hand, was thick as a tree stump and had skin that looked as if it had been weathered for decades before it had ever been wrapped around him.

Having been in plenty of scuffles for plenty of different reasons, Red didn't mind stepping up for this one. Luke's experience in that arena was much more limited. More often than not, if he had a dispute with someone, he talked his way out of it. A couple of times, he'd settled a troublesome matter by circumventing all of the normal procedures and thrown a punch without setting up a time and place for a real fight. Those times were rare, but they kept any following incidents down to a minimum.

"Come on, then," Red said. "Let's do this thing."

"I don't want to fight you," Luke told him.

"It's not a fight. It's just a stupid tournament."

"Right. It's stupid."

"If you're too yellow to fight," Joseph said, "then you can just go right back home to your mama."

Luke's eyes narrowed and he weighed the consequences of both his choices. As much as he didn't like the thought of going through with the fight, it would be less painful than being needled for having walked away. "Fine," he sighed. "Let's get this over with."

Red laughed under his breath and showed his friend the sort of grin he always wore when he took the role of protector. The fact that Luke didn't need much protection wasn't the issue. Mostly, Red seemed to enjoy looking out for him as if the difference in their ages were at least triple the actual number. It was also the grin that came around when Red vaguely admired something Luke was about to do. Much like, Luke thought to himself, someone watching a child toddle over to try his hand at a task that was well over his head.

"I'll take it easy on you," Red said.

"The hell you will." With that, Luke stepped up to the other boy and grabbed him by both arms.

The two pushed and shoved each other in a fashion similar to the other bouts they'd seen that day. When he tried to shove Red toward the same bale of hay that had tripped up Marty Paulsen, Luke was unable to make more than a few inches of progress. Red planted his feet and put some of his muscle into moving Luke back. Although he started to slide on the dirty floor, Luke shifted his weight until he could find a spot from which he could make a stand. Once he gained some footing, he halted Red's surge.

"Not . . . bad," Red admitted. "But you won't be able to beat me."

"Why not?"

"'Cause you don't . . . have it in you. That's why."

"Well," Luke said between strained breaths, "you'll have to beat me to prove it."

The next couple of seconds dragged on for what seemed like hours in Luke's mind. Every bit of it was spent with him trying desperately not to get humiliated by the somewhat larger boy. They might have been friends, but this wasn't the first time Red had asserted himself as the tougher of the two. Luke wasn't one to argue such banal points, so he usually let it go with a shrug. He was still a young man, however, and wasn't about to roll over and be dominated just for the sake of moving on to other things.

As Luke gritted his teeth and tried to shove Red back, he felt the other boy step forward and place a foot behind his. Red then pushed him and forced Luke to trip over that foot. Since Luke wasn't about to let go, he dragged Red down with him and both boys headed for the floor. They landed and immediately scrambled to try to get over on each other. In the end, Red's natural quickness and strength put him in a superior position a second or two before Luke could get there. The older boy wound up grabbing one of Luke's wrists and using his other hand to press down against his chest. Luke wedged his hand against the floor so it wouldn't be moved and strained to keep from being forced all the way down.

"Go ahead and give up," Red said. "You put up a good fight."

"The fight . . . isn't over."

They struggled for a while longer before Luke became aware that he couldn't move an inch from that spot. He didn't have the power to force Red back and wasn't about to allow Red to push him down. Judging by the sweat and strain showing on his face, Red had arrived at a similar conclusion.

"Come on, Red!" Joseph Paulsen shouted. "I got two dollars that says you can take him down easy!"

"Don't listen to him, Luke," Marty said. "My money's on you. Put Red in his place and we'll split the winnings!"

The rest of the crowd whooped and hollered as if they'd found themselves at a prizefight.

It was some time later and Luke could barely hear much of that over the rush of blood through his ears and the straining breaths surging in and out of his body. Still wedged into a vaguely stable position between defeat and victory, he and Red both refused to give an inch.

The stable had become quiet. In fact, the younger boys had already found somewhere else to be. Although the Paulsen brothers were still there, they'd started talking to each other without casting more than an occasional glance at the continuing struggle on the floor.

"Just give up so we can leave," Red snarled between tired breaths.

"You give up!"

Red thought about it for a few seconds and then steeled himself. "I should win this. I'm the one that took you down."

"You don't know anything about wrestling."

"I know I got the drop on you easy enough!"

"Oh yeah?" Luke grunted. He then clenched his eyes shut and pushed with great effort against Red's shoulder in an attempt to turn the tables. Although he moved Red an inch or two, he couldn't do much more than that.

Red pressed more of his weight down on him, straining to put an end to the match once and for all. He took back the inch or two he'd lost, gained maybe a fraction of another inch, and was stopped cold.

The struggle between them shifted ever so slightly back and forth for a few more minutes. Although the effort took every bit of focus the boys could muster, it didn't make for a very good show. But Luke or Red didn't seem to notice even as their small audience drifted away.

"You gonna give up?" Red asked.

"N-no."

"You ain't gonna win."

"I won't give up," Luke insisted.

The stables were quiet apart from the two boys' voices and the occasional shifting of hooves from one of the horses in the two occupied stalls.

For some of that time, Luke wondered if he would get to leave that drafty structure on his own two feet or if he would have to be carried out. His strength was fading and his thoughts shifted toward the ever more attractive possibility of giving in just to put an end to the senseless contest. That thought alone, however, might as well have been a sharp set of spurs jabbed into his sides. His will flared up and when he thought of how Red would flaunt his victory, the rest of his body followed suit.

Luke shifted his weight until he felt Red attempt to compensate. At the right moment, Luke escaped from the deadlock by pushing in another direction entirely and started to climb to a more tenable position. In the end, his fighting and scraping bought him less than another three inches. Before he could feel the oppressive weight of a seemingly impossible task settle upon his shoulders, it all came crashing down. Both boys fell over as their limbs collectively gave out at the same time. Red wound up on his side and Luke pulled himself up onto all fours. The instant he saw what had happened, Luke placed a hand flat on Red's chest and held him down.

"I . . . got you," Luke wheezed.

"The hell . . . hell you do."

Putting all of his weight behind that single arm, Luke shoved Red down even harder as he struggled to his feet. He only managed to get one boot on the floor before his arm was slapped aside. The grin Luke wore might have been tired, but it remained in place even when he realized he couldn't get up.

"I just got tired, is all," Red said.

"I put you down and kept you there," Luke announced. "That's how to win a wrestling match."

Propping himself up on his elbows, Red said, "Take a bow, then. Looks like them two horses enjoyed the show."

Sure enough, those horses were the only other living things in that stable with them. As much as he would have liked to think the pathetic excuse for an audience was entertained by the spectacle, Luke couldn't find the first hint of amusement in either animal's eyes. When Luke ran his hands through his hair, they came away covered in enough sweat to fill one of the troughs in those stalls. "I did win, though. At least admit that much."

"If it's so damn important to you, I'll admit it."

"It's not so important. It's true!"

Red scowled at him and scooted back until he found

a wall he could lean against. Once there, he stretched his legs out and slicked back the hair that had fallen into his face. "What's gotten into you?"

"Nothing. What do you mean?"

"Like a bolt from the clear blue sky, you get a burr under your saddle and want to pull my head off my shoulders. That's what I mean!"

Luke was going to protest one more time but stopped himself. Suddenly he didn't feel like looking his friend in the eye. "Remember Mike Miller?"

Twitching as if he'd been blindsided by a quick jab, Red rested his head against the wall. After taking a few seconds, he replied, "The kid that lived out on the old Keeler spread?"

"That's the one. His family lived in Maconville for a year or two before they moved on."

"What about him?"

"Mike got it in his head to push me around and challenged me to a fight," Luke explained. "I didn't want to, but—"

"You was about to bust into tears at the thought of fighting him if I recall," Red chuckled.

Even though the potential dustup was when both of the boys were much younger, Luke still blanched at the memory. "I wasn't gonna cry," he said. "I just didn't want to fight him."

"I don't blame you. He packed a wallop."

"You'd know that because you fought him."

Red shrugged. "Mike had a big mouth."

"Is that why you fought him?"

"Probably."

"Or was it because you wanted to keep him from picking another fight with me?"

"Every little thing wasn't about you, Luke."

"It seems to me that you protect me sometimes."

"That's what friends do. You've helped me more times than I can count."

Turning to face Red, Luke stared him straight in the eye and said, "I'm not weak."

"No one ever said you was."

"If you think I can't handle myself, then you must think I'm weak."

"Is that what all this was about?" Red asked as he waved a hand in a sweeping motion encompassing the stable floor. "'Cause if it was, then you made your point."

"Did you let me win?"

The hint of a grin flickered across Red's face, but disappeared just as quickly. "Why would I do that? Joey Paulsen was betting on me."

"I know. He wouldn't shut up about it."

"Those Paulsen brothers really get under my skin sometimes," Red grunted.

"I thought they were your friends."

Red shrugged. "They're around lots of times and it's easier to just leave it that way. Joe's so thick I'd have to waste all my breath to explain I just want him to leave me be."

"Wasn't it their idea to do this stupid wrestling thing to begin with?"

After taking a few moments to think it over, Red scowled. "I think you're right! They got us all fired up about it and started calling everyone yellow if they didn't want to tussle in this damn stable."

"They always shoot their mouths off," Luke grumbled. "Seems like they just like the sound of their own voices. The only reason they left this time was that you and me weren't gonna rip each other's heads off."

Chuckling, Red said, "Wasn't as if you didn't try, though."

"I got wrapped up in the moment."

"You was trying to prove yourself."

"If that's so, then I did prove myself," Luke said. "I won."

"You keep tellin' yerself that."

Luke's eyes were trained on the wall directly in front of him. Slowly, he glanced around to where each of the other boys had been standing. When he got to the place that had been occupied by the Paulsens, he narrowed his eyes as if he were trying to burn a hole into the old wooden slats. "Marty bet on me."

"That's what he said," Red replied. "But that was just more hot air."

"Didn't they say something about splitting the take with whoever won?"

Red's eyes rolled around in their sockets. "You honestly think you'll see any of that money?"

"Why shouldn't we?"

"We?"

"That's right," Luke said with a nod. "They're the ones who started this whole mess. Why should they be able to just walk away from it without honoring their word?"

The grin on Red's face could have been peeled off the Devil himself. "They did say they'd pay up."

"And we did follow through with our end."

After getting up and dusting himself off, Red offered a hand to Luke. "Them Paulsens really do grate on me," he said while helping his friend to his feet. "Someone ought to at least keep 'em honest."

Chapter 3

It wasn't difficult for Red and Luke to find the Paulsen brothers. All they needed to do was listen for the sound of boisterous taunting and follow it back to its source. If the brothers weren't giving each other a difficult time, they were extending the favor to anyone else in their vicinity. For the last few months, the younger boys who'd been at their wrestling tournament had been trying to get in the brothers' good graces. Desperate for friends, especially older ones, the younger boys had followed them around like puppies without seeming to mind that they were getting treated more like mangy dogs.

"You know what you two should try?" Joseph asked the skinnier of the two younger boys. "Boxing! I heard that's a sight to see!"

"Yeah!" Marty chimed in. "We could even sell tickets. I bet we could scrounge up some other guys to have a fight and we could split up the profits!"

The four of them were clustered near the corner store that sold candy sticks and sarsaparilla. Across the street were a dress shop and a laundry, which gave the air the bitter scent of bleach at certain times of day. There wasn't any steaming going on at the moment, but the odors still lingered from earlier on. A pair of horses was led down the street toward John Vassilly's blacksmith's shop, providing more than enough noise to mask the approach of the two young men who insinuated themselves into the conversation.

"Before you think about more profits," Luke said, "you should settle up the debts you already have."

The brothers turned around to get a look at the other two boys, and the younger pair seemed happy to have been removed from the spotlight. "Well, well, well," Joseph said. "Seems you two finally got finished rolling around on the floor. How'd it turn out?"

"I won," Luke said.

Joseph scowled and when he glanced over to Red, he got a subtle nod to confirm the story. "Guess I should've stayed around to see what happened," Joseph said. "Since the two of you barely look scratched, I suppose we didn't miss much."

"You can say that again," Marty laughed.

Red took one step forward, causing Marty to reflexively take one step back. "What would you have preferred? Me and him knock the hell out of each other?"

"Would've been more fun to watch."

"Well, it's not our job to entertain the two of you," Luke said. "And it's not our problem that you wandered off. You did mention something about a wager, though."

Marty's eyes widened. "That's right!" Turning to his brother, he said, "You owe me some money!"

"And then you owe *me* some money," Luke said. "I recall you saying you'd cut me in if I won."

"That's right, little brother," Joseph said as he smacked Marty's shoulder. "I recall you saying that as well. Best pay up."

The two brothers threw a few halfhearted punches at each other while laughing and making idle treats. When they were done horsing around, Marty turned to Luke as if he was surprised he was still there. "Yeah, well, I can get that money to you later."

"No. I'll take it now."

Marty was still smirking as he looked back and forth between Luke and Red. Slowly the grin faded and he straightened up to his full height, which was roughly comparable to Luke's. "I don't got it now. I'll get it some other time."

"Nah," Red said. "I think we should take it now."

"Why?"

"Because you're a loudmouthed little weasel who can't be trusted any farther than he could be tossed." Red then looked over to Joseph and added, "That goes for the both of you."

"I thought we were all friends," Marty said.

"And there's no reason why we don't have to be friends," Luke told him. "Just pay me what you owe."

"What brought this on?"

"It's like he said," Luke replied while nodding toward Red. "I don't think you'll pay up. If you do, I'll apologize."

"And what if I don't?"

"Then you'll prove to be every bit the little weasel Red thought you were."

The two youngest boys backed away from the other four. After they'd put a certain amount of distance between themselves and the rest, they took off running so they could watch what happened from afar.

Marty started to inch forward but was pushed back by Joseph. The older brother was a bit taller than Luke and considerably more muscular. Glaring at him from beneath smooth eyebrows, Joseph said, "You'll take that back."

"I will as soon as I'm proven wrong."

"We don't owe you a damn thing and you know it."

"I beg to differ," Luke replied with a smirk. Joseph was drawn tighter than a bowstring, and the quick wink Luke gave him was more than enough to make him snap.

Joseph's hands balled into fists and he lunged at Luke. Before he could get close enough to swing, he was tackled by Red, who slammed his shoulder against the older Paulsen's midsection.

Still blinking in surprise at how quickly that had happened, Luke looked over to find Marty in a similar state. As his older brother struggled with Red, Marty sputtered, "You gotta have someone else fight your battles?"

Not one for threats, Luke struggled to find something to say that would get his point across. Hearing those words, along with seeing the petulant look in Marty's eyes, sparked something in him that he'd never really known was there.

"You've always been a yellow little coward, Luke," Marty said as his brother shoved Red aside. "Everyone knows it."

When he'd convinced Red to march over to the Paulsen boys, his intention had been to stand up to them and let them know they couldn't just start trouble and walk away from it. Too many times, Luke had seen blowhards get away with whatever they pleased simply because nobody bothered calling them out for what they were. Also, as he and Red had both mentioned, the Paulsen boys weren't exactly their favorite people in town. Hearing Marty say those things to him at that particular moment caused Luke's eyesight to blur around the edges like a poorly taken photograph. Before he knew what was happening, he was no longer standing in the spot he'd once been.

Marty said something, but Luke didn't hear it. He didn't even hear the yelp that came from Marty when Luke punched him in the mouth.

A few steps away, Joseph threw a punch at Red. Ducking beneath the incoming fist, Red grabbed the front of Joseph's shirt, pulled him in close, and drove his knee into the other boy's stomach. Joseph groaned and staggered back as Red stalked forward in pursuit.

"Wait a second!" Marty said.

But Luke was too far along to stop now. In fact, the louder Marty pleaded, the more Luke wanted to stomp him into the dirt. When he snapped a quick jab into the side of Marty's face, it was mostly to get the other boy to fight back.

Nearby, Red had a hold of Joseph's shirt and was tossing him around like a rag doll. The other boy tried to fight back, but Red pulled him down and slammed his knee into his face. Joseph straightened up as blood flew from his nose. The pain from the blow made him unsteady on his feet and a surprised expression showed beneath a spreading crimson mask. Not as surprised, however, as Red himself.

"I'll get the money for you!" Marty said. "I swear!"

"Get it right now," Luke demanded.

"I don't have it!" When Luke cocked his head and drew a fist back, Marty quickly added, "But we got other things. Maybe something we could trade."

"Anything worth as much as you owe?"

"Sure! Sure!"

Realizing that Marty was anxious to appease him, Luke asked, "What about more than what you owe? You got anything worth that much?"

"Why more?"

Luke surged toward the other boy and bared his teeth like an animal. "Because the deal wasn't for a trade! It was for money and if you can't scrape it up, you'll have to make up for it and then some!"

All Marty had to do was look over to his brother. Joseph pressed both hands against his face and moaned as blood seeped from his nose. Standing nearby with a good amount of blood on himself as well, Red calmly turned to look at how the other two were doing.

"I—I got some things I could trade," Marty whimpered. "Please. Just don't kill us."

Luke recoiled at that and looked over to Red. His friend wasn't about to say anything, but it was plain to see that he was fighting to keep from busting out in laughter. Motioning for his friend to keep holding his tongue, Luke said, "That depends on what kind of trade you can make."

The Paulsen brothers scampered off like a couple of whipped dogs. Although the arrangement was for them to meet Red and Luke at an empty lot the older boys in town had claimed as their own, there were only two souls on that patch of land almost an hour after the agreed-upon time had passed.

Red sat on an overturned bucket that had been in that spot for so long it had sunken roots into the dirt. His elbows rested upon his knees, and his hands worked to whittle down a short stick with a pocketknife. "They ain't comin', you know."

Standing at the edge of the lot with his arms folded and his eyes pointed in the direction of the Paulsen home, Luke replied, "They'll come. Marty will, at least."

"What makes you say that?"

"Because he was too scared to do anything else."

Shaking his head, Red asked, "What did you tell that boy?"

"To pay what he owes."

"I thought we were just going to give them two some grief for shooting their mouths off all the time."

"We were," Luke said.

"So what happened?"

"Things got . . . out of hand."

"They sure did," Red chuckled. "Why did you tell Marty you were gonna kill him?"

"I didn't! Why did you bust Joseph's nose?"

Shifting his focus back to his whittling, Red said, "It's like you said. Things got out of hand."

Luke looked over to his friend. "Why did you do that to Joseph?"

"He's always gotten under my skin. He thinks he's so tough . . . I guess I showed him he's not the big man he thought he was. What about you?"

"What about me? I barely even touched Marty."

"But you put more of a fright into him than I did with Joe," Red told him. "And I could tell you liked doin' it."

"Yeah? Well, Marty flaps his gums plenty as well. Guess it was good to take both of them down a notch or two."

"Did you have to threaten to kill him, though?"

Luke sighed. "He came to that conclusion all on his own and I got no idea how he got there."

"All he had to do was look at you," Red said as he sharpened the stick in his hand to an even finer point. "I even thought you were gonna send that little weasel to meet his maker."

"You know I could never do something like that."

"Sure. I know that. If I hadn't known you since we were in short pants, though, I wouldn't be so sure."

Luke turned his back to his friend so he could watch for approaching visitors. That way, Red couldn't see the little smirk on his face when he said, "Let him think what he wants. Just as long as he follows through."

"And what if he don't?" Red asked.

"Looks like we won't have to worry about that. Have a look for yourself." Luke pointed west of the Paulsen home. Maconville was a tame little place under most circumstances, and any movement had a tendency to stick out. The pair of figures Luke had spotted walked directly toward the empty lot. One of them was shorter than the other, and judging by how they carried themselves, if they'd had tails, they would be tucked between their legs.

"Guess I'd better put these away," Red said as he stood up from his grimy seat with the stick and knife in his hands. "There's no telling what they think I'll do with 'em."

Red stuck the stick into the ground and was folding his knife when Joseph and Marty Paulsen entered the lot. Joseph did his best to keep his chin up, but his younger brother was rattled all the way down to his core, which made it difficult for him to pretend otherwise.

"You got our money?" Luke asked in a voice that was steady, if not altogether forceful.

Marty's eyes flicked over to his brother, and his lips clenched tightly together.

"No," Joseph said. "We don't have any money lying about. If you wanna wait until we get paid from Deke Harrold, we'll be able to take care of it then."

"You working at the mill?" Red asked.

When Joseph looked over to him, there wasn't an ounce of malice in his eyes. On the contrary, he seemed downright respectful when he replied, "Yeah, for a few weeks now. He's hiring on a few more hands if you need some work."

"I'll think it over."

"You already wanted to cheat us once," Luke pointed out. "That means we're not likely to let you do it again. Let's just settle this matter right here and now."

There was a silence between all four boys, which ended with a quick jab from Joseph's elbow into Marty's ribs. Startled into speaking, the younger Paulsen said, "Sorry about what I said before. I shouldn't have called you them names."

Throughout his life, the only other boy to apologize to him was Red Connover. Other than that, he'd either been ignored or shoved aside by everyone else. Hearing those words come from Marty and seeing the sincerity in his eyes truly struck a chord within Luke. Since he didn't know what else to say, Luke nodded and replied, "All right."

"If you still want us to settle up," Joseph continued, "that's what we'll do. We shouldn't have promised to pay you anything that we couldn't deliver, and our pa always taught us to stand up and answer for our own mistakes. So here," he said while pulling up the tail of his shirt to reveal the belt around his waist.

When Luke saw the pistol tucked there, he froze in his tracks. Red had a much different reaction and immediately dropped down to pluck the sharpened stick from the ground with one hand while digging into his pocket for the knife with the other.

Squinting his eyes and tensing his muscles to try to hold back the shakes that he felt creeping through his body, Luke snapped, "What are you doing with that?"

Oddly enough, the two brothers seemed even more nervous than Red or Luke. Marty held out both hands in a placating gesture as he said, "That's what we brought to trade! Honest."

Joseph nodded. "He's right. It used to belong to my uncle."

"Is it loaded?" Red asked.

"Yes." Keeping his hand an inch or two above the pistol's grip, Joseph asked, "You want to take a look for yourself?"

"Yeah," Luke said quickly. "Hand it over."

"Maybe you should take it from him," Red warned.

Before Luke could take that precaution, Joseph had already drawn the pistol from where it had been tucked beneath his belt. The pistol's barrel was at least twice as long as Luke had been expecting. The lines were smooth and the grip looked as if it had been through six different kinds of hell.

"What a piece of junk!" Red said.

"What are you talking about?" Joseph snapped. "My uncle was in the army. He carried this gun against a band of Apaches in the Dakota Territories!"

"Looks like he dropped it into a river about that long ago too. Did you just fish it out yesterday?"

Luke reached out and took the pistol from Joseph. "How can I tell if it's loaded?"

"That right there," Joseph said as he showed him how to open the cylinder.

It wasn't easy, but Luke rolled the cylinder all the way around. He then closed it up and got the weapon situated within his grasp. A smirk snuck onto his face, which he wouldn't have been able to hold back if he'd tried.

"Unless you've got another couple of those things stashed somewhere, I'd say you still owe us," Red told him.

"That's a good gun," Marty said. "I fired it myself."

Red laughed loudly. "I know that's a damn lie. If you fired more than two rounds from that thing, you'd be missing a piece of your hand."

The iron was partly rusted, but its weight felt good in Luke's hand. He hefted it and nodded in satisfaction as he rested his thumb against the hammer. After taking a breath, he pulled it back to hear the invigorating clack of the firing mechanism. "What kind of gun is it?"

"It's a genuine Colt," Joseph told him.

"There's two shots in the cylinder ready to go." Eyeing the other boy suspiciously, Red asked, "You won't shoot us, will you?"

Glaring at Marty, Luke said, "I never said I was gonna kill anyone. I just want to see if this thing really works or not."

"Don't do it," Red warned. "I've heard of men getting their whole hand blown off when a pistol misfires."

"I'll be careful."

"Don't matter how careful you are! Something goes wrong and that gun could blow up in your face."

Luke's eyes were glassy and transfixed upon the weapon in his hand. "Just get me something to shoot at."

"Are you gonna take that gun as a trade or not?" Marty asked. "We wanna be done with this."

Luke glanced over at him and was about to fiercely tell the boy to mind his manners when he realized Marty was already stricken mute. Without meaning to, Luke had pointed the Colt at the boy. Reluctantly he lowered the pistol and forced himself to sound innocent when he said, "I never shot a gun before. That's all I'm after." Luke wasn't much of an actor, but he was convincing enough to get the Paulsen boys to relax a bit.

"There's some bottles over there," Joseph said. "Marty, go set them up on that fence."

As Marty hurried away to complete the task he'd been given, Red walked over to Luke and whispered, "Just take the gun and be done with it. We can probably sell it to get the money we were after."

"Don't you want to try to shoot it?" Luke asked.

"I shot a gun before. My pa has one. Hasn't yours ever taken you hunting?"

"I've been hunting, but this isn't like any hunting rifle. This has been through Indian wars," Luke said as he turned the Colt over to see how the light reflected off its rusted surface from different angles. "This is like a pistol carried by gunfighters."

"It's one carried by a soldier," Red reminded him.

"Plenty of gunfighters used to be soldiers." Looking up to find a trio of bottles lined up on the fence separating the lot from the strip of land behind the neighboring store, Luke grinned and opened the Colt's cylinder.

"You wanna bet that thing won't blow off your hand?" Red asked.

"It won't."

Seeing that he wasn't about to sway his friend from the course he'd chosen, Red threw his stick at the ground with enough force to bury its point several inches into the dirt. He stormed off a few steps before turning and placing his hands on his hips to watch what transpired next.

Luke squared his shoulders, planted his feet, and straightened his elbow. Bringing that arm up, he felt as if the Colt had gained a few pounds in the last few seconds. Adjusting his stance and ignoring the tension in his muscles, he sighted along the top of the barrel and pulled the trigger. The Colt let out a haggard bark and kicked against his palm without so much as nicking the bottle.

"That's got some punch!" Luke said while smiling as if he'd sent glass flying in every direction.

"It sure does," Joseph said. "Try it again."

Although he could hear Red sighing behind him, Luke didn't bother turning to see the scowl on his friend's face. Instead he brought the gun up again and took his time while aiming. As he stared down that barrel, he swore he could see every flake of rust, every nick in the iron, and every speck of dust within the structure of the firearm. Luke took a breath, held it, and pulled his trigger again. The gun sounded even louder than the first time, but he didn't come any closer to knocking a bottle from atop that fence.

"The thing's probably bent," Red said. "Satisfied?"

Luke thumbed the hammer back again, took quick aim, and pulled the trigger only to hear the dry slap of iron against an empty chamber. Before he could ask for another bullet, someone called to them from the street.

"What's going on over there?" a man asked in a gruff voice. "Who's doing that shooting?"

"That's the sheriff!" Red said.

For a moment, all four boys froze. They looked at one another, waiting to see if any of them could come up with a good plan. The only one that had anything to say was Luke, and he just managed to get out one word.

"Run!"

That was plenty of incentive to scatter the boys like dry leaves in a stiff breeze. As soon as they got moving, the shouting that had started it all came at them with even more intensity.

"I see you boys!" the lawman shouted as his heavy steps brought him closer to the lot. "You best not have a gun or I'll tan all of your hides!"

Luke's legs pumped for all they were worth. His ears were filled with the thump of his heart and the quick wheeze of excited breaths. Only when he'd found an empty alley did he stop and take a look around to see where he'd wound up.

The Paulsens were nowhere to be found.

From what he could see, the alley he'd chosen was between a shoe store and a leatherworker's shop. Sure enough, when he pulled in his next breath, it was laden with the scent of polish and cowhide. Suddenly hurried steps closed in on the alley. Luke raised the Colt to hip level to greet whoever had chased him down.

"Put that thing away, you idiot!" Red said as he

charged down the alley. "Hasn't that hunk of scrap already caused enough trouble?"

"Where's the sheriff?" Luke asked.

"He's hightailing it after Marty Paulsen. The damn fool ran straight back to his own house. We just gotta hope he doesn't speak a word about us to the sheriff."

"He won't," Luke said.

Taking a gander out of the alley, Red looked up and down the street. There were a few locals out and about who were taking interest in the commotion nearby, but none were looking in his direction. He moved back into the alley before he was seen. "He won't, huh? You think you scared him that much?"

"He's too scared to speak his own name. Doesn't much matter what it is that got him that way."

Unable to refute that logic, Red leaned against a wall and ran his fingers through his coarse mane of hair. When he let out the breath he'd taken, a nervous laugh came out with it. "What in blazes were you thinking? The least you could've done was take that gun somewhere it wouldn't attract so much attention."

"You say that now, but you didn't think about the sheriff coming along before he started shouting at us."

"I still say you could've blown your hand off."

"But I didn't," Luke said quietly. The Colt was still in his grasp and he angled it so he could view the barrel from several directions.

"Joseph or Marty was probably just looking to unload that thing," Red said as he approached his friend. "They might have stole it, even."

Luke laughed once and shook his head. "Neither of them lilies has what it takes to steal anything. I'm gonna clean this up and get it working properly."

"Then what?"

"Then I'm gonna show that sheriff what trouble really is!"

The boys looked at each other quietly for a few seconds before breaking into laughter.

"Who's that over there?" someone shouted from outside the alley.

Luke wasn't sure if the voice belonged to the sheriff or not. He and Red ran in the other direction and didn't look back.

Chapter 4

1864

Most of Luke's days were spent either with Red or on his own. As the war spread throughout the entire country, everything else seemed to become smaller. Fighting was all anyone could talk about and death had become all too familiar for young and old alike. If a family member hadn't been scarred or killed by enemy fire, someone had a friend or acquaintance that had been touched by the terrible hand of conflict. Having left school behind earlier that year, Luke tended to his own studies by reading books or honing the skills he thought he would need. With the world in its current state, one of those skills involved a friend that had grown closer to him in recent months.

The Colt Navy revolver had been disassembled, cleaned, reassembled, polished, taken apart again, and repaired as best Luke could manage. There was only so much he could do for the old pistol, but the weapon was firing better than it had at the start. Either that, or all of his practice with the gun had done him a lot of good. He could hit more targets than he missed. When bullets had gotten too expensive to buy, he'd begged the town's blacksmith to teach him how to press his own using supplies paid for with the sweat of his brow.

John Vassilly was a stout man with a bald head and thick, burly arms. As he'd been a blacksmith for over half his life, nearly every bit of exposed skin was scarred from heat, bruised from his hammer, or callused by thick layers of petrified skin. Not one given to smiling, John showed the same expression for every occasion. He knew Luke well enough to give the young man a crooked smirk when he did a good job and a slap on the back when he was particularly proud of his unofficial apprentice.

"You about to head on home?" John asked

The autumn sun was still lingering in the sky, but it was well past the time when customers would be accepted into the little shop attached to an old barn that had been converted into John's workspace. Luke sat in a corner where he toiled at learning the blacksmith's trade and tried his hand at a few of the smaller jobs that came into the shop. He even had a small square window within inches of his head, which he now looked out to see nothing more than an empty street.

"I can stay," Luke replied.

"I'll need you to go. Gotta lock up for the night."

"I can do that."

"You've been here long enough, boy. You need to get on home so your mama don't fret about where you are or what you're doing."

Luke rolled his eyes and set down the set of tongs he'd been repairing. "Did she tell you to keep an eye on me?"

"As long as you're in my shop, I'm keeping an eye on you. Don't forget that," John said sternly. In a somewhat softer tone, he added, "But yeah. Your ma did come around and ask that I don't keep you for so long. She said something about you needing to get home to read more."

Ever since Luke had put his schooling days behind him, his mother had been yapping at him to dive back in. She wanted him to go away to some fancy university school she'd heard about in Illinois. He didn't know how she'd gotten the money for him to go and it didn't matter. He wasn't about to leave her in Maconville.

"Go on, now," John said as he picked Luke up by the collar as if he were lifting a cat by the scruff of its neck. "I told you to git and so you'll git. Give my best to your ma and pa."

"He's not my pa," Luke said.

Even if John didn't know everything that went on in the Croft home, he had eyes in his head that told him plenty while looking at the young man in front of him. "Kyle seems like a good enough sort."

"That's what everyone says."

"Well," the blacksmith said as he gathered up the things he needed to take home, "isn't it the truth?"

Luke shrugged and stood up. "If I gotta go, I gotta go." The Colt lay in its regular spot on an empty crate he used for a table. He picked it up and tucked it under his belt.

"What about that friend of yours?" John asked while trying not to stare at the weapon that was never out of Luke's sight. "How's Red doing these days?"

"He's fine. I'll see you tomorrow, Mr. Vassilly."

Stepping aside to let Luke pass, John gave him a pat on the shoulder. "Bright and early. Maybe we can get Barry Hogan's team shoed ahead of schedule."

"Sounds good." Luke didn't look back as he left the blacksmith's shop. He did, however, pause for a few moments before turning in the direction he needed to go if he meant to head home. Despite having reached the height of a man some time ago, Luke shrank a bit as he started walking the familiar path that would lead to his front door.

The house at the end of that path was the only one Luke had known his entire life. He'd been born in Missouri but was brought to Kansas when he was still an infant by his mother and father. His birth father had died some years ago, and memories of him faded more and more no matter how hard Luke tried to hang on to them. For better or not, he'd learned, everything faded.

As usual, the Croft house was quiet. And, as usual, that silence was shattered the moment Luke walked in through the front door.

"Where have you been?" his mother asked. She was a short woman with dark blond hair and a crooked nose. She always smelled of freshly baked bread, and it had been years since the hint of worry had left the corners of her eyes. She rushed forward to place her hands on his arms to hold him steady as she looked him over.

"I'm not hurt, Ma," Luke said.

"I know. I just missed you. I hardly ever see you anymore."

"He's working, Virginia!" said the man who stomped out of the kitchen with a fresh layer of chicken grease on his face. "Leave him be."

"He's my son," she said proudly. "I won't leave him anywhere."

"How much did you bring home today, son?"

Wincing at being called that, Luke couldn't help thinking of his real father. The man who bore the kind face from his fading memories had died of a fever. It was a quiet, forgettable death compared to the gruesome sacrifices being made during the brutal days of war. The passing of one good man seemed even less significant since nobody mentioned his name any longer. Ever since Luke's mother had met Kyle Sobell, it was as though the man that had brought Luke into this world had been erased altogether.

"I asked you a question," Kyle said. "How much did you bring home?"

"Nothing," Luke told him. "I'm still working on a few things."

"What kind of job is that?"

"It's an apprenticeship," Luke's mother said. "He's learning a trade and John Vassilly is a fine teacher."

"If he was learning a trade, he'd be bringing home some pay or otherwise finding a way to help us make ends meet," Kyle groused. "At least that way he'd be of some use around here."

"Don't talk to him like that." Before she was finished speaking those words, the back of Kyle's hand was on its way to meet her cheek. It was a light slap compared to the others that had been given to her over the years, but it rang out like a thunderclap in Luke's ears.

"Don't do that!" Luke said.

Kyle barely acknowledged him with half a glance. "Just get out of my sight," he said to the young man.

Luke stood up straight. "I won't go anywhere. You will."

Slowly, Kyle turned to face him. His eyes angled downward as a wicked smile eased onto his face. "Oh, you're the big man now, are you? What are you gonna do, big man? Draw that pistol and shoot me down?"

Luke hadn't even realized his hand had drifted toward the Colt. Looking down, he saw his fingers were less than an inch from touching the weapon's grip. "Just . . . stop hitting her."

"Or what?"

Rushing forward to grab Kyle with both hands, Virginia pleaded, "Leave him alone! He's just upset, is all. Things are hard for Luke. He's always been alone."

"That's because he's a freak with dead eyes," Kyle said. "Ain't that right, boy? You look like some kind of ghoul. Maybe you should be an undertaker. Go learn a trade that suits you better."

Dead eyes.

That had always been a peculiar little insult that Kyle had thrown at Luke ever since the three of them had gone to pose for a family photograph six Christmases ago. Luke had blinked at the wrong time and the resulting photograph showed only empty white spaces where his eyes should have been. Of course, that space was a reflection off his eyelids, but Kyle picked up on the fact that it looked more like a ghost's eyes. Whenever Luke kept to himself or seemed particularly withdrawn, Kyle brought up his dead eyes. Since those sorts of instances were frequent, Luke had learned to let the insults roll off his back. The same could not be said about his mother.

"Don't call him that!" she said. "It's a terrible thing to say."

"He knows I'm only fooling about," Kyle said through a smile. "Besides, I thought you always liked my jokes."

"That was back when you were amusing," she replied. "Now you're just cruel."

"Am I? At least I'm not the one that's about to draw a gun on the man who's put a roof over his head all these years."

Kyle was right. Luke's hand was still within easy reach of the Colt. His mother waved that off without a second thought. "He's just scared," she said. "He won't hurt anyone."

"Scared as a church mouse," Kyle grunted. "He should've outgrown that a long time ago. Guess it ain't his lot in life to be a real man."

If he hadn't already heard those things from Kyle as well as so many others over the years, Luke would have been angered by such words. Instead he saw them for what they were: the feeble rants of an ignorant man.

When Luke's mother drew herself up to defend him, he rubbed her back and said, "It's all right."

"No. It's not," she said defiantly. Before she could get another word out, a heavy set of knuckles pounded against the front door.

Virginia looked toward the door as if she'd been caught in a sin and Kyle strode over to answer it while shaking his head in silent disgust at the rest of his adopted family. He opened the door to reveal a tall man wearing a rumpled waistcoat over a dusty white cotton shirt. A wide-brimmed hat sat atop his head, casting a shadow that was almost dark enough to obscure his entire face.

"Did I come at a bad time?" the man asked.

"No, Scotty," Kyle replied. "Come on inside and make yourself at home. We was just having a discussion."

Emory Scott was lean and had sunken features. He wore a double rig around his waist carrying two finely polished pistols that looked to have cost him a pretty penny. After removing his hat, he gazed at Luke's mother for just a bit too long. "Evening, Ginny."

She averted her eyes and patted her son's arm while making her way to the bedroom. Without a word to anyone, she shut herself inside.

"She's a quiet one, huh?" Scott said.

Kyle grunted and crossed the room to grab a bottle of whiskey from the top shelf in the kitchen.

The tall man looked over at Luke and then to Kyle. Luke's stepfather grunted once and said, "Don't pay him no mind. He's about as useful as teats on a bull. What brings you around to this neck of the woods? More work from the captain?"

"Do you always discuss business with others around?" Scott asked.

"What does it matter? This is my home, ain't it?"

"Yes, but it's not everyone's business."

"I didn't say nothing about the move to Wichita, if that's what you mean." When Scott let out an irritated sigh, Kyle added, "Not that it matters anyhow. I can trust them."

"Maybe we should do this some other time," Scott said.

Carrying the bottle and two glasses over to a table in the front room, Kyle said, "Nonsense! You came all this way. Have a drink at least."

Reluctantly Scott accepted the glass that was handed to him and held it out to be filled.

"Now," Kyle said. "Have you got another job for me?"

"I do . . . if you have something for me."

"You know I do," Kyle said through another smirk. Angling his head toward the bedroom, he shouted, "Virginia! Bring that valise out here! The one under the bed."

Scott's eyes narrowed and his face darkened in a way that made Luke feel like an intruder in his own home. The lean gunman remained quiet until Luke's mother emerged from the bedroom carrying a leather bag that had been under her bed longer than most of the dust that had collected down there. Although he'd always known it was under his mother's bed, he'd never been inclined to open that bag. The fact that this stranger wanted to do just that struck him as very peculiar indeed.

"Hurry up and get over here with that," Kyle demanded.

Scott watched her without the salaciousness that had been in his eyes when he'd first arrived. Now he studied her the way a hawk studied mice scurrying around on a desert floor.

As soon as he got the bag in his hands, Kyle opened it. "Here you go," he said while reaching inside.

Scott moved forward to block Luke's view of the bag's contents. Grabbing the bag in one hand, he pulled it away from Kyle and took a look inside for himself. "What in the hell is wrong with you?" he snarled. "You keep this here where everyone in this house can know about it?"

"They're my family," Kyle said. "I already told you. They ain't about to—"

"There's no telling what they might do," Scott cut in. "The fact of the matter was that you were told to keep this safe."

"It is safe!"

"Safe from the law as well as safe from prying eyes, you blasted fool."

Kyle shook his head and opened his mouth without saying anything. As much as Luke liked to see his stepfather at a loss for words, he couldn't help feeling an even greater desire to get out of that house. If not for the fact that his mother was on the other side of the room, he might have done that very thing.

"They don't know everything," Kyle insisted. "But they live under the same roof as me. They're bound to know something. All that matters to you or anyone else is that they're no danger to anyone."

"You willing to stake your life on it?" Scott asked.

Without hesitation, Kyle said, "Yeah. If you hadn't stormed in here the way you did, they wouldn't know much of anything at all."

"Stormed in here?" Scott asked with a humorless laugh. "You were told to expect me."

Virginia eased her way across the room toward her son. "We can just leave you men be," she said. "No need for all of this fuss on our account."

Stopping her with a sharp glare, Scott asked, "What do you know about what your husband does for a living?"

"I know he's gone for weeks at a time every now and then," she said. "I also know he provides what we need. The rest is none of my concern."

Scott nodded and shifted his gaze to Luke. "What about you?"

Unable to meet the man's predatory stare, Luke replied, "I don't care what he does. I prefer it when he's away."

"Doesn't sound like a lot of loyalty to me, Kyle," Scott mused. "You call this a family?"

"Ain't nobody's perfect," Kyle said.

As Scott's hand drifted toward his holster, he said, "Even so, what did Granger say about how we're to conduct ourselves between jobs?"

"Like we was nothin' more than ordinary folks . . . which is just what I've done."

"Ordinary folks don't have this kind of thing stashed under their bed," Scott said as he held the valise so it fell open enough for Luke to get a look at the bundles of money inside. His heart skipped a beat and his breath caught in his throat as his mother's hand tightened around his arm. She pulled him toward the door, but Luke's feet were rooted to the spot.

"Damn it," Kyle sighed. "They never knew that bag was under there and they surely didn't know what was inside!"

"Your woman knew the bag was there," Scott said in a voice that sent chills beneath Luke's skin. "She's the one who fetched it for us. Did you think I forgot about that so soon?" His eyes narrowed and his hand came to a rest upon one of his holstered pistols. "Is that the problem here? You think I'm stupid?"

A silence fell upon the entire house that was so complete, Luke couldn't even hear any noise from the world beyond its walls. He stood there with his mother hanging on his arm, waiting for Kyle to turn the situation around, praying that he wasn't making a mistake in choosing this moment to put the first lick of trust in the man.

Holding both hands out, Kyle spoke in a voice that was so soft it could barely be heard. "You know that ain't true. You're just making a big thing out of this."

"Am I?" Scott asked.

"Yes. I swear on everything that's holy . . . you are. Everything that's supposed to be in that bag is there. Take it. Send my regards to our mutual friend and come see me when there's another job to do."

"Maybe you've outlived your usefulness."

"And maybe you're wound too tight today." Putting on a shaky grin, Kyle added, "Or maybe you've had a nip of whiskey with your supper? Lord knows you wouldn't be the only one to indulge that way. Tends to make a man cross, though."

Scott moved his hand away from his holster. "Maybe you're right. I could have been making too much of this."

"That's right," Kyle sighed. "We've worked together long enough to know where each other stands."

"Perhaps you did pick some good folks as a family."

"I sure did."

And as quickly as Scott's relaxed demeanor had come, it was gone. "The matter still stands that this here woman knew more than she should have and now so does the boy."

Kyle gritted his teeth and said, "If that's anyone's fault, it's yours! Everything was fine before now."

"Maybe it was my fault to put you on the spot," Scott admitted. "But we're in something of a bind here. It's got to be set straight. You want to do it or should I?"

Shaking his head, Kyle said, "You're mistaken. Nothing needs to be set straight."

Luke's pulse sped up and he suddenly regained control of his legs. When he tried to get his mother moving with a gentle tug on her arm, he found she was now the one frozen in fear. He tugged a bit harder, which was enough to snap her out of the spell that had come over her.

"This ain't the first time you've put us all at risk," Scott said. "But I can tell you it'll be the last."

"Don't do this!" Kyle yelled.

"Too late," the stranger said. "It's already done."

When Scott drew a pistol from his holster, it was in a motion so fast that Luke barely saw it. The thunder that followed would follow him for the rest of his life.

Chapter 5

Luke thought his stepfather was dead after the first pair of shots blasted through the house. But Kyle had jumped to one side, grunting as he hit the floor. The moment all four limbs were beneath him, Kyle crawled toward the wall where his hunting rifle was set upon two pegs above the kitchen door.

"You've got to get out of here!" Virginia said to her son.

All Luke could do was nod and hurry with her toward the front door.

Without a word of warning, Scott turned and fired a round at them. Even compared to the gunshot itself, the thump of lead drilling into flesh was deafening to Luke's ears. He felt his mother's entire body jerk as her steps became a falling stagger toward salvation. She reached toward the door leading outside, only to push Luke toward it in front of her.

"Go on," she gasped. "Get the sheriff."

Another shot caught her in the back. Her eyes glazed over and she fell into Luke's waiting arms.

Luke stared down at her as she grew heavy and limp. From the corner of his eye, he could see Scott coming toward him. He knew the other man had more bullets to fire, but he simply didn't care. The only thing that surprised him was the bellowing sound of Kyle's voice before another torrent of gunfire was unleashed.

Pivoting smoothly, Scott fired the gun in his right hand while drawing the second pistol with his left. All the while, the familiar bark of the hunting rifle exploded within the house. Glass shattered. Furniture was overturned. Lanterns were knocked from the wall and tabletops. The room that was so familiar to Luke, unchanged throughout most of his life, was destroyed in seconds. A storm raged around him and a large part of him didn't care to get out of its way. If he was to be stricken down by the chaos, then so be it.

What the boy felt wasn't bravery.

It wasn't even anger.

What Luke felt was a vast, clawing cold stretching out from his stomach to claim every inch of his body.

His eyes absorbed the unfolding horror without focusing on one thing for more than a fraction of a second. He saw blind rage written across Kyle's face as he fired the hunting rifle and levered in another round. He saw smoke bellow into the air between the two men. He saw Scott toss an empty gun from his right hand to calmly replace it with the second one he'd drawn a few moments ago. After moving to one side, Scott dropped to one knee before firing the round that put an end to Kyle's fight.

Falling backward, Kyle was swallowed up by the gritty smoke that had filled the air. Although Luke's ears were ringing too badly to hear the body hit the floor, he felt the impact through the boards. He felt the sudden need to get away from his mother's body, so Luke backed toward the door.

Scott walked toward the spot where Kyle had fallen and fired another round into him. He then scooped up the valise and turned toward the front portion of the house. "What are you fixing to do with that, boy?" he asked.

It wasn't until that moment that Luke realized he had the old Colt in his hand. The gun no longer felt heavy or comfortable in his grasp. His body was still too numb to feel itself.

"Shame this had to happen," Scott said. "But it's your daddy's fault. You probably know he wasn't a very good man."

Although he had some vague ideas of what line of work Kyle was in, he never much cared to hear any details. Kyle kept his business to himself, making it clear that he preferred it that way and Luke was only interested in the next time Kyle would be leaving town. That had always been the way of things, which suited Luke just fine.

"I can see you're frightened," Scott said. "No one can blame you for that. What happened here wasn't your fault. It's over now, though. We can part ways here and you won't never see me again."

Luke believed that as much as he believed pigs could fly. He brought his gun up and fired before he had a chance to take proper aim. To his clouded ears, the shot sounded muffled and far away. The stranger wasn't trying to talk any longer. Also, there was something written in his features that hadn't been there before.

Surprise.

Still holding his pistol the way he'd practiced when trying to knock bottles from a fence or empty cans from hitching posts, Luke pulled his trigger again and again. The Colt spat fire and smoke while sending shock waves all the way up his arm. Scott got a shot off as well, but Luke didn't care much about that. He paused just long enough to finally look at the other man through his sights and continued sending rounds through the air.

Scott's arms splayed out to one side and he twisted around in a tight circle. He jerked again, folded over, and squatted in place with his weapon dangling from a shaking hand.

Luke's finger tightened around the trigger, but the Colt no longer bucked against his palm. He turned his hand over to inspect the gun as if something was wrong. All he could see was blurred iron and his own hand as if it had been drawn in smeared paint. Every breath was filled with acrid scents mingled with a bitter, coppery odor he could not place. Scott still squatted where he was, so Luke pointed the Colt at him and pulled its trigger again.

The hammer slapped against another empty casing. His gun was empty. It seemed like a simple revelation, but Luke had just now figured it out. Instead of trying to reload the Colt, he held it as if he'd just forgotten what he'd learned a second ago. Unwilling to let the gun go or even lower it, Luke walked toward the stranger.

Scott let out a grunting breath, like a piston that had expelled its last gout of steam, and collapsed. He didn't fall like Kyle or Virginia. Instead he lowered himself to the floor and leaned back against something that allowed him to sit upright. The gun slipped from his right hand to clamp tightly against his chest. His other hand reached down to the floor to support his weight. "I guess," he grunted, "... I had that coming."

Staring down at him, Luke felt his muscles tighten. It was unfair that this man got to speak while his mother's voice would never be heard again. Even Kyle deserved to say his hurtful things more than this piece of filth. As he thought that over, Luke found himself pulling his trigger again. He knew the gun was empty and felt embarrassed that he was so out of sorts.

Scott's next breath came out in a haggard laugh.

"Don't worry. You done . . . all you needed to do. You ever . . . fire that gun before?"

Luke nodded. His mouth opened and the words "Yes, sir" escaped his lips before he could stop them.

The stranger's nod was an awkward up-and-down motion similar to a toy in need of grease. "You . . . you'll fire it again, I reckon."

At that moment, every part of Luke's body came back to life. He could feel the gun in his hand, the pain in his chest, and the weight on his shoulders. His vision was swiftly clearing.

The front of Scott's shirt was wet with blood, most of it centered in his midsection. Every time he tried to draw a breath, tremors rocked his frame. "Next time," he wheezed. His hands scraped at the floor and his legs stretched out as if they were trying to move on their own to get the rest of him moving. "Next time . . . it'll be . . . easier."

And then the house became silent once again.

This was a silence unlike the one that had come before when everyone was alive and hoping not to spark anything. The silence surrounding Luke now was thick enough to suffocate him and strong enough to crush him beneath its mass.

Now that his body was awakened, Luke's mind started to churn with dozens of random thoughts.

There could be more gunmen waiting to hear from Scott.

Someone could have heard the shots.

The law might be on its way.

His mother . . .

That last thought stopped all the others.

Luke allowed the gun to fall from his hand and staggered over to the spot where Virginia was lying. His steps blended together until he found himself hunched over her body. She was quiet and peaceful. Instead of trying to lift her into his arms, Luke bent down to gently place a kiss on her forehead. In his mind, he could see the warm smile that she usually gave him when he showed her affection and he turned away from the body on the floor before he saw something that would rob him of that gleaming memory.

There wasn't much time. As he worked his way through the house, Luke kept that at the front of his mind. It kept him going and gave him something else to think about other than the haze of gun smoke and the stench of death in the air. He went to his bed and collected as many clothes as he could stuff into the old carpetbag that Kyle used when he went away for so long. He rounded up all the food that was fit to toss into the bag and then made his way back to the carnage in the front room.

Luke kept his eyes above the bodies and didn't think about the reason the floor was slick beneath his boots. He gathered up all three pistols: the old Colt and both of Scott's guns. When he tried tucking them under his belt, Luke stopped and looked down at the gunman's body. He took a breath to steel himself and then hunkered down to unbuckle the gun belt from around Scott's waist. All of those things, guns and all, were stuffed into the carpetbag, which was now too full to be properly closed.

Finally Luke found himself staring down at the valise that had been at the heart of this terrible storm. He picked it up, looked inside, and shook it to see if he could get a rough estimate of how much money was in there. His brain was spinning in too many circles for him to count, but he knew it was a lot. Taking both bags with him, he started toward the front door. Instead of walking past his mother and Kyle to step through that door, he turned around and walked through the kitchen to leave through the back.

As soon as he was outside, Luke felt as if he'd rejoined the world. Voices were hollering back and forth. There was a commotion in the street near the front of the house. Luke knew most of that was probably in response to the sounds of shooting, but his most powerful instinct told him to take what was his and put some distance between himself and that house.

It wasn't his house any longer. He didn't want to step foot inside or set eyes on it ever again, and there wasn't anything strong enough to make him change his mind. He'd been given a horse that Kyle had bought from Cam Eberhauser, an old farmer who worked a plot of land a few miles to the north of town. That horse waited for him now and was always grateful to be saddled up for a ride. Luke hurried through the motions and loaded that horse with everything he'd lugged away from the place that used to be home. Instead of hopping onto her back and riding away, he led her out to the shed behind the Croft home and tethered her there.

"Don't you worry, Missy," Luke said to the horse. "I won't leave you here for long. When I come back, you'll get to stretch your legs for a good long while."

The horse nuzzled him gently and looked at him with eyes that seemed to know more than they possibly could. He rubbed her neck for a bit longer and then headed back to the house. Rather than go inside, he ran around to the street where a small herd of folks was gathering.

"Luke!" one of his neighbors said. "Where's your ma and pa? Was there a shooting?'

More of his neighbors swarmed toward him, each of them asking question after question.

"Was anyone hurt?"

"What happened?"

"What was that noise?"

"Who was that man that rode up to your house?"

"Where did that blood come from?"

When he heard that last question, Luke looked down at himself to find dark red stains on his hands, shirt, pants, and boots. His vision had been so clouded by smoke that he hadn't noticed the gruesome filth until that moment.

The neighbor lady who'd started the cascade of questions grabbed hold of him and looked him in the eye when she asked, "Are you all right?"

"Yeah," he said in a meek tone. "I wasn't shot or nothing."

"So those were gunshots?"

"Of course they were gunshots!" the lady's husband snapped. "What else could they be? What happened, son? Where's Kyle and Virginia?"

"They're . . . inside," Luke said.

"Are they all right? Were they shot?"

Luke knew the answers and meant to say them, but suddenly he couldn't form the words. It was as if his brain was a machine that had just popped a spring and ground to a halt. Some of the other men who lived nearby were approaching the front door, and when Luke tried to stop them, he was held back and wrapped up in the neighbor lady's arms.

Luke had lived in the house next to her for as long as he'd been in Maconville, and just now he couldn't recall her name. He recognized all the faces surrounding him, but only as familiar shapes from another life. One of those shapes was a star made of dented tin.

"I heard there was a shooting here," the sheriff said as he and two deputies approached the house. "What happened?"

"I think the Crofts are hurt," the neighbor lady said. "Except for Luke Croft here. I'll keep an eye on him."

The sheriff nodded and looked over to Luke. He was only an inch or so taller than the young man, but he looked down at him as if he were speaking to a child. "Anything we should know before going in there, son?"

Absently, Luke shook his head.

The lawmen drew their weapons. "Stay put and don't worry," the sheriff said. "Everything's gonna be all right."

Chapter 6

The narrow ribbon of water that wound its way through the weeds southwest of town was called Double Bend Creek. After a long string of summer nights spent catching tadpoles and their kin when he was too young to go to school, Red took to calling it Froggy Crick. He and Luke might have grown too old to draw much pleasure from scooping up tadpoles, but they still visited Froggy Crick whenever they could. Usually it was a place to escape from chores and the people intent on making the young men do them. Today, it offered much simpler pleasures.

It was quiet.

"Here," Red said as he handed over a bottle that was less than a quarter full. "I swiped it from my old man."

Luke took the bottle from him and sniffed its contents. It wasn't the first time he'd tasted whiskey in his seventeen years on this earth, but it was the first he'd drunk it down for reasons other than pure rebellion. The liquor cut through his body, washing away the horrible tastes that had collected in the back of his mouth. He took another pull from the bottle, which gave him a hint of warmth at the bottom of his chest. "Thanks," he said while handing it back.

Red took the bottle but didn't drink. He closed his eyes and lifted his head to the inky black sky above him as if he were basking in the light from the half-moon. Crickets chirped in the distance and water from the creek rustled through some of the thick bunches of weeds. He sat with his back against a rock that he'd dragged up and set there years ago for that very purpose. "We've been here for a while, Luke. You ever gonna tell me what happened?"

"I already told the sheriff and a bunch of the neighbors. I don't wanna tell that story again."

"I don't want to hear the same story," Red told him. "I asked about what happened."

Luke smirked and shifted his weight upon the stump where he sat. His boots were pressed firmly against familiar ground, feeling as if the waters from his youth had finally washed them clean. "Some man came to talk to Kyle. Some fella he works with, I guess."

"Another salesman?"

"Kyle wasn't a salesman like he told everyone. I think he was an outlaw."

"Are you kidding me?"

Luke shook his head. "Nope."

"How do you know?"

"Because the man who came looking for him was a killer. He asked for something and Kyle had it. A bag full of money. Ma knew about it too. She must've known about everything. Could be what they were always fighting about."

"So . . . you think Kyle stole that money?"

Luke shrugged. "All I know for certain is that he was holding on to it for the man who came along to collect. I don't think Kyle was ever any kind of salesman, though."

"I thought he only had that hunting rifle." When Luke looked over to him expecting a point, Red shrugged. "It's just that outlaws carry something other than hunting rifles, don't they?"

"He hid a lot from me. They both did. A stash of guns wouldn't be too hard."

"Suppose not." Red held the bottle to his mouth as if he was going to take a drink. Before he did, he asked, "How did you get out of there?"

"I told everyone. I hid under a table until the shooting started."

"Sure, that's what you told them," Red said. "You're telling me now. I know when you're lying. You're not very good at it."

Smirking, Luke said, "Since you're the only one who can tell when I'm lying, I'd say I'm pretty good at it."

"Well, I can tell right now. There's more to it."

"Why do you want to know?"

"Look, I'm not like the rest of them that flocked to that house so they could get a look for themselves on account of nothing worth seeing ever happens around here." Using the bottle as a pointer, Red told him, "All the rest of them may just want something to talk about, but I ain't all of them. You should know that!"

Luke gazed around at the creek, the weeds, and the trees scattered for miles in front of him. "He meant to kill us."

"Who did? Kyle?"

"No," Luke said. "The stranger. Kyle called him Scott. He got mad when my ma went to fetch the money that was supposed to be hid and he told Kyle he made a big mistake. Kyle tried to tell him otherwise, but . . ." Luke shook his head. "In the end, after all the grief I gave him and all the bad things I said and thought about him, Kyle did his best to save me. To save my ma."

"He stood up to that stranger?"

"Tried to. Only, he wasn't armed. He got to the hunting rifle, but the stranger had two guns. That man fired like it wasn't any kind of burden to shoot a woman in the back or cut a man down in cold blood. Funny thing is, I didn't hide."

"There wouldn't be no shame in it if you did," Red told him.

Luke shook his head. "I just stood there. I couldn't do much of anything to help. Before the shooting started, and plenty of times before today, Kyle said I wasn't much use to anyone. Today, when I was needed more than ever, he was right. I was useless."

"What were you supposed to do?" Red asked.

"Shoot that stranger."

"With that Colt of yours?"

"Yes. Once I got a hold of myself . . . when it was too late to do my ma or Kyle a lick of good . . . that's exactly what I did."

Red not only tipped the bottle back for a drink, but he nearly held it there until all the whiskey had been poured down his throat. He handed the bottle over to Luke, who took it and finished it off.

"You killed a man?" Red asked.

"That's right. And I was still too late to save either of them."

"Did you tell the sheriff?"

Luke shook his head. "Why would I do that? So I could get hung?"

"He wouldn't have hung you. That stranger killed two people right in front of you! It was self-defense."

"Maybe so, but I didn't want to tell him or anyone." Glancing over to his friend, Luke added, "Until now."

"Yeah, well, I ain't exactly honored. You have to tell the sheriff what really happened."

"Why?" Luke snapped as he jumped to his feet. "It's over! It's all over. *They're* over! You think the sheriff needs to know so he can see justice is done? I'm the one that handed out justice, but it still wasn't enough. I could never kill that bastard enough to have any real justice!"

Red looked up at him silently. When Luke had finished talking, he climbed to his feet and said, "Justice don't have anything to do with it. We both know there ain't no such thing. If there was, your ma wouldn't have been knocked around by a piece of trash like Kyle and my little sister wouldn't have died after being thrown from a horse that she cared for since it was born."

"That's all just hardship," Luke said.

"Then I suppose I don't know anything about justice. According to my daddy, there's a lot I don't know about."

"That's about to change."

"How do you know?" Red asked.

"Because I decided I'm leaving this town and striking out on my own."

Red couldn't help laughing. The more he tried to stop himself, the more it took him over. Fortunately his laughter spread to his friend, who cracked the first genuine smile he'd worn since his world had been turned onto its ear. "Striking out on your own?" Red said. "Is that why you brought Missy along with you? So you could just ride off and not look back?"

"Actually . . . yes."

Red looked over to the horse that was grazing nearby. He tried to laugh a bit more but found he no longer had it in him. "That's crazy."

"Staying here would be crazy. I have to get away. Why would I want to stay after all that happened?"

"Because there's matters to settle. Your family's house is here. Kyle had some business dealings with the dry goods store. Outlaw or no, he had something worked out with the owner of that place."

"The house will get sold," Luke said. "Kyle's business will get taken care of. There are plenty of people in town who can't wait to divvy everything up, and I don't want a part of it. I took what's mine and that's that."

"That's that, huh? Then why does it look like you're busting at the seams to tell me something else?"

Luke walked over to his horse and motioned for Red to follow him. When both of them were standing close enough to pat the animal's flank, Luke took the valise that had been hanging from his saddle horn. "You can't tell anyone about this," he said.

"About what?"

Opening the valise to show Red its contents, Luke said, "This."

Red gazed down at the money inside and his jaw dropped. Reaching into the bag, he dug his hand in to pull some money out. "Is this what that stranger came to collect?"

Luke nodded. "He won't need it anymore."

"And you could live for a while on it. Hell, if you play your cards right, you could stretch this much out for years!"

"I guess that's true."

Placing the money back in the bag, Red asked, "What do you mean you *guess* that's true? One thing I knew about you from the first time I sat next to you in that schoolhouse was that you don't guess about much of anything."

"When did you start scrutinizing every little thing I say or do?"

"You've just walked through hell and lost everything you hold dear. No matter what families we're from, you're my brother in all but blood and it's my job to make sure you make it through something like this as best I can." Leaning in closer while tapping Luke's forehead, he said, "I know you're tore up after all of this, but I can tell there's more going on in there. I can see the wheels turning."

"I got a lot to think about."

"I know that. I just want to make sure you're not thinking of doing anything crazy."

Luke turned away and took a few steps in the opposite direction.

"I'll be damned," Red groaned. "You are thinking of doing something crazy. And if *you* think it's crazy, I'm really worried."

"Don't worry about a thing."

Storming around to stand in front of Luke, Red planted his feet to block him from going any farther. When Luke attempted to walk around him, Red grabbed hold of his arm and pulled him back. "You think you're the only one that wants to get away from Maconville?" Red snarled. "You think you're the only one who wants to do something other than what he's expected to do by all the farmers and shopkeepers around here?"

"No."

"You and me have an understanding. We're fighters. Even back when we were nothin' but kids, we were fighters. What you're doing is runnin' away."

"I'm not just running away."

"So tell me what's got your wheels turning."

Luke stared into his friend's eyes and prepared to lie to his face. When it came time to start talking, he just couldn't do it. Instead he turned away from Red and pulled free of his grasp. He tried to think of other lies to tell him that were slightly smaller than what he'd originally planned and therefore might be easier to sell. He couldn't say those either.

All this time, Red stood his ground and waited.

Finally Luke said, "When that stranger came to the house, he and Kyle spoke about a few things."

"Uh-huh."

"Mostly, they were trying to dance around what they

really wanted to say. Probably on account of me and Ma standing right there."

"Whatever it was, there's no reason to believe any of it," Red told him. "You told me yourself that the stranger didn't want any of his and Kyle's business known."

"Yeah, but after a while, the stranger started saying plenty of things. I think . . ." Luke had to pause to steel himself. When he turned to face Red again, his eyes were cold as two pieces of stone. "I think he'd already made up his mind on what he was gonna do with us. In that stranger's head, we were already dead. Me and Ma anyhow. There's no reason to watch your tongue around dead folks."

Red nodded and immediately stopped himself so as not to inadvertently pour salt into the fresh wound.

"They talked about someone moving to a place outside Wichita," Luke continued. "Struck me as someone important. Name of Granger."

"Granger?" After thinking it over for a second, Red asked, "Granger who?"

Luke shrugged. "I don't know. At least . . . not yet."

Red studied his friend for a short while as his own wheels started to turn. Glancing back at the horse, which was loaded and ready to make a long ride, he looked at the valise, which was stuffed with more than enough cash to get Luke just about anywhere he wanted to go. His eyes dropped down to Luke's waist, which was mostly obscured by the jacket he wore. Red grabbed the jacket and pulled it open to reveal the double-rig holster that had come into town strapped around Scott's waist.

"No!" Red snapped.

"What do you mean, no?"

"You heard me! No, you're not going to Wichita!"

"You can't tell me what to do," Luke said.

"What would you do once you get there? Just walk around and start asking for any outlaws by the name of Granger?"

Luke hooked his thumbs over the gun belt. "I'll think of something."

"No, you won't. There's nothing you can think of that will make that a good idea."

"What would you have me do, Red? Just stand back and let everything keep rolling on as if nothing ever happened?"

"I've known your mother for years! She always treated me like one of her own. It tears me up to know what happened to her! But it just happened."

"You weren't there," Luke said in a low tone that rumbled up from the bottom of his soul. "You barely even know what happened."

"Maybe not, but that stranger is the one who killed your ma and Kyle. He's dead now and you killed him. Your ma wouldn't want—"

"She doesn't want anything anymore," Luke cut in. "She's gone. I'm all that's left and I don't intend to stay in this town to let the rest of my years slip away."

"Before you do anything, just give yourself some time to think it through."

Luke let out a tired laugh. "Something's definitely not right if you're the one telling me to be patient. You're the most hotheaded person I ever met."

"Exactly! So if I'm saying this to you, it must be true."

Although Luke wasn't completely appeased by that, he did seem to cool off a bit.

"Give it a little time," Red pleaded. "All this is still fresh. My head is still spinning from hearing about everything, so I can barely imagine what's going on inside yours. Just rest up and come at it once the smoke has cleared." Seeing that he was making some ground with his friend, Red added, "It's not like you can take off to Wichita in the middle of the night anyway."

"I could use some sleep," Luke admitted.

"That's right."

"But I don't want to sleep in that house."

"Nobody would expect you to. Come on home with me. We'll scrounge up something to eat and you can come up with something to say to my daddy when he smells the whiskey on our breath."

Luke's tired grin returned. "I'm the one that's been through hell, so I've got a good excuse. You're the one that'll be in trouble for drinking liquor."

"You got that right."

"I can sit and stew all I want, but that won't change a thing. Fact is, I've got the rest of my life to miss my ma and I'm sure I'll be doing plenty of that throughout the years. I can tell you right now I won't ever come around to thinking I want to stay here and let the rest of my days trickle away."

"You could at least give it some time," Red told him. "You've at least got to be here to see your mother put to rest."

Shaking his head, Luke replied, "It don't matter if I'm here or not for that. I said everything I could to her when she was here. From now on, it don't matter what I say because she won't hear it. And if she does, she'll be able to hear me no matter where I'm at. All that business about putting her in a box and watching as she's . . ." His eyes clenched shut as if to fight away the images that his imagination was conjuring up. When he opened them again, he was even more somber than he'd been before. "What I have to do . . . it'll take time. I can't waste any of it."

"What is it you intend to do?"

"I'm going to Wichita and I'll find whoever that Granger person is."

"Do you have any notion on how to do that?"

Luke nodded. "Yeah."

"When do you mean to leave town?"

"First light tomorrow morning."

"And there's nothing that'll change your mind," Red asked in a tone that said he already knew the answer.

"No."

"How long do you think it'll take?"

"A few days to ride to Wichita. If I can't find who this Granger is within a few more days after I get there, I doubt I'll ever find him. After that . . . I don't know yet."

"All right, then," Red said decisively. "We head out tomorrow morning for Wichita."

"We?"

"That's right. A ride that long, you shouldn't go it alone. Anything happens out there and you could die without a soul knowing about it. Well, your ma would know, but I doubt she'd be too happy about you going off and doing such a foolish thing as that. Also, wherever she is, she'd find a way to haunt me for the rest of my days if I let such a thing happen."

Luke started to laugh. "I reckon she would. She always did believe in ghosts."

"Remember when she wanted to visit that traveling spiritualist? Kyle threw a fit."

"And she went anyway," Luke recalled. "She said that spiritualist wasn't nothing but a huckster. But that fellow who came along to hold séances last year, the one who got the spirits to rattle them bells and such on that wall he had, she said he was the genuine article."

"Your ma was funny."

Luke nodded. He then looked over to his friend and said, "She wouldn't be happy if she knew I was getting you into trouble. She always told me you got into enough of it on your own."

"She never knew the half of it."

"She knew about you robbing that first spiritualist blind."

Red's eyes grew so wide that they were clearly visible in the faint moonlight. "What did you just say?"

"All right," Luke admitted. "I think she knew about both of us robbing that spiritualist."

"How could she know about that? We snuck into his tent, stole his lockbox, and was out again before anyone was the wiser."

Luke shrugged. "I don't know how, but she knew. She just couldn't prove it, so she lectured me for hours about how wrong it was that anyone should steal or otherwise break the law."

"I never heard about that before!"

"Because I wasn't about to give you up."

"It was your idea to rob that fella," Red pointed out.

"Exactly. And when I didn't admit to any of it or cave in while she was raking me over the coals, Ma let it be known that she would never lift a finger to help anyone who got caught stealing."

Letting out a breath as if he'd just escaped from a posse, Red said, "I'm surprised she still didn't tan your hide and then come after me."

"She . . . she said that . . ." Luke had to pause to take a breath. Keeping his head down, he said, "She told me that if that fella was any sort of spiritualist at all, he would have known in advance that he was gonna be robbed. For bilking good folks out of their money, he got what was coming to him."

"She once told me something along those lines," Red said. "After I got caught trying to steal one of the Johanssens' cows."

Luke turned just enough to look at him and see Red

smirk. “The sheriff did his part to scare me. He even put me in his jail cell, but I was only . . . what . . . ten years old?”

“Thereabouts.”

“He scared me good. I’ll give him that much. My mother and yours came down to bring me home. While the sheriff was talking to my mother, your ma took me aside and told me how what I did was wrong. But, more than fearing the law, she told me I should fear divine retribution.”

Luke’s brow furrowed. It wasn’t the first time he’d heard those words, but they struck a chord at that moment.

“She told me,” Red continued, “that folks always get what’s coming to them. Good or bad. It might take a while and it might come in strange ways, but what they do always comes back to them. I never forgot that.”

“Then how come you kept stealing?”

“’Cause I figured it was already too late for me.”

“We’re a bit young to be thinking such grim things.”

Red nodded. “And we’re also too young to be giving up on our lives. It’s time we started them. That’s what I’ve had in mind for a while now.”

“That so?”

“Yep. Thought I’d join the army. Soldiering is a good career and it gets me out of Maconville.”

“Puts you on a battlefield,” Luke told him. “Most men that see those fields either don’t live to tell about it or leave a piece of them there. From what I’ve seen in the newspapers, they’re usually mighty big pieces that get left behind.”

“Like what you’re proposing is so much less dangerous?” Red scoffed.

“At least I’d be fighting and dying for my own cause and not someone else’s.” He reached out to put a hand on his friend’s shoulder. “Don’t pay attention to what I just said. I think that's real honorable of you, Red. You'll make a fine soldier."

"I sure will. After I get back from Wichita."

"That's my job to do," Luke said. "You've got yours."

"We're brothers. We fight together. We ride the same trails."

"And what if I'm making a mistake?"

"Then we make it together." Red placed his hand on the side of Luke's face. What seemed like a tender gesture quickly took a more familiar turn when he pushed Luke's face to one side as if he'd slowly slapped him. "Besides, you don't think it's a mistake. Otherwise, you'd never do it. You're too smart for anything less."

"This isn't your fight."

"If you believe that, then maybe you're not so smart after all."

"I don't want you getting killed on my account."

"You don't have any say in the matter," Red said. "I'm coming along with you whether I'm riding beside you or following you all the way to Wichita."

"All right, then. I'm too tired to argue anymore."

"Come along home with me. If folks know where we're at, they won't watch us so hard and we can skin out of town that much easier come the morning."

Luke nodded and followed his friend back to the Connover place. Once there, he received some heartfelt condolences from Red's kin, a hot meal, and a warm bed for the night. It was the last taste of a real home he would feel for quite some time.

Chapter 7

When morning came, Red woke with a start. The house was quiet and the sun's rays were only starting to warm the old curtains hanging in the window beside him. He sat bolt upright, pulled those curtains back, and found only one horse tethered to the post outside. Before he could mutter the curse that sprang to his mind, he recalled Luke's horse had been tied to the post on the other side of the house because the troughs on either side needed to be filled and there was just enough water in each of them to keep one horse happy. Red looked toward the door to his cramped room and found Luke curled in a ball on the floor between two blankets and a little square pillow.

When they were smaller, the two of them had fit much better inside that room. Now they seemed less like two peas in a pod and more like a pair of boulders stuffed into a marble bag. Red swung his feet over the side of his bed, which wasn't much more than a sturdy cot, and rubbed both hands over the top of his head. By the time he'd pulled his fingers from the tangle of red hair, Luke had thrown off the blanket covering him.

"You ready to go?" Luke asked.

"Can't we at least have breakfast first?"

"I said first light. It's already past that. I thought this town would be miles behind me by now."

"And I thought I would have gotten Becky Walsh alone in the loft of her barn by now, but we don't always get what we want. I smell griddle cakes. If you can walk past those without stopping for a bite, then you don't have a soul."

Scratching his haunches as he shuffled from his room, Red pulled open his door and stepped into the short hallway leading to the front of the house. The floorboards were cool beneath his feet, and it wasn't until he was a few steps away from the kitchen that he heard the sizzle of a frying pan.

Red's father always looked as if he'd just tumbled out of bed. He looked over at his son and said, "About time you decided to wake up. Where's Luke?"

"Right here," Luke said as he entered the kitchen.

"Glad to have you, boy. Fix yourself a plate. You know where to find what you need."

After having spent almost as many nights in that house as he did his own, Luke did know where everything was. He found a plate and fork and then helped himself to some hotcakes and butter. By the time Red was digging in to his own stack, his mother had arrived to fix them all coffee. From then on, Red's parents engaged in a whole lot of small talk with Luke that flowed like so much rainwater through a gutter.

Yes, he felt better than he had the day before.

Yes, he missed his ma and Kyle.

Yes, he knew things would be better.

No, he didn't think he was alone.

Actually Red thought that last answer was earnest enough. When Luke gave it, he'd looked over to him for silent confirmation that he truly wouldn't be alone as the day wore on. Red nodded and piled some more griddle cakes onto his plate. Even his mother's coffee, which usually smelled like hot glue and had the consistency of mud, was something to be savored that morning.

"Well, now," Red's father said as he slapped the table and stood up. "There's work to be done. You'll come along to lend a hand as soon as this mess is cleaned up, you hear?"

"Yes, sir," Red replied.

"And you," Mr. Connover said while turning toward Luke, "rest up and feel free to come and go as you please. You're welcome to stay here as long as you like, but you'll do your part just like everyone else. Ain't no grief in the world couldn't be cured by rollin' up your sleeves and keeping yourself too occupied to fret about it."

Luke nodded. "Thanks for your hospitality, sir. Ma'am."

Accepting his gratitude with a warm smile, Red's mother busied herself by collecting dirty dishes and scooping up knives and forks. She'd used to have a lot more to say, but that was before Red's brother, Matt, went off to join the Union army last year. Since then, she'd become quiet as a sheep and twice as complacent.

After all he and Luke had been through together, Red never wanted him to know what a mean drunk his father was or how it made him sick to his stomach that his mother had given up on stepping in when things between him and the old man had gotten rough. Even before Matt had gone off to war, things had been strained in the Connover household. When Luke was around, everyone was on their best behavior. Red was often grateful for that. Other times, he resented the fact that an outsider was needed to buy him some peace inside his own home.

Red stepped outside to find his father pulling on the gloves he wore when chopping wood. A spot in the fence near the back of the property needed to be mended, and today was the day when that job would be finished. Like a cat responding to the slightest scrape of a mouse's foot against a floor, the old man wheeled around to find his son.

"Git your lazy hide over here and help me carry these rails!"

Red nodded at his father's words but didn't take another step in his direction. "Luke needs help with some things," he said. "We gotta ride over to his place and—"

"Do whatever you like," his father said with an exasperated wave. "I stopped thinking you'd serve any purpose years ago. If your brother was here, this fence would've been done by now."

That was normally the time when Red would fire back with a spiteful remark about how Matt would have been appreciated for his labor because he was the only one who was treated better than a stray dog in that family. He held his tongue, however. Knowing he was leaving town in a matter of minutes made such things easier to bear.

"Good-bye, Daddy," Red said.

The old man grunted to himself without bothering to look over his shoulder.

Red went back inside, where his mother was fussing over Luke, headed to his room, and threw some clothes into his brother's old saddlebags. No longer caring about leaving things the way they should be, he stripped his bed of sheets and pulled up the old, paper-thin mattress to find a gun belt wrapped in a dirty pillowcase. The holster had belonged to his father's brother and had been a gift to Matt on his thirteenth birthday. It had been left behind so Red could learn to shoot and protect the house if trouble rode in when their father was passed out drunk in a saloon somewhere.

The pistol was a Smith & Wesson revolver with a polished barrel and cylinder. The wooden grip was smooth as silk and stained to a rich black. Red opened the cylinder and turned it to confirm that three of the seven chambers were filled with .22-caliber rounds. Compared to the old Colt Luke had been working on, Matt's pistol felt more like a cork gun. It would get the job done well enough as long as it was used properly, and the holster fit comfortably around his waist. Before buckling it there, he reminded himself that he still had to walk past his parents and didn't want to explain why he was doing so while heeled. After bundling the gun belt, pistol, and the spare ammunition he had inside an old shirt, Red held the package under his arm and left the room that had been wrapped around him for most of his childhood.

"You still want to tend to them matters you told me about?" Red asked as he turned toward the kitchen.

Luke was eager to get moving, but not so eager to leave the company of Red's mother. He looked at her with a genuine smile and said, "Thanks for everything, ma'am. It really means a lot."

She patted his cheek. "You're part of this family, Luke. Don't ever forget that."

"I won't."

With that, Luke and Red walked out of the house, where they split up to saddle their horses. Before long, they were riding through town, heading in the general direction of Luke's house.

"You sure you want to do this?" Red asked.

Without a pause or a lick of emotion in his voice, Luke replied, "Yes."

Luke kept riding without casting an eye toward his old house. Red tugged back on his reins just enough to slow his horse a bit to see what his friend was missing. The front door of the Croft home was wide open and a fat man in a long black coat waddled from a long black wagon to step inside the house. Recognizing the fat man as the town's undertaker, Red was glad Luke had the sense to keep his head turned away. He shuddered to think what was inside the home and, a few seconds later, wished he'd followed Luke's example by not glancing over there at all.

Several neighbors and other familiar people waved at the young men as they rode by. None of them seemed surprised or offended when they barely got a response in kind. They simply looked to Red, gave him a sympathetic nod, and went about their business.

Plenty of things flowed through Red's mind as Maconville thinned out into empty prairie and a wide trail leading south to Wichita. Foremost among them was a pang of regret that he hadn't given proper farewells to anyone before leaving. For all he knew, he and Luke could be returning in no time at all and they would resume where they'd left off. Red couldn't be absolutely certain about anything, but he felt the odds of that coming to pass were particularly slim.

He wondered if they should have taken more time to plan before saddling up their horses and riding away from most everything they knew. Of course, he'd heard plenty of stories of miners and homesteaders who set out to go a lot farther without being truly prepared for what they would find. Stocking up on provisions might serve its purpose, but they couldn't prepare someone for the things that would truly put them to the test. Try as he might, Red couldn't think of anything he might have done that would have genuinely prepared him for the ride he'd agreed to take with his friend.

When Red shifted to get comfortable in his saddle, he couldn't really find a comfortable spot until he was seated with his back straight, his chin high, and his eyes pointed directly ahead.

Maconville was behind him.

Wichita lay a few days' ride ahead.

Everything else would be decided when it came. There was a good amount of comfort to be taken from all of that.

Chapter 8

The ride was more enjoyable than either of the young men had expected. Without familiar surroundings, their eyes could soak up the swaying fields of wheat and tall grass for what they were instead of being reminded about some day from years gone by.

They reached a little town named Wendt Cross toward the end of the second day. Although both of them had passed through there once or twice in their lives, the place wasn't familiar enough to spark any memories. After buying some supplies and watering the horses, Luke was ready to move on. Red, on the other hand, had other ideas.

"What's the hurry?" Red asked.

While Luke had climbed into his saddle and was getting situated, Red still walked beside the gelding that looked as if it had traveled more miles than both boys and the other horse combined. Even when the gelding had first been purchased, its coat resembled faded brown paint that was about to start peeling off after having seen too many rains. No matter how many times it was washed, that animal always looked dirty. As soon as Red's family scraped together enough to buy a stallion in much better condition for his brother, Red took the horse as his own and cared for it as though he could win every prize a horse could earn. Its mane was coarser than the oldest brush, much like its tail. The gelding had lost his right ear some time before the Connovers had bought him, and the nub that remained was so gnarled that it looked as if it had been chewed off. Because of that, Red's mother took to calling him Vincent. She said that was the name of some fancy artist, but Red didn't know much about that.

"We need to get to Wichita," Luke said. "Did you forget?"

"No, I didn't forget. There's no reason why we can't stay here for a spell."

"The more ground we cover before nightfall, the quicker we'll get there."

"Yeah," Red said. "I know how that works. I just think we'd be better served getting a hot meal and a good night's sleep in a proper bed than by spending another night stretched out on the cold ground."

"It hasn't been that cold."

Red responded to that with a furrowed brow and a hard stare.

Although Luke didn't exactly fold under pressure, he did take another look around at the little town. There wasn't much to see. Apart from a barebones assortment of storefronts scattered along the one street they'd ridden, the remaining places were either boarded up or unmarked or were offices that held no spark of interest for young men striking out on their own. After turning down another street, they did find one clearly marked as a hotel. Looking at that place, Luke said, "I think we'd be better off sleeping on the ground than on any bed we might find in there."

"What about in there?" Red asked while nodding toward a place a bit farther down the road.

Luke shifted his focus in that direction to find a wide

storefront marked only as STORMY'S. "How do you know that's a hotel?" he asked.

Leaning over to him while dropping his voice to a whisper, Red said, "Look at them girls sitting on the front porch. By the looks of them, I'd say we can definitely find some warm beds inside. Know what I mean?"

"Not really."

"Look at them girls!"

When he'd first looked over there, Luke had only seen a few people sitting on the front porch. At first glance, they were two women sitting on either side of one man. There were two more chairs placed on the other side of a set of doors leading inside. One of the doors was open and there didn't seem to be much movement beyond them. Now that he took a closer look, Luke saw that one of the ladies was fairly pretty. She had long black hair and an inviting smile that was plainly seen, thanks to her brightly painted lips. The other girl had black hair as well, but was much skinnier and had sunken cheeks. Both of them were paying plenty of attention to the fella who was lapping it all up like a kitten in front of a saucer of milk.

"That scrawny lady doesn't look too healthy," Luke said.

"Maybe, but I reckon there's more inside to choose from." Red wore a beaming smile that grew wider as he waited for Luke to respond. When he didn't get anything apart from a blank stare, he said, "They're whores, Luke. Have you got rocks in your head?"

Luke looked at them again. "How can you tell? Have you been here before?"

"Haven't you ever seen a whore before?"

"Just Patsy and Dinah at the Ox Yoke Saloon back home. They weren't anything like that."

"I know. These ladies are a whole lot better! Well . . . the first one is."

"If you're so interested in whores, I wager there's some to be found in Wichita."

"They'll be cheaper here," Red told him.

"When did you become an expert on soiled doves?"

"Matt worked as a hired hand on a cattle drive that went all the way to Texas. He came back with some mighty good stories, and one thing he said was that ladies like them charge less in small towns than they do in big ones. Although the ones in Wichita might know some more colorful ways to curl yer toes."

"Good Lord," Luke sighed.

"What are you? A preacher? You don't like girls no more?"

"I didn't ride all this way to waste money on whores."

"They ain't evil, you know," Red said. "They're just working girls trying to get by."

"I think there's more to it than you feeling sorry for them."

"Yeah! There is. And if you gotta keep asking me about it, then there must be something loose inside you after all." Giving his friend a nudge, Red added, "Besides all that, a sweet little distraction could be just what the doctor ordered to get your mind off'a things for a spell."

Luke rolled his eyes, knowing all too well how difficult it would be to steer his friend away from something once he'd sunk his teeth into it. More than that, there would be plenty of misery down the road if they did keep moving since Red wouldn't exactly let the matter drop. "Fine," Luke said. "But we're leaving good and early tomorrow."

"Yes, Pa," Red chided.

"I mean it. And we'll stock up on supplies while we're here. There's got to be a gun store or some such around here. Both of us could use something better than what we've already got."

"I like the sound of that," Red said with genuine enthusiasm.

"And, for the love of God, don't let on about the money I'm carrying."

"You mean *we're* carrying."

Patting the bag still hanging from his saddle horn, Luke said, "I'm the one who took it and I'm the one carrying it."

"And if things go badly in Wichita, we're both the ones that'll die for it."

"I never asked you to come along."

"And yet," Red said with a grin that Luke often found to be particularly maddening, "here I am."

Luke shook his head and muttered, "Here you are."

"I thought we agreed to split some of that money. Not down the middle," Red hastily added. "But that I'd get some sort of share."

"I remember." Luke dug into the bag while glancing from side to side. There were only a few other folks walking past on either side of the street and none of them seemed interested in what the two young men were fretting about. Having removed a bundle of cash, Luke counted what was in his hand and gave it to Red. "Take it and don't ask for any more until we get to Wichita."

"This is . . . sixty dollars!"

"Seventy-three. I swear you were asleep every day we were in that schoolhouse."

"I was too busy watching Mrs. DeLoach bend over to pick up them little pieces of chalk I tossed onto the floor."

The darkness that had settled onto Luke's features cleared up considerably. "That was you tossing chalk onto the floor?"

"Yep."

"I didn't know that."

"Figured I had to be sneaky about it," Red admitted. "Did you ever see the size of Mr. DeLoach? He's a bear!"

"Anyway, don't throw all that money at one woman."

"That's right. We gotta save some for the saloons. Think we could get a poker game going?"

"Oh yeah. Watch the whiskey, though. We're moving on to Wichita tomorrow even if you're too drunk to sit in your saddle. I'll just tie your feet to that sorry excuse of a horse of yours and ride toward the roughest stretch of road I can find."

Rubbing his horse's neck affectionately, Red said, "I won't hear that kind of talk about Vincent. Now let's get ourselves to that cathouse so you can see me sweep a lady or two off their feet. If'n I don't get one of them to bed for free, I bet I at least convince them to give me a mighty fine discount."

Rather than try to burst his friend's bubble, Luke held his tongue and followed Red toward the place with the busiest front porch in town. "Shouldn't we find a place for the horses?" he asked.

"There's a hitching post and trough right here."

"If we're staying, I want someplace better than—"

Having caught the eye of the prettier of the two ladies in front of Stormy's, Red tipped his hat and said, "Excuse me, ma'am. Could you tell me where I might find some feed for this fine horse of mine?"

She stood up from her chair, allowing one hand to linger on the shoulder of the man sitting beside her. The fellow looked to be in his forties and had a finely clipped set of sideburns. His dark blue suit was slightly rumpled after being rubbed by both women, but he didn't seem to mind that nearly as much as he minded losing one of his companions to the two young arrivals. The girl on his other side brushed up against him a bit more to take up the slack.

"There's a nice little stable out back," the prettier lady said. "Just go right down that alley and around. You won't be able to miss it. Of course, that's for our paying customers." Slipping her fingers through the raven black hair flowing over one shoulder, she added, "You will be staying on with us for a bit, won't you?"

"Indeed we will, ma'am," Red said in a hurry.

The woman smiled, which made her skin seem even smoother and her face even more beautiful than before. "Good," she said. "Why don't I show you inside? Just one thing. Don't either one of you call me ma'am. Makes me sound like some kind of spinster."

"Yes, m— I mean," Red chuckled. "I'll call you whatever you like."

"You two put your horses up and I'll meet you inside." When she turned toward the building's front door, she captivated every man within eyeshot. Her hips swayed. Her hair swung against the creamy curves of her shoulders and neck that were bared, thanks to the plunging lines of a dark green dress that clung to her like a coat of oil paint. When she opened the door, a few bars of music drifted from inside. Whatever song it was, it did a mighty fine job of accompanying her enticing gait.

"I might need some more of that money," Red mumbled.

Although he tried to put on a stern front, Luke didn't have any trouble sympathizing with his friend. He'd seen a few women that drew him like a cat tugging at a bit of string, but none of them had the polish of that black-haired beauty. Even knowing that she was just trying to bring them in to spend their money, he couldn't help going along with it. In some respects, that didn't seem like such an outlandish request. Luke didn't mind paying for a show, and her walk alone was one unforgettable performance.

The stable was a narrow building that was just over half as long as the main structure. Its twin doors were tended by a bald man with tired eyes and a waistcoat that looked to have been plucked from a heap of trash. From the grime on his face, it was difficult to discern whether he had a dark complexion or was just in need of a good scrubbing.

"We need two stalls," Red announced.

"They's for paying customers only," the tired man said.

"That's us, sure enough."

"If'n one of the managers comes out to check and you ain't a customer, your horse and gear will be kept for a fee."

"Held for ransom, sounds to me," Luke grumbled.

"Call it what you like," the stable man said. "I'm just providing fair warning, is all."

Red slapped the older guy on the back hard enough to get him to wobble where he stood. "No need for the warning, old man," he said. "We're both headed in there to see some of them fine ladies."

The stable man wasn't outwardly impressed. "Fifty cents a day, then. That's for each horse, including feed and water."

"Not charging for water?" Luke said. "How generous."

"Don't pay no mind to my friend," Red said as he handed over a dollar. "He's just desperately in need of Stormy's services."

"Ain't we all?" the older man grumbled.

Already in high spirits, Red laughed while unbuckling his saddlebags to drape them over one shoulder. "There any places in town where I could purchase a gun?" he asked while handing over the reins.

The stable man looked at the pistol tucked under Red's belt, but his eyes lingered on the double-rig holster strapped around Luke's waist. "Looks like you already got guns."

"It's a dangerous world out there," Red said. "And we don't intend to stay here for long."

"Best place would be Jordan Bickle's store down on Westminster. The Eastern Trading Company. He gets a good supply of just about anything you might need."

"Much obliged." With that, Red sauntered toward the back door of Stormy's, which was currently being held open by a curvaceous redhead in a black dress with lace trim.

Luke took the bag from his saddle horn and then removed the ones attached to his saddle.

"You two headed to Wichita?" the stable man asked.

Luke became still and studied the man's dirty face carefully. "Why do you ask?"

"Lots of folks pass through here looking like you."

"Looking like what?"

Obviously not concerned with his own outward appearance, the stable man replied, "Carrying guns."

Luke's hand drifted toward the old Colt when his fingers brushed against one of the pistols he'd taken from Scott. The extra weight on his hip had taken some getting used to and was now second nature. Being reminded of where he'd acquired the shooting irons and what he intended to do with them still hadn't sunk all the way in.

"Men of all sorts make their way through these parts," the stable man continued. "The cattle barons and gunmen tend to favor Wichita or Dodge City."

"I suppose they would." After the stable man took hold of Missy's reins, Luke started to walk away. At the back door to the main building, Red was already being sweet-talked by the woman who'd come out to greet them. Luke was about to head that way as well when he stopped and turned back around. "You said lots of gunmen come through here?" he asked.

"They do."

"You ever heard of a man named Granger?"

The stable man pulled in a breath and looked up as if the memories he was looking for would be drifting among the clouds that wandered above him in the pale blue sky above him. "Name does strike a chord. He a friend of yours?"

As much as it pained him to say it, Luke replied, "Yeah. I've been hoping to catch up with him."

"I believe he may have passed through this way, but it was some time ago."

"How long?"

Once again, the stable man's eyes wandered. Instead of the sky, he gazed over toward the backside of the closest neighboring shop to Stormy's. "I'd say at least three months or so. Maybe longer."

"What did he look like?"

"Ain't he your friend?"

"Sure he is," Luke replied with a smirk. "But it's been a while. A man grows a beard, maybe gets his hair cut real short, he looks different. If I know how he's keeping himself nowadays, it'll help me ask around once I reach Wichita."

The stable man seemed suspicious, but that didn't keep him from saying, "I suppose I could recall his features and such. A favor like that usually comes along with a gratuity of some kind."

"Gratuity?"

"You know what that is, right?"

"Yeah," Luke replied. "If you can help me, I'd be mighty grateful."

When the stable man smiled, he somehow looked

even filthier than before. "You truly are new to this, boy. Money. I'm talkin' about a payment. You pay me and I'll tell you what I know. Lord Almighty, you're thick in the head."

Luke reached into his pocket where he'd already put a few dollars for expenses. "How do I know you have anything good to say?"

"You're talkin' about Bose Granger, ain't you? The killer that derailed that Union Pacific train on its way to Rock Island?"

"You heard about that job?" Luke asked, hoping his question wouldn't be as transparent as it felt.

Apparently Luke's ignorance didn't shine through, because the older fellow quickly nodded. "Course I heard about it. A man who does something like that just to get his hands on a few dollars becomes famous real quick."

Luke's stomach tied into a knot. He'd guessed that Granger was some sort of outlaw, but he hadn't considered the possibility that he was a killer of that caliber. Looking back with that in mind, he saw it made a little more sense why Scott had wanted to be so cautious when talking about the money that had been stolen. The fact that he could better understand the man that had slaughtered his own mother only made the sick feeling in Luke's innards that much worse.

After pulling out three dollars, Luke handed it over. The stable man took the money greedily and looked real pleased with himself until he saw that Luke's hand was now resting on the grip of his holstered Colt.

"Easy, now," the old man said. "I didn't mean to offend."

"Just tell me what you know about Granger."

"You're no friend of his, are you?"

"No, sir," Luke replied since he doubted he could lie well enough to right that particular ship.

"You a bounty hunter?"

Luke was more than pleased to go along with the stable man's guess if it meant less explaining was required from him. One nod was all it took to get the old man to continue.

"Granger is about my height, dark hair, and a bit wider in the face. He's got scars or marks in his cheeks. Both of 'em. When I saw him, he had his hair long and a mustache with a . . . bit more here," the stable man said while tapping a finger to the spot directly beneath the middle of his lower lip. "Not a full beard, but just a patch there."

"I know what you mean. How many men were with him?"

"I think maybe that's worth a bit more."

Rage swelled within Luke's chest as he thought about the man that had been sent to spill blood all over the floor of the Croft house. Even though Scott had been the one to pull the trigger, he'd been taking orders from someone and it looked as if that someone was Granger. As his heart slammed within his chest, Luke's vision became dimmer and clearer at the same time as though the color had drained away but he could see every grain of dust on the stable man's face. "Just tell me," he snarled.

The stable man nodded hastily. "All right, all right. There were two or three men with him. One rode back through here not too long ago. Less than a week. Skinny fellow. Looked like death warmed over."

"I know him."

"That's it. I keep my eyes open and listen to what the girls talk about. Them ladies sit outside and watch every little thing that goes on around here. Other than that, I ain't exactly taken into the confidence of men like Granger or any other gunman for that matter. Please believe me."

The stable man's eyes were full of fear and every ounce of it was directed at Luke. The thrill of it soaked in much deeper than when the Paulsen brothers had turned into quivering little rats.

"There had better not be anything else you should tell me," Luke warned.

"That's all. I swear!"

"And if anyone else comes asking about—"

"I won't tell anyone about you or that any bounty hunter was even here," the stable man sputtered. "So help me God."

Luke had been so wrapped up in finding Granger before anyone else that he hadn't been thinking about anyone finding him and Red. Thankful for the accidental reminder from the stable man, Luke nodded and said, "Good. Here," he added while pulling out another couple of dollars from his pocket. "Take this for your trouble."

The stable man reached for it with a trembling hand and stopped less than an inch away from the crumpled bills.

"Go on," Luke said.

"M-much obliged," he squeaked while snatching the money and tucking it away with the rest. "I'll take real good care of your horses too. Don't you worry."

"Thanks." Luke turned toward Stormy's to find the tall woman with the black hair standing at the back door. One hand was propped upon a shapely hip and she stared at him with a cool expression on her face. When he walked toward her, she stepped aside so another girl could take him by the hand. She looked to be three or maybe four years older than him, had long, stringy blond hair and wide, full lips.

"Hello there," the young blonde said with a friendly smile. "Come along with me and I'll take real good care of you. My name's Emma. Are you Luke?"

"How'd you know that?" he snapped.

She placed a small hand on his chest as if she could will his heart to slow down a few beats. Surprisingly enough, her touch was soothing enough to do just that. "Your friend is in here with Rose. He told me you'd be following him in here."

"Where is he?"

"Busy," Emma said with a wink.

Before Luke could ask her again, he felt another hand on him. This one was only slightly larger than Emma's, but was much stronger as it rested on his shoulder. "Take it easy, cowboy," the brunette who'd greeted him out front and let him in through the back said. "He's in good hands. Knowing Rose the way I do, I'd wager he's going to be in those hands for a while yet. Would you rather wait for him in the sitting room?"

Luke was being taken down a hallway that led to a large parlor filled with padded chairs and little round tables. There was a small bar at the far end of that room, and the air was laden with the distinct odor of pipe tobacco.

"I can wait with you if you'd like," Emma offered. "Or you can be alone."

Now that he'd settled down a bit and taken in his surroundings, Luke felt his muscles loosen up. He hadn't realized his hand was still on the Colt and when he took it away, both of the women accompanying him relaxed as well. "No," he said. "I'd like the company."

"Oh yes," Emma cooed. "I know you will."

Chapter 9

A year ago, Luke had grown closer to a girl he'd known for most of his life. Jennifer Moss was the older sister of a boy that Luke used to skip stones with before they started going to school. She was a sweet girl with a cute face and a pretty smile. A few nights during the course of one spring, she and Luke had snuck up into the loft of an old barn to spend hours kissing and exploring each other with nervous hands. After that, Luke's shyness had kept him from getting very close to another girl. He'd always consoled himself with the fact that he'd at least been with one in his lifetime. After spending less than an hour with Emma, he realized that he and Jennifer hadn't had the slightest idea what they were doing in that loft.

The room Emma had brought him to was small, but cozy. The space that wasn't taken up by the bed was occupied by one chair, a small dresser, a bathtub, and a tall oval mirror held in a chipped wooden frame. After shutting the door and locking them in, Emma had set him on the bed and slowly disrobed. Luke watched her, entranced by the slow dance performed by her swaying hips and expertly moving hands. She'd then turned her attentions to him, taking him to the tub, undressing him, and cleaning him off. Once he was mostly dry, she took him to the bed and made him forget all of the brutality that had so recently filled his life.

Her touch was constant and gentle, never leaving his skin or letting her warmth fade from him. She'd kissed him intently at first, but quickly adjusted to his hesitance and took a slower pace. When it came time to go further, she let him put his hands wherever he pleased. It wasn't long before he reached the limits of his knowledge in regards to a woman's body and when he got there, she took over without making him feel awkward or ashamed.

In that short span of time, Luke felt excited, worried, eager, timid, strong, and weak. The weakness he felt when she was through with him, however, was anything but bad. She lay beside him in the dark when it was over, resting her head on his shoulder as her hand slowly rubbed his chest. Luke stared up at the ceiling, illuminated by one candle that had been sputtering on the verge of going out, lost in the simple patterns of wood grain and the lines where one board met another.

There was no sorrow in his heart.

No killers in his thoughts.

No struggling to find his way.

No plans to make.

Just him and Emma, warm beneath a wrinkled blanket, their feet sticking out from the edge that had been pulled up from beneath the mattress somewhere along the way.

"How are you doing, honey?"

"Good," Luke told her. "I'm doing . . . really good."

Emma propped herself up on one elbow. Her hair was a mess and her cheeks were flushed. "You sound surprised by that."

"It's . . . been a while since I've felt good."

"How long?"

"I guess it really hasn't been much if you were to count the days. Still, it seems like a really long time."

She nodded and traced a design on his skin. "I've had times like that. All things must pass."

Luke blinked. "What?"

"It's something my mother used to tell me. Good things, bad things, everything will pass sooner or later. I always thought it was a comfort. At least when she was talking about the bad things."

"Good things shouldn't last forever. I wouldn't want them to."

"Is that so?" she said while mischievously poking him with her finger. "Then I must not have done something right."

Luke rolled onto his side to drape an arm over her and smiled when she didn't pull away. "No," he said. "You did everything right. It's just that, if the blessings weren't mixed in with the rest, you couldn't really appreciate how good they are."

"That's beautiful."

"I don't know about that," he said as he flopped onto his back. "It just came to mind."

"So . . . do you think you're ready for another go-around?"

Luke's response came to him in an instant, but he still wasn't fast enough to answer her before the door to Emma's room was rattled by a key turning in the lock. He sat up and looked around for his gun. The holster had been slung across the back of the only chair in the room, which was just out of reach. The door swung open as he silently cursed himself for being so foolish as to get wrapped up in the moment at the expense of his own well-being.

Fortunately the only person standing in the doorway was the beautiful brunette that had drawn him to

Stormy's in the first place. "Are you two through?" she asked.

"I hope not," Emma replied.

"Then you can pick up where you left off in a while. I'd like to have a word with our guest."

Luke felt Emma's hands on him before he was treated to the sight of her slipping out from beneath the blanket to get to the pile of her clothes. "We could both probably use a chance to catch our breath," she said.

The brunette stood staring at him, reminding Luke of Mrs. DeLoach when she'd been displeased with a smart-mouthed answer or some other form of mischief in her classroom.

"Mind if I get dressed?" he asked.

The brunette sighed. "I'll wait outside. Please hurry. I'd just like to have a word with you." She took a step back and closed the door.

Jumping from the bed, Luke gathered up his clothes and started pulling them on. While hopping on one leg to get into his pants, he nodded toward the room's only window. "Get that open for me, will you?"

Emma stayed put and shook her head as if she suddenly didn't know where she was. "What's wrong?" she asked. "What are you doing?"

"Getting out of here, that's what."

"Why? Because of what Stormy said?"

"Stormy?"

Emma nodded. "That woman who was at the door just now. She's Stormy. This is her place."

"That's just great." Now that he was partially dressed, Luke pulled his gun belt around his waist and buckled it. Before he could take a step toward the window to open it himself, he was stopped by Emma, who'd crawled over the bed to get in front of him.

"She just wants to talk to you," Emma insisted.

"Are you certain of that?"

"Yes."

The tone in her voice left no room for misunderstanding. Emma was as certain of what she'd just told him as she was certain that the sky was blue. Luke looked at her carefully as he asked, "How are you so sure that's all she wants?"

"Because if there was any trouble, she wouldn't have come here alone. There are some men who work here that are a whole lot bigger than you who would have introduced you to a shotgun or club before you had a chance to skin out through a window. And even if none of those fellas were around, she surely wouldn't have stepped outside to give you a chance to get away if she wanted to do you any harm." Placing her hands flat on his chest, Emma said, "She's a good woman and if she tells you she just wants to talk, that's all there is to it. Please, just give her a chance."

Against his better judgment, Luke gave up on trying to escape. Now that he had a chance to think, he realized that not only would he be scurrying off like a coward, but he'd also be abandoning Red in the process. "What does she want to talk about?" he asked.

"I don't know. I've been a little preoccupied for the last hour or so."

He waited for a few seconds while mulling over what she'd told him. What put his mind somewhat at ease was the fact that nobody had made another attempt to get into the room. Luke was being given some measure of trust. It only seemed right that he return the favor.

"All right," he said. "I'll hear her out. It's not like I'd get very far anyway."

"You got that right," Emma told him with a relieved smile. "The last man to try jumping out one of these windows broke both legs when he hit the ground. I've got plans for you, cowboy. Best keep yourself intact."

"I'll do my best."

Once he'd buttoned his shirt, Luke walked over to the door and opened it just enough to get a look outside. The pretty brunette stood there with her hands clasped in front of her in a way that reminded him once again of his schoolteacher. There was nobody else with her. No armed men waiting to pounce. Not even any other girls trying to get in or out of one of the other rooms. Gathering his strength with a deep breath, Luke pulled open the door while wearing the sternest expression he could manage.

"You're Stormy?" he asked.

"That's right. I hope I didn't interrupt anything."

"Not as such. I just didn't know I had to clear out of the room so quickly."

She smiled, but it was nothing like the beaming display she'd put on when was sitting on the front porch. "Like I said before, I'd just like to talk to you for a moment. When we're done, you can go right back and keep Emma company."

"All right, then. Go ahead and talk."

"Not here. Follow me." With that, Stormy turned and walked down the hall without once looking back.

Luke followed before he had a chance to think otherwise. Once he realized how easily he'd fallen in line, he stopped and asked, "Where's Red?"

"Is that your friend?"

"Yes. Where is he?"

Stormy turned back around and said, "Room Four, but I don't think you want to go in there without knocking first."

"Mind if I see for myself?"

"Be my guest. I'll be right in here," she said while motioning toward a door marked OFFICE. "Come right in when you're through with your friend." Stormy used a key to unlock the door, stepped inside, and shut it behind her.

Luke stood in his spot for a few seconds. All he heard was some music and voices from downstairs as well as some scuffling from one of the nearby rooms. His hand rested on his Colt, only this time it was there on purpose. Instinct had become habit in no time at all. Since it seemed to be just him in that hallway for the time being, Luke checked the numbers on the doors and moved along until he got to room number four.

Even before he was close enough to knock, he could hear more than just scuffling coming from inside. Initially, he wanted to move away and let Red have his fun. Then he reminded himself that he couldn't be absolutely certain who was inside that room. There was always the chance that Stormy had sold him a bum steer just to put his mind at ease.

Tapping his knuckles against the door, Luke said, "Hey, Red. You in there?"

The only sounds he heard were grunting and groaning. A man and woman were in there all right. As for who they were was still anyone's guess. Wincing in embarrassment, Luke knocked harder. "Hey, Red!"

"What?" a man roared from the other side of the door. Luke still couldn't be sure it was Red since the voice was strained and breathless.

"It's Luke."

"Whatever you're after, it'd better be good."

After hearing a complete sentence, Luke was able to recognize his friend's voice. "You all right in there?" he asked.

"He's just fine," a woman replied. Luke recognized it as the redhead who'd corralled Red at the very start. "And he's about to get a whole lot better."

There was some giggling and laughing from both of them, followed by more scuffling.

Luke had heard plenty and didn't want to hear whatever was coming next. "Just checking. See you later."

"Don't wait up!" Red said.

More than happy to leave them be, Luke walked back down the hall. When passing Emma's room he felt a pull to go back inside and forget the rest of the world existed for a while longer. As tempting as that was, he was fairly certain that Stormy would only come along to collect him again. She had a sternness about her that spoke of a woman who was accustomed to getting her way. She wasn't a sweet talker like the other women in the place, but someone who carried herself with genuine strength. If there was one lesson Kyle Sobell had taught him, it was that genuine strength should always be respected.

Luke made his way to the office door, reached out to knock, and then retracted his hand so he could just open the door and step inside. The room was smaller than Emma's bedroom, containing a desk, several small cabinets, and a few chairs. Two oil lamps lit the confined space, and their dark green shades made Luke feel as if he were stuck several feet underground. Stormy sat behind the desk without so much as flinching at his unannounced entrance.

"Glad you decided to see me," she said while standing up.

"I said I would, didn't I?"

"There was always the chance that you might leave as soon as you had the chance. I appreciate you giving me your time. Please sit down." When Luke sat, he watched the brunette for any hint that he might be in harm's way. The only move she made was toward one of the cabinets beside her desk. She removed a pair of glasses and a small, strangely shaped bottle.

"Would you like a drink?" she asked.

"Sure."

After pouring out two measures of liquor, she handed one glass to him and then sat back down. Stormy raised her glass and took a drink. As soon as Luke brought the glass near his lips, he could tell it wasn't whiskey. Not wanting to make himself look foolish or timid, he took a drink. Luke's wishes to maintain his composure went out the window when he almost coughed up every drop of liquor that had trickled down his throat.

"It's brandy," she told him. "The taste takes some getting used to."

"Never heard of it," Luke said.

"It's not a common sight in most saloons around here. I don't even serve it downstairs. I save it for special occasions. I can have some beer or whiskey brought up if you'd prefer."

Luke looked her in the eye, took another drink, and forced himself to maintain a straight face. Not only did he keep from coughing again, but he actually found himself enjoying the taste. "You're right," he said with a bit of a rasp left over from the first sip. "It does kinda grow on you."

She smiled at him and sipped from her glass. Closing her eyes, she savored the taste of the drink as well as the heat it brought.

"So, you own this place?" Luke asked.

"I have partners, but yes. I run the day-to-day operations."

"Is your name really Stormy?"

Her eyes opened and locked on to him. "As far as you're concerned, it is. But I'm guessing someone in your line of work is accustomed to folks living under assumed names."

Luke took another drink. His mind filled with possibilities of what she was talking about. Rather than show how desperate he was for a hint of what he should say next, he bought himself some time by mimicking the way Stormy had lingered over the exotic liquor.

Finally she asked, "You are a bounty hunter, right?"

Lowering his glass, Luke felt his temper flare. "Where did you hear about that?"

"From Wayne. He's the man who looks after our stable."

Luke's teeth ground together and a curse rumbled up from the back of his throat.

"Before you get too riled up," she said, "let me assure you he didn't come running to me with this. I understand you wanted to tend to your affairs without everyone knowing who you are."

"But you found out anyway," he snarled.

"That's right. Only because I overheard you two talking when you were outside."

"So you eavesdrop on the folks you call guests?"

"In case you didn't see the name on the sign, this is my place," Stormy told him sternly. "I can come and go as I please, wherever I please, on this property. But no, I wasn't eavesdropping. Your friend had already been brought inside and you were lagging behind. I came out to see if you required anything, only to find you and Wayne engaged in a rather heated discussion. I stayed put in the event you drew your pistol and Wayne needed my help."

"All right. So you heard me talking. Now what?"

Stormy poured another portion of brandy into her glass. "Would you like some more?"

"No," Luke replied.

Holding the glass a few inches beneath her nose, she swirled the liquor around while staring over her desk at him. After a few seconds, she said, "You look rather young to be a bounty hunter."

"Do I?"

"Of course, we get young men in here all the time. Mostly, they want to get their first taste of a woman or feel what it's like to indulge in some of the finer things. Lots of times, it's the sons of rich landowners or ranchers."

"The ones without all that money probably just go to a saloon for their women, right?"

"That's right. To a saloon or an establishment without my high standards. That being said, I still say you seem too young to be the man you claimed to be. Was that just some tough talk to a frail old stable hand or are you truly someone who hunts men for money?"

"What's it matter to you?" Luke asked indignantly.

"How many men have you captured?"

Throughout the years, Luke found that he had a penchant for lying. Although he didn't have the stony face of a poker player, he could weave his words around his situation and surroundings to seem as convincing as possible. He didn't lie unless it was necessary, but so far, Red had been the only one to ever catch him in one. He thought about what Stormy had heard, what she probably knew, and what she could see. Since she already doubted him, he figured trying to talk himself up wasn't the way to go.

"I've brought in a few," he said.

"Who were they?"

"Nobody you would have heard of. I'm just getting started in my line of work, but I've brought in some dangerous men."

"How dangerous?" she asked.

"Dangerous enough to have a price on their head," he told her with a healthy amount of anger in his voice. "If you brought me in here to call me a liar, then I don't have to sit here and take it. All you should be concerned about is whether or not I can pay for what I've gotten here." Standing up, he added, "I assure you I can, so I'd like to get back to some more pleasant company."

"Please, sit down."

There was respecting strength and then there was being shoved around by someone who thought they were stronger. Luke had spent too much of his life being on the receiving end of the latter, and when he heard the tone in Stormy's voice just now, he was ready to show her just how much he hated it.

"You won't tell me to do anything," he snapped. "I don't care how many men you've hired to watch this place. None of them will be able to get into this room before it's too late to make any difference."

Even though he hadn't made a move toward his gun, Luke's voice alone had an effect on the woman in front of him. She wasn't petrified, but the superior glint in her eye was gone as she said, "I'm sorry. It's just that . . . you do look rather young. Most bounty hunters tend to be more experienced."

"And how many bounty hunters do you know?"

"A few."

"You want to know something? The men I did get the drop on made the same mistake you did. They underestimated me on account of how I look. They stood just as tall as you please until I burned them down."

"Have you killed men?" she asked.

"What's it to you?"

Stormy was more shaken than he'd previously thought. She did a good job of keeping her chin up, but when she picked up her brandy glass, her hand was trembling just enough to create ripples in the liquor. She took a sip, set the glass down, and folded her hands on top of her desk. "I didn't mean to offend you. You just are not like most men in such a dangerous line of work."

"I can pull a trigger just fine."

"That's good to hear." Clasping her hands a little tighter, she looked him dead in the eye and said, "I have a business proposition for you."

"Business?"

Stormy nodded. "There's a man in town, not from around here, who owes me a good deal of money. He's apt to leave any day now and doesn't intend to pay. I'd like you to collect it for me."

"And you think a bounty hunter needs to do this?"

"Not a bounty hunter specifically. Just someone willing to shoot this man if push comes to shove. Is this the sort of business you're interested in?"

Chapter 10

It was some time later when Red finally came staggering into the room toward the front of Stormy's that had been made into a small saloon. There was a bar, a few tables, and several ladies lounging about batting their eyelashes at the fellows who came along. Emma must have had a word or two with those ladies, because they didn't try very hard to tempt Luke. Instead they smiled and gave him friendly pats as they walked by as if he'd been taken off the menu. Red was still pulling his suspenders over his shoulders and halfheartedly tucking in his shirt as he approached the bar. He had a few words with one of the girls there, who steered him in the direction of Luke's table. Red went to tip his hat, found he wasn't wearing it, and gave the helpful woman a lazy salute.

"Hot *damn*!" Red exclaimed as he pulled up a chair and dropped himself onto it. "Coming here has got to be the best idea I've ever had. Maybe the best idea anyone's ever had."

"Do you have any money left?" Luke grunted.

"Sitting in paradise and money's all you can think about? There must be somethin' wrong with you. Somethin' up here," Red chided as he tapped Luke's forehead. "Or maybe a little lower. Didn't you get yourself a woman?"

"I did, actually."

"Well, good for you." Twisting around in his chair, Red asked, "Which one is she?"

"Never mind that. I saw Stormy."

"Stormy? She's that sweet little thing that brought us in here, ain't she? Rose told me about her. Said she owns the place. Is that why you're askin' me about money? Did she sweet-talk you out of everything you had?"

"Will you just shut up and listen to me?" Realizing he'd spoken loud enough to be heard throughout most of the room, Luke dropped his voice to a harsh whisper and said, "I was with a lady and Stormy came to find me."

Red's eyebrows shot up and the lewd remarks he wanted to make became so obvious that they might as well have appeared as writing on his face.

"Not for that," Luke quickly said. "She offered me a job."

"Just you?"

"Well . . . us. She overheard us telling the old man outside that we're bounty hunters."

"And she believed it?" Red straightened up and nodded proudly. "We're actually pullin' this off."

"The job sounds pretty simple and the pay isn't bad."

In a matter of seconds, Red's high spirits took a dive. "You took the job?"

"I told her we'd think about it."

"Why?"

"What was I supposed to do?" Luke snapped.

"You were supposed to turn her down flat. I shouldn't have to tell you, but we ain't bounty hunters."

"I know that."

Composing himself quickly, Red took a look around the room to find the few other men in there were too preoccupied by the ladies to take notice of him or Luke. There were two ladies without company at the moment, who were eagerly looking toward the front window, where some new arrivals were being lured inside. Studying Luke a bit more carefully, Red asked, "How long have you been sitting here?"

"An hour or so. Maybe a little more."

"You been drinking?"

"No!"

"Just checking," Red told him. "That might explain a few things if you'd had too much whiskey."

"I'm not drunk. I've been thinking about taking her up on her offer."

Red laughed under his breath as if he'd just caught on to an inside joke. When Luke looked back at him without a trace of a smile on his face, Red snapped right back to the intense scowl he'd had before. "Sometimes it's hard to tell when you're joking."

"I'm not joking."

"Why would you consider something like this? Going to Wichita is crazy enough, but at least I can see what brought that on. Taking on a job, pretending to be something we ain't . . . that's just plain loco."

Instead of getting angry or defensive, Luke knocked his hand against the top of the table and insisted, "It's nothing of the sort. If anything, it'll only help us do what we need to do in Wichita."

"How do you figure?"

"It was going to be hard for men like us to go in and find Granger, but we could have done it."

"So you say," Red grumbled.

Luke continued unabated. "Finding someone like him is easier for someone who's more *like* him."

"First we're bounty hunters, now we're outlaws. If that ain't loco, I don't know what is." When he saw Luke glaring at him across the table, Red eased back into his seat and said, "Go ahead. I won't interrupt no more."

"All she wants us to do is collect some money from a fella who owes her," Luke said in a rush while he still had the floor. "She's got men around here who protect the girls and such, but she's worried that this man she's after will see one of those men coming and get away before any of them get close."

"Is that all she's worried about?"

Reluctantly Luke said, "She also told me there might be shooting."

"So she thinks one of her boys will get shot on sight and instead she sends someone like us to get shot on sight. Sounds real inviting. I see why you'd want to sign on for this job."

"We're not talking about some mad-dog killer," Luke explained. "He's just some blowhard who thinks he can pull one over on a woman. He doesn't have a reason to gun down anyone that comes along. If he doesn't recognize us, we can think of any story we want to have a word with him somewhere private, and when we get the chance . . ."

"What?" Red asked.

Luke was still wearing the expectant smile he'd put on when he thought he'd spelled out his intentions. "When we get the chance, we get the drop on him and take the money away from him."

"So you really do want to be an outlaw."

"That money ain't his, Red. He stole it and we're taking it back."

"How do you figure this will help us in Wichita?"

"That's what I've been sitting here thinking about," Luke said. "We do this job, it gives us something to tell to Granger or one of his friends in regards to our qualifications."

"What qualifications?"

Speaking quickly in much the same way he'd explained countless math problems while they were in school together, Luke said, "It's the same thing we're pulling on this fella who owes the money. We say whatever we got to say to get in close with Granger. Once we're there, we finish the job."

"It sounds to me like you still don't know what this job is."

"I know well enough."

"You're ready to kill this Granger fella?"

"Yes," Luke replied. "I told you already."

"That was when you were still angry and the blood was pounding through you after what happened at your house. I thought you might come to your senses after you had a chance to simmer down."

"If you want me to ease up on my ma and Kyle being killed, then you'll be waiting a long time."

"Then maybe you're eager to join 'em," Red offered.

"Your problem is that you still think I'm this defenseless little kid you once knew. I don't need protecting anymore. If you don't want a part of this, then you're welcome to leave."

Red shook his head. "I said I'd see you through this and that's what I aim to do. I'm just making sure you still know which way you're headed. This trail you're takin' might lead to someplace you don't wanna go."

"It's my trail. I'll go wherever it leads. Besides, it could wind up being good for both of us."

"How do you figure?"

"Something else I been thinking about is this fella who took Stormy's money. If he's done this to her, odds are pretty good he's probably done it to some other folks. That means he'll have more money than just what Stormy's expecting us to bring back."

"We've already got money," Red said.

"The more we have to hand over to Granger, the better our chances are of getting to see him face-to-face."

"Is that something else you've been thinking about?"

"Yep," Luke replied. "Even if this fella Stormy is after doesn't have one penny more than what he took from her, going up against him still buys us plenty. It's something we can talk about that makes us look more like dangerous men because it's a true story that can be backed up. Also, it'll give us a bit of practice before we go up against a man like Granger or anyone riding with him."

"Now, that," Red said while pointing across the table, "is the first sensible thing you've said since I sat down."

"If we can't go against a man like this thief, we don't have any business sniffing after Granger or stepping foot into Wichita."

"What happens if we get whipped by this thief you're talking about? That is, if we walk away from him at all?"

"Then we go home. Leastways, we don't go to Wichita."

Red's eyes narrowed as if he were squinting through his friend's surface to get a look at what was boiling underneath. "I don't think you believe that."

"I don't," Luke told him without a twitch. "Because I think the two of us can do this job and do it well. Even though I was heeled when I went in to talk to Stormy, she told me I was too young to be who I was claiming to be."

"She was right about that."

"My point is that us looking the way we do will work in our favor. If we can get this thief to underestimate us the same way, then getting up close to him will be even easier."

"What did you do to convince her that you could handle this job?" Red asked.

"Honestly, I don't know. She changed her tune real quick, though."

"You think she might be throwing us to the wolves?"

That stopped Luke in his tracks. "What do you mean?"

"I mean maybe she's trying to get someone to go after this thief or whoever he is as some kind of distraction or . . . I don't know. We only met these people a couple hours ago. They could be angels or they could be devils. Who can tell what they're really after?"

After a pause, Luke said, "Then we'll have to be careful. Besides, it's not like we're talking about some desperado who's wanted in five states."

"You don't know that either!"

"If he was so dangerous, he'd have better things to do than cheat some cathouse out of a few dollars." Seeing that he was making some headway, Luke added, "I bet you could think of a pretty easy way to get a look at this fella to see what sort of man he is."

"You know where to find him?"

Luke nodded. "Stormy told me right where to look."

The wheels were turning within Red's mind. Luke could tell as much by the way his friend drummed his fingers against the table in a steady pattern of dull taps. All around them, women were laughing, men were boasting, a banjo was playing, and bottles were clanking against the tops of glasses. "What's his name?"

"Carlo Procci."

"Never heard of him," Red grunted.

"In this case, that's a good thing."

"Where do we look for him?"

"Stormy told him where he was staying," Luke said. "It's a hotel not too far from here."

"You know which room?"

"Yes, but she also said he's moved on from there. Been hiding out since he stole that money."

"When do we have to get to him?" Red asked.

"Soon. He's leaving town pretty quick."

"He may already be gone."

"Then we should hurry," Luke shot back.

Red's expression became intense as if he was locked in some sort of contest with the young man sitting across from him. "If he's not at his hotel, then where do we find him?"

"Stormy told me he's a cardplayer and that he favors two saloons here in town."

"If he ain't at either of them?" Red asked.

"Then we go look at the stable where he's keeping his horse. Before you ask, yes, I know which stable it is and, yes, I know what kind of horse he rides."

"This lady was mighty thorough."

Luke nodded. "I'd say she spends a lot of time sitting outside and sizing men up just like she did with you and me. She sees a whole lot and makes it her business to remember as much as she can."

"You put all that together while I was with Rose, didn't you?"

"Mostly."

Red sighed. "What if things don't go well?"

"Then you won't have to worry about Wichita anymore because we'll either be dead or too hurt to ride."

Even though Luke barely flinched when he said that, Red knew him well enough to tell when he was joking. "You think it's funny now, but it might be a whole different story when things get rough."

"We've already seen things get rough."

"Not with someone who might be a real killer."

"If we can't handle this, I'll forget all about Wichita," Luke said.

"You swear?"

"Yes."

Red held his hand in front of his mouth, spat on his

palm, and stuck it out toward his friend. Luke spat on his own palm before shaking Red's hand.

"There's no going back now," Red told him.

"I agree."

"What I mean is, you break a promise after this and that makes you no better than a mangy dog in the street."

"How many times do I have to tell you?"

"Once more."

"We don't pull this off," Luke vowed, "we go home." Tightening his grip on his friend's hand, he added, "But if we *do* pull it off, we ride from here on without looking back or otherwise second-guessing ourselves. That makes us look weak."

"This is all my fault," Red groaned as he took his hand back. "I ain't gonna leave you with so much time to think anymore."

Chapter 11

Before leaving Stormy's later that afternoon, Luke and Red had another drink. They passed it off as a way to bring them good luck for the venture they'd decided to undertake, but both of them knew they needed the extra dose of firewater to steel themselves for what lay ahead. Luke wasn't about to turn back for any reason whatsoever because he was too invested in the outcome and Red just wasn't cut from the cloth of a quitter. They tipped back their drinks, slammed their glasses down, and, better or worse, good idea or not, marched outside.

After heading down the street and turning a corner, they were close enough to see the place that Luke had been searching for. Pointing to a shabby carriage house next to a cluttered lot, Luke said, "That's the place where our man is keeping his horse."

"What's his name again?" Red asked.

"Carlo Procci."

"He an Italian?"

"I guess," Luke snapped. "What's that matter?"

"I don't know. Just asking." Dropping to a knee, Red ground his hands into a pile of mud and smeared some onto his face.

Watching him with a mixture of confusion and disgust, Luke asked, "What are you doing?"

"I'm gonna go in and say I'm a friend of his or some angry fella looking for him. I haven't decided which. Either way, I can't go in smelling like all that lilac water Rose rubbed on me. They'll think I'm a dandy."

"Nobody would have mistaken you for a dandy," Luke scoffed. "A ranch hand who wandered in to get his toes curled, maybe, but not a dandy."

"You want to do your own scouting? Just let me do this my way."

Luke took a step back and raised his hands, allowing his friend to approach the stable without another word.

As he headed toward the stable, Red patted his belt to feel the Smith & Wesson still tucked where it always was. Although he'd fired the pistol plenty of times and knew it as well as he knew his own hand, the gun's presence wasn't inspiring the normal amount of confidence. Fortunately someone was already emerging from the stable so Red didn't have to think about whether or not he was ready for a confrontation.

"What can I do for you?" asked a lanky man in dirty brown pants and a dusty blue shirt. "Since you don't have a horse with you, perhaps you're interested in buying one? I got a few for sale."

"I don't want to buy nothing," Red snarled with a bit more ferocity than the words required. "I'm looking for someone."

"I don't know what I can do about—"

"He's a customer of yours," Red cut in. "Carlo Procci. You know him?"

"I do know him."

Pulling his shirt from where it had been hastily tucked into his waistband, Red made sure the skinny fellow could see the Smith & Wesson as he said, "Tell me where to find him!"

The other man hopped back as if he'd just found himself at the wrong end of a cannon. His eyes grew wide and his hands shot out to either side. "No need for that! He's inside. Just go and see for yourself. I wasn't about to make any trouble. Go on inside!"

"That's right. You ain't gonna cause any trouble. That includes you going and fetching anyone else, you hear?"

"I don't know your business with that man inside and I don't wanna know."

"You don't wanna get no law either," Red warned.

The other man shook his head so vigorously that it seemed close to rattling off his shoulders. "There ain't no trouble. I got no reason to stand in your way."

Now that the other man had proven so easy to shove around, Red didn't quite know what to do with him. "All right, then," he said while trying to maintain the same intensity he'd had a moment ago. "Sorry about the cross words."

Now the other man was confused. He squinted at Red and lowered his hands. "Ummm . . . you're sorry?"

"Just go."

"You want me to go now?"

Too irritated with himself to say another word, Red grumbled angrily and stormed into the stable. As long as the skinny fellow didn't follow him, he didn't much care what he did.

The stable was much longer than it was wide, which meant it was considerably larger than he'd first thought. Sunlight shone in through several large holes in the roof. Dust trickled down from various loose boards overhead as well as from a loft that seemed barely sound enough to hold the few bales of hay being stored there. The straw on the floor was so matted that most of it was stuck to the boards. Of the five stalls sectioned off by low walls, three had functioning gates and only one of those was occupied by a horse.

Red stepped inside wearing a terse expression. His arms were at his sides, and his right hand was close enough to the Smith & Wesson to draw it the moment he thought it was needed. So far, the only distressing thing he encountered within the stable was the stench.

"Hello?" he called out.

There was no reply.

Cautiously moving forward, Red glanced back and forth at what was on either side. He saw the usual assortment of tools, feed bags, harnesses, and such that could be found in any stable and not much else. One trough was filled with water that would have made a swamp look like a crystal-clear stream. One stall must have been rented recently because it was almost fit for an animal to use. Midway through, he came upon the occupied stall. The light gray horse inside was chewing lazily on its feed and barely took notice of Red with its large, dark eyes. Its coarse mane was a mix of gray and black. After taking stock of Red, it snuffed and got back to its chewing.

Red's eyes were drawn to the saddlebags piled in one corner of the stall. Before he had a chance to wonder about why those bags had been left there, he spotted a man lying propped against the wall beside them. He was mostly covered by a blanket meant for the horse. Enough straw and dirt had either fallen onto him or been kicked onto him that he would have been easy to miss by an unaware passerby.

"Hey," Red barked.

For a moment, Red thought the man half-buried in the straw was dead. Not only wasn't he moving, but his entire body was twisted at such a strange angle that it seemed most likely he'd been tossed there like so much refuse. When Red tried to push open the gate to get inside, it rattled noisily on its hinges. He pulled the rusted latch and eventually had to kick the gate before it would swing aside for him. Only then did the man in the stall behave like anything more than a corpse.

"Wha . . . ?" the man groaned.

Red stood just inside the stall. "Are you Carlo Procci?"

After making one attempt to lift his head, the man on the floor grunted and shifted beneath the blanket. His upper body was still skewed at a different angle than his head, and the one hand protruding from beneath the straw was balled up so tightly that it was hard to tell if it was his right or left.

"I'm talkin' to you!" Red said as he stomped forward. "You'd best answer me."

"Or what?" the man asked in a haggard voice.

"Or . . . there'll be hell to pay!"

The man shifted some more until he was more or less lying on his back. Using the exposed hand, which now could be seen as his left, he pushed his hat back away from his face so he could get a less obstructed view of the other person in the stall with him. His nose was long, angular, and had been broken at least twice throughout his thirty-some years. Thin eyebrows and high cheekbones framed a pair of clouded blue eyes. The rest of his face was covered in thick layers of greasy whiskers that were too scattered and wild to be considered a proper beard. After looking at Red for all of two seconds, he let out a gurgling belch and set his head back down.

"Did you hear me?" Red asked.

"I'd be deaf if I hadn't."

"Are you Carlo Procci?"

"If I say yes, will you let me get back to sleep?"

Red stood his ground and watched the man get situated on the floor. So far, his scouting plan hadn't only backfired, but left him painted in a corner and unsure as to whether or not the man in the stall was answering his question or just trying to get some peace and quiet. "Is this Carlo Procci's horse?" Red asked.

"Yeah."

"What would you say if I took it?"

"He drinks more water than a fish and doesn't like the rain," the man replied.

Red walked over to the horse, who barely acknowledged him as he reached out to take hold of its mane. Since his actions weren't sparking much of anything from either of the other souls in that stall, Red let go of the coarse, wiry hair and moved back through the gate. From there, he went all the way to the rear of the stable to examine the other stalls.

Unless there was another man hidden even better than the first one he'd stumbled across, it seemed that the one sharing the stall with the gray horse was the only other person in there. Red went back outside to find the skinny fellow right where he'd left him.

"You say Carlo Procci is in there?" Red asked.

Suddenly looking as if he was regretting staying put, the stable man said, "That's right."

"Scraggly-looking man with a gray horse?"

"Yessir. He paid extra to bunk down in that stall with his horse. I suppose he couldn't afford no room at a hotel."

Red glanced back inside the stable as if someone else might appear, shrugged, and walked away.

"You conduct your business with him?" the skinny man asked.

"We'll see about that."

Chapter 12

"So," Luke said as soon as Red was close enough to hear him, "was his horse in there?"

Red crossed the street to where Luke was standing and took a look over his shoulder as if to make sure the stable was still there. "I guess so."

"What's that supposed to mean?"

"It means I asked where to find Carlo Procci and was told he was inside."

"That was your big plan?" Luke asked. "Ask if he was there? Anyone could have done that."

"Then you should have done it yourself!"

"So, what did you find out? You think he'll be a problem?"

"Nah," Red told him. "If that's Carlo Procci in there, he won't be any problem at all. He ain't much more than a vagrant sleeping in a dirty horse stall."

"*If* that's Carlo Procci? You're not even sure?"

"I was just supposed to go in and scout. That's what I did. Far as I know, that's Carlo Procci and his horse in there." Red stepped aside and swept his arms toward the stable. "You want to proceed with the rest of the job you took for no good reason? Be my guest."

Rather than start fighting about why he'd taken Stormy up on her offer again, Luke walked past him and headed straight for the stable. After a few more steps, he could hear his friend keeping pace behind him.

By the time he'd made it to the stable, Luke had worked up quite a head of steam. Red was only chuckling under his breath behind him, which got under his skin to no end. The skinny fellow who was touching up the paint of a sign advertising the stable's daily rates saw them coming and immediately became nervous.

"Excuse me," Luke said in a choppy, impatient tone. "You know a man named Carlo Procci?"

The skinny fellow started to say something, but choked it down again. He then glanced over to Red and closed his mouth tight. Looking back to Luke, the fellow set down his can of paint, placed his brush on top of it, turned around, and walked away.

Luke pulled open the narrow door built close to the larger twin doors at the front of the stable. Wincing as he was hit by the smell of manure that needed to be cleaned out and moldy hay that needed to be swept away, he looked to his friend and asked, "Where is he?"

"In the stall with the horse," Red replied.

Before asking which stall that was, Luke saw there was only one with a horse in it and walked over to it. The gate to that stall was still ajar after Red had been there, and the gray horse on the other side of it didn't seem the least bit interested in taking a run for its freedom. The man who'd been lying on the floor had since kicked off his blanket and was sitting with his back against the wall and his long, lanky legs bent so his feet were flat against the ground.

"Are you Carlo Procci?" Luke asked.

"Why's everyone so damn interested in me today?" the man grunted.

"Are you or aren't you?"

The man snapped his eyes up toward both young men

and said, "I'm him. What do you want that's so important I can't finish the sleep I started?"

"You owe Miss Stormy some money."

"Miss Stormy, huh?" Carlo chided. "Did she send you over here promising a discount to put a scare into me? Go on back and tell her you did just fine. I'm petrified."

"Whatever her real name is, you know who I'm talking about. She's the one that owns the cathouse down the street."

"Hard to miss that place," Carlo said.

"You owe her some money," Luke continued. "And I'm here to collect."

Placing his hands on his knees, Carlo looked back and forth between the two young men. "You're the best she could find?"

Luke nodded. "We're bounty hunters."

That brought Carlo to his feet in a rush. It wasn't a scramble to pull himself up, but more of a flicker of motion that ended with him standing at his full height before either Red or Luke could do much about it. Although he was still filthy, Carlo didn't seem nearly as scattered as he had a moment ago. Instead of the tired vagrant Red had found sleeping with his horse, Procci was an armed man who stood several inches taller than both of the younger men.

It took a moment for Luke to digest the fact that Carlo was on his feet. The fact that Carlo wore a gun strapped around his waist sank in a moment later.

"How much money do I owe Miss Stormy?" Carlo asked in a tone that made the last two words sound like a lewd joke.

"Five hundred dollars."

"What's your cut? Ten percent? Twenty?"

"Twenty," Luke replied.

"Guess it stands to reason," Carlo said. "You get what you pay for."

Tired of being regarded as if he was something better suited to drink from one of the dirty troughs in another stall, Red pulled himself up by his bootstraps and said, "It don't make one bit of difference what you think of us."

"Good, because I sure don't think you're bounty hunters."

"All that matters is that we're here," Red told him. "And that you owe a lady some money."

"Lady?" Carlo sneered. "Have you met Stormy?"

"Yes," Luke said sternly.

Carlo eased his hat back far enough to scratch beneath it. "I suppose she conducts herself a lot better than some of the dogs in heat that work for her. There's a piece of work named Rose who makes a rough stretch of road look like a primrose path."

Red's brow furrowed and he took half a step forward. "What did you say?" he growled.

Grinning, Carlo said, "And she insists on dousing her boys with lilac water. The kind of stuff that still stinks to high heaven no matter how much mud gets on you afterward."

Luke extended an arm to keep his friend from going any farther. "We're just here for the money. Hand over what you owe."

"Or what?" Carlo asked. "There'll be hell to pay?"

"Something like that."

As the three of them squared off, the air within the stable became still. All was quiet apart from the rattle of a wagon passing on the street outside and the gray horse's occasional shift from one hoof to another. Luke's guns were within easy reach, but he suddenly wasn't eager to draw them. It was plain to see that Carlo Procci wasn't to be taken lightly. Beneath the layers of filth and rumpled clothes was a coiled snake, tensed and ready to strike. Although Luke felt the need to tread lightly, he could tell Red wasn't thinking so clearly.

Sure enough, Red made a grab for his Smith & Wesson. Carlo lunged forward to take hold of Red's wrist so he could force him to pull the pistol from where it had been kept and point it away. Either out of surprise or desperation, Red pulled his trigger. The shot cracked through the air, sending a .22-caliber round whistling past Carlo's head to knock another hole into the wall behind him. Without reacting much to the shot that had just been fired, Carlo twisted Red's hand until he had to drop the pistol and then caught it before it hit the floor.

"This all you brought?" Carlo scoffed as he tossed the Smith & Wesson into the hay where he'd been sleeping. "Sorriest excuse for a bounty hunter I've ever seen."

Luke cussed under his breath and drew one of the pistols holstered at his side. Before he could clear leather, Carlo's leg came up and his boot thumped into Luke's gut. If he hadn't already been tensed, Luke wouldn't have been able to breathe. As it was, he still felt a good portion of the wind spout from his lungs as he was knocked a step back.

"You still think this is worth a hundred dollars?" Carlo asked. "That's only fifty for each of you."

Neither of the younger men responded with words. Luke struggled to catch his breath and regain his footing while Red lowered his shoulder and charged at Carlo like a bull.

Carlo was grinning from ear to ear as he turned toward Red and opened his arms as if to wrap him up in a warm welcome. He grunted as Red plowed into him and forced his back to a wall. After they'd come to a stop,

Carlo pushed against both of Red's shoulders to gain enough room to bring his knee up into Red's chest. Although he wheezed after taking the blow, Red responded with renewed vigor as he grabbed Carlo's legs and pulled them out from under him. Both of them toppled to the floor and started fighting to gain the upper hand.

"I got him, Luke!" Red said as he placed his forearm across Carlo's neck and leaned down on it. "You get the money!"

"You sure?" Luke asked.

"Just get it!"

Luke had drawn one of the pistols from its holster and was surprised to see it wasn't the Colt. In his haste to arm himself, he'd skinned one of the pistols taken from Scott. The gun felt uncomfortable in his grasp, which was what troubled him about taking it in the first place. If he needed to use a weapon to defend himself, he knew better than to take his chances with one that wasn't familiar. Rather than waste time in switching guns, he went over to the saddlebags piled near the tethered horse.

The other two were making plenty of noise but didn't seem to be making much headway. As soon as one appeared to be coming out on top, the other would sneak in a quick punch or squirm in such a way that gave him a fleeting advantage. Red was just about to be tossed onto his back when he planted one foot squarely in place and pushed off to put some extra power behind the fist he slammed into Carlo's side. Carlo let out a strained moan and curled into a ball.

"Red!" Luke shouted. "Catch!"

Red looked toward his friend as Scott's second pistol sailed toward him. Although he was quick enough to catch the gun before it cracked him in the face, Red needed a moment to get a proper grip. By the time his finger had found the trigger, Carlo was on his feet.

Procci might have looked unruly before, but now he was a battered, bloody savage covered in sweat and glaring at Luke with wild eyes. Instead of diving for cover or even drawing his own pistol, he rushed straight at Red as if the gun in the younger man's hand were a toy. "Come on now," Carlo said through gritted teeth as he slapped the gun aside. The pistol barked loudly and sent a round through the neighboring stall. "You've got to do better than that!"

Red was quick to pull his gun back, but not fast enough to track Carlo as he surged forward and to one side. When he pulled his trigger again, Red's bullet sailed through empty air.

"Some bounty hunter," Carlo said as he flicked a powerful jab into Red's stomach.

Even though the punch landed in a spot that had been tenderized earlier in the fight, Red swung his hand in a chopping blow that knocked the pistol against the side of Carlo's head. Staggering like a drunk, Carlo moved out of Red's reach and then turned around. Red fired one more time, snapping Carlo's head back.

Red's breath caught in his throat when he saw a bit of blood fly through the air. Carlo remained upright for a second before his knees buckled and he fell onto the horse blanket lying on the floor behind him. "I . . . got him," Red said between labored breaths.

"Is he dead?" Luke asked.

Without turning his eyes away from the fallen man, Red said, "Just find that money. I'll have a look."

Red's gun hand was steady as he approached Carlo. His eyes burned with a mixture of sweat trickling from his brow and grit from the gun smoke in the air that stuck to his face. His heart was pounding hard enough to make his breath jumpy and irregular.

So far, Carlo hadn't moved. He lay on his side with his

limbs splayed like a dog that was taking a nap. A small amount of blood was smeared on the floor near his head, and there was surely plenty more beneath it. Red shifted his focus down to the man's chest to look for a sign of life. "He ain't dead. Looks like he should be comin' to soon."

The door swung open and smacked against the front wall of the stable. "What's going on in here?" the skinny man from outside asked. "What's the shooting about?"

Red turned to tell the skinny fellow to get lost, only to find him brandishing a shotgun. Both barrels were pointed at the stall where everyone and his horse were gathered.

"Leave us be!" Carlo said as he pulled himself up off the floor.

The skinny fellow brought the shotgun to his shoulder and took a few steps closer. "This is my place and I'm through with being shoved around by everyone that comes along. You men get out or—"

Propping himself up on one arm, Carlo lifted his other arm to point a gun toward the stable's entrance. He fired a shot that burned a path well above the skinny fellow's head before saying, "Go on and git!"

The skinny fellow turned tail and went.

Bending his arm so his pistol was now aimed at the roof, Carlo grunted, "I'm through with being threatened by ultimatums from lesser men."

"Who're you callin' a lesser man?" Red demanded.

Slowly, Carlo shifted his gaze toward him. Smoke still curled from the barrel of his gun to form a crooked halo near his head. "Don't test me, boy. Leastways, don't test me any more than you've already . . . aw, just help me up, will you?"

Red looked over to Luke, who was now sifting through the second saddlebag in the pile. Since he didn't get anything helpful from him, he pointed the gun in his hand down at Carlo and thumbed back the hammer. "Put your gun away first," he said.

"Sure, sure," Carlo muttered while stuffing the pistol back into its holster.

"No, I mean drop the gun. Toss it away."

Carlo sighed, removed the gun gingerly, and threw it toward Red's boots.

Even though he'd been the one to make the request, Red didn't seem to know quite what to do now that it had been obeyed. Carlo extended his hand toward him, but Red took a step back and straightened his gun arm. "On second thought, help yourself up," he said.

"Finally thinking before you act," Carlo said as he climbed to his feet. "That's a step in the right direction."

"Mister, you don't know anything about me or what direction I need to go. Luke, did you find what you're looking for?"

Having already reached the bottom of the second saddlebag, Luke upended both of them and dumped their scant contents onto the floor. Looking down at the various things, he replied, "No. There's nothing here worth any amount of money."

"So you were really sent here by Stormy?" Carlo asked.

"That's right," Red told him.

Rubbing the side of his head, he winced and checked the tips of his fingers. There was some blood on his hand and when he touched his left ear, he grimaced. "That was a close shave," he said good-naturedly while turning to show that side of his head to Red. His ear was slick with blood, and a small piece of it had been chipped away by the bullet from Red's gun. "If your aim was a little better or if you had shown up a little earlier, I guess I would have been in real trouble."

"Do you have the money or not?" Luke asked. "We're tired of wasting time with you."

"Then by all means," Carlo said, "be on your way. I'd be just fine if I never saw the two of you again."

Drawing the old Colt gave Luke some comfort. He pointed the familiar pistol at Carlo's head and said, "Stormy wanted me to hurt you if you put up too much of a fuss. I thought we'd just get the money and be through with it, but now I'm warming up to her idea."

After scowling in thought for a few seconds, Carlo said, "Yeah, that does sound like something she'd say."

"So start being helpful before you run out of time."

"I'd say we're both on borrowed time," Carlo warned. "After all the shooting and such, it won't be long before someone else comes along to make sure the trouble don't spread. Maybe even the law."

Although Red became more anxious at the mention of having to answer to the law in a strange town, Luke didn't flinch.

"Something tells me you'd have more to lose than we would if you had to face a lawman," Luke said.

Carlo shrugged without giving away much. "Maybe."

"And those same lawmen would probably understand if a man like you wound up dead in a pile of filth like this."

This time, Carlo was the one who twitched.

Luke nodded, recognizing he'd gained the upper hand. "We may not be bounty hunters, but I bet we'd still get more than fifty dollars each if we put you down and waited here for those lawmen to show up."

"There's an idea," Red chimed in. "That way, we wouldn't even have to drag his carcass anywhere to cash it in!"

"You want the whore's money?" Carlo growled. "You can have it."

"That's better," Luke said. "Where is it?"

"It ain't here."

Luke shook his head and sighted along the top of his barrel. "No more games, mister. Tell me where it is."

"If I had known how much trouble would come along with that little bit of cash, I never would have taken it. Aw, who am I kidding?" Carlo continued as though he weren't talking to anyone in the stable with him. "I would've taken it."

"Start telling us what we need to know," Red demanded.

Looking around to survey the entire stable, Carlo said, "We need to get out of here. That is, unless you really do want to speak to the law. That fella outside had the look of a simpering little rat that's bound to go scampering off to fetch help."

"Aw, to hell with this," Red groaned. "I say we cut our losses and be done with this job. It's gone too far south as it is."

"Carlo's right," Luke said. "We can't have the law sniffing after us. We started a job and I aim to see it through. Besides, we came this far. Sounds like we don't have much farther to go. There's a back door. Let's get out of here."

"Finally, someone who listens to reason," Carlo said.

After scooping up Carlo's gun and jamming its barrel into his back, Red shoved him toward the door and said, "Don't get yer hopes up."

Chapter 13

"You might want to put that gun away," Carlo said as he was shoved down a narrow street with nobody else on it and only a few shabby buildings on either side. The way he kept looking around, he might have been expecting a parade to march down it at any second.

"Why?" Luke asked. "You worried about upsetting the rats?"

The street narrowed to a dirt path. On one side, a slow trickle of sewage made its way to a small, stinking pool behind them. Rodents and a few mangy dogs stared at them from the shadows, none of them willing to budge from the territory they'd staked out unless absolutely necessary.

"I'm just saying we did well to avoid the law before," Carlo said. "No need to draw attention now."

"Just tell us where we're headed and let us sort out the rest," Red said as he shoved Carlo along.

The three of them formed a strange procession as they moved toward a corner that emptied onto a much larger street. A few more people were walking there, but nobody displayed any panic arising from the disturbance in the stable. Red walked beside Carlo, and Luke was behind them, holding the Colt.

Turning to look at both men as he continued walking

at his leisurely pace, Carlo said, "I'm not exactly sure where, but I know who."

"What are you taking about?" Red asked.

"The money I owed to Stormy—"

"*Still* owe to Stormy," Luke corrected.

Carlo rolled his eyes. "You're a real stickler. I bet you were a lot of fun in school."

"You have no idea," Red chuckled.

Jabbing the pistol into Carlo's spine, Luke snapped, "Get on with it."

"That money I owe," Carlo said, "it wasn't just to Stormy. It was to a few other folks in this town and a few others besides. I've been paying them off as best I can, but it's been slow going. Times are hard with the war and all. When it comes to paying folks back, a man's gotta pick and choose."

"You mean Stormy's behind someone else in the chow line," Red said.

Carlo stopped and turned around. "And here I thought he was the smart one," he said while nodding toward Luke.

Making sure the Colt was front and center, Luke said, "You sure aren't very smart if you think you're calling the shots here."

"I told you to put the gun away, boy. There's no reason to wave it about."

"I can come up with plenty of good reasons."

"It's just going to get you into trouble," Carlo warned. "Seems to me like it already has."

"I'm not going to let you walk about free as you please."

Carlo looked as if he was genuinely amused by that. While turning to look at Red, he snapped one hand out to grab hold of the Colt around the gun's middle. With a twist and a pull, he'd forced Luke to let go of the pistol and taken it clean away from him. The entire process was over in less than two seconds.

"There, now," Carlo said as he spun the Colt around so he could slip his finger beneath the trigger guard. "See what I mean about this gun getting you into trouble?"

"Give it back to him," Red warned. His gun was in hand and pointed at Carlo.

The older man didn't move as he asked, "Do you honestly think I can't put a bullet into you if I choose?"

"Maybe," Red said. "But not before I put one through you. This time I'll hit something more vital than your ear."

Carlo's only response to that was a skeptically raised eyebrow.

"So you can come and go as you please," Luke said. "We've established that. What now?"

"Now I'll see about getting Stormy's money for you," Carlo said.

"You'll help us? Why?"

"Because I said I would. Besides," Carlo added, "that money isn't in my pockets now and it won't be in my pockets if Stormy has it. I'm served better by settling things here and moving on to somewhere else that I can work without so many so-called bounty hunters nipping at my heels."

"We won't get much farther if we stand here pointing our guns at one another."

In another series of motions that was almost too quick for Luke or Red to see, Carlo spun the pistol around so it dangled from his finger instead of being aimed at anyone. "I was right," he said. "You are the smart one." When Red tried to take the gun away from him, Carlo spun it again and dropped it into his holster. "Why don't I keep this for now? That is, unless you want to trade me for my own firearm."

"Might as well," Luke said.

Red looked over at him and asked, "What is wrong with you?"

"He's got a gun now," Luke replied. "Doesn't much matter which it is. Just give it to him as a show of good faith. If he doesn't give us what we're after, we can go back to threatening each other."

By the time Red had retrieved Carlo's pistol, Carlo offered the gun he'd taken in an open hand. The exchange wasn't as quick as Carlo's draw, but was over swiftly and all three of them were soon walking toward the busier street.

"So, where are you leading us?" Luke asked.

"The man I came to town to pay is named Jordan Bickle. I met up with him at a saloon and don't rightly know where to find him again, but I do know someone who should be able to point us in the right direction. He's got that money you're after."

"And you're willing to get it back for us?" Luke asked suspiciously.

"Let's just say it doesn't serve my purpose for anyone to know I had that money to begin with. Since you two, Stormy, and God only knows how many others know about it, I'd rather he be cut out altogether. Besides," he added with a wry smirk, "you two got the drop on me and are calling all the shots."

"There's more to it than that."

"All right," Carlo replied. "I paid this man more than I owed to Stormy. We get that money back, you take her share back, I take the rest, and we go our separate ways. Sound good?"

Luke looked over to Red, got a noncommittal shrug, and said, "Sounds fine to me."

When they reached the corner, it was as if they'd stepped out of a dreary tunnel and back into the above-ground world. There were people to be seen instead of just rats and dogs. The buildings weren't as close to falling over, and most of the windows in sight weren't busted.

Carlo had just found his stride when he realized he was walking all by himself. "What's the matter?" he asked. "If you think I'm doing all this walking alone, you're mistaken."

"Jordan Bickle," Red repeated. "Why does that name sound familiar?"

Luke was thinking as well but arrived at his conclusion in no time at all. "He's the owner of the Eastern Trading Company."

Red snapped his fingers. "That's where I heard it! That fella watching our horses mentioned it!"

"The Eastern Trading Company? Are you sure?" Carlo asked.

"That's what we were told," Luke said. "We'll start there."

Carlo blinked a few times, glanced around at the rest of the street, and then shrugged. "Let's go and see if that information you got was accurate or not."

"Why would an old stable hand lie about something like that?" Red asked.

"If I need to answer that question," Carlo replied, "then you need all the help you can get."

Chapter 14

The Eastern Trading Company wasn't hard to find. Luke only needed to ask more than one person about it because the first had been too drunk to point in the right direction. The second local only had to wave toward a nearby corner. By the time the three men had walked halfway there, they could see the large building situated behind piles of lumber and other supplies that were too large to be moved inside. Three wagons were parked in the street directly in front of the place where half a dozen burly men worked to unload various other items packed in crates, sacks, and bundles wrapped in paper and twine.

One man who wasn't unloading a wagon or carrying something into the store was being very noisy about overseeing the process. He had a moon-shaped face that was reddened from the labored breaths he was spewing and a plump body wrapped in sweat-stained clothes. "You there," he called out to one of the workers. "Bring that over here and set it down."

The man at the receiving end of that order was half the size of the moon-faced man and carried a stack of no fewer than five small crates. He was more than happy to set them down near the front of the store so he could stretch his back and wipe his brow.

"Is this the shipment from San Francisco?" the moon-faced man asked.

"Yes, sir, Mr. Bickle."

"Get a pry bar."

The worker went to a wagon and scrounged for the tool. When he tried handing it over, Bickle looked at him as if he'd sprouted horns.

"Well, go on and pry it open!" Bickle snapped. "You don't think I'm just going to sign for something like this without checking it first?"

Surely the worker had some things in mind he wanted to say, but he kept them to himself as he levered the top crate open.

The crate was about twice as long as it was wide. Despite its only being around a foot deep, he had to remove a few more slender pieces of wood that were used to keep the contents from shifting during shipment. When he was able to reach a little deeper, Bickle smiled and removed a slender brass candlestick from the crate as if he were handling a newborn child.

"Look here," Bickle said. "This is some of the finest craftsmanship this side of the Atlantic Ocean."

When the worker started reaching out toward the crate to see a sample up close, his hand was promptly smacked aside.

"I said to look here," Bickle said. "Look! Not touch. Now go get a hammer so you can seal this up again."

"Seal it up? It just needs to go inside that door."

"And I don't want anything to happen to my merchandise before it gets to where it needs to be."

The worker glanced at the door, which was less than three paces away, and then back to the stack of small crates. Instead of arguing with the man who was already flushed with anger because someone had almost touched a candlestick, he shrugged and went back to the wagon to retrieve a hammer.

Bickle put the candlestick back in its crate and carefully set the thin wooden support slat on top of it before replacing the cover. He took a step back and grew impatient with the worker's progress in a matter of seconds. The longer he stood by and watched the other workers move back and forth, the more anxious he became. When one of the workers actually nudged the stack of crates as he walked by, Bickle grabbed the open one on top and clutched it to his chest so he could walk it into the store himself.

When he turned toward the doors that were propped open, he got a look straight down Westminster Street. That was a busy part of town on most days, but he made it a habit to examine every face that came along. After all, the entire town and the world beyond were filled with potential customers. When he saw one of those faces, however, his first thought wasn't what he could sell to the person attached to it.

"Hey there, Jordan!" Carlo said as he waved from the street. "I see you've got some roots in town after all."

Bickle wanted to run. His feet were more than happy to comply and his arms started to ditch the load they were carrying before his greed kicked in to overpower it all. He fumbled with the crate and frantically searched for a direction he could go that was unobstructed. The store's front entrance was filled with workers on their way to pick up another load. The street behind him was blocked by wagons. Directly across from the store was a row of smaller shops and a bank. A farmer driving a cart down the street was moving slowly enough to pose the least of all threats. At least, that's what Bickle came up with before running in front of the cart while clutching his precious merchandise.

"Look where you're goin', you bleedin' fool!" the farmer in the cart shouted as he pulled back on his reins.

After running a scant couple of yards, Bickle was already sweating profusely. He veered to one side before hopping onto the boardwalk and shoving past a young couple and a little girl dressed in a bright yellow skirt.

"Mr. Bickle?" the young woman said after narrowly escaping being knocked over by the large man. "Is something wrong?"

He twisted around to find Carlo stepping onto the boardwalk about twenty yards behind him. "That man . . . he . . ." Before he could come up with anything else to say, panic swept through him and he bolted in the opposite direction.

Carlo strode down the boardwalk but wasn't about to start running just yet. Judging by the grin on his face, he was enjoying the spectacle of watching Bickle stumble and sputter like a broken windup toy.

The couple escorting the girl in the yellow dress weren't the only ones who'd taken notice of the frantic shopkeeper. A few of the other folks walking nearby tried to question Bickle, only to get a few hastily spat syllables in response. Some of the curious locals looked around for the source of Bickle's frenzy, and when they couldn't see a maniac with a gun or a pack of wild dogs, most of them shrugged and went about their business. One had a keen enough eye to pick out what had caused Bickle's distress and stepped in to assert himself.

"Just what do you think you're doing?" the man with the little girl in yellow asked.

Having been stopped by the young fellow, Carlo started moving by without a word and was blocked once again.

The man stepped in Carlo's path and asked, "Is there a problem?"

"This doesn't concern you, mister," Carlo said. To emphasize his point, he reached down to pat the holster at his side.

The sight of the gun so close to Carlo's hand was enough to take the wind from the local man's sails. Since Bickle had already hurried out of sight, the man stepped back to gather up his family and glare sternly at Carlo.

"Good day to you, now," Carlo said as he gave the family a polite nod and followed in Bickle's wake.

The shopkeeper had ducked into one of his competitor's establishments, a small place stuffed to the rafters with finery of all kinds. Bickle was immediately recognized by the old woman behind the counter, who stood up from her stool behind the cash register to greet him.

"I thought I told you not to come in here bad-mouthing my wares!" the old woman yapped.

"Shut up, May!" Bickle said. "I'm just passing through."

"What's that in your hands? Did you take that from one of my shelves?"

Bickle kept moving toward the back door while shouting, "It's mine!"

"Put it down!" she hollered. The old woman was still shaking her cane at the rear of her store when the bell above her front door jangled again.

Luke stepped inside and took a quick look around. "Did a man just come through here carrying a box?" he asked. "Thick around the middle. The man, not the box."

Hearing that, she turned around to set her eyes on Luke. "You're after Jordan Bickle?"

"Yes, ma'am."

"He went out that way," she said while pointing to the back door with her cane. "When you get him, bring back the box he stole from me. There'll be a reward in it for you."

Luke tipped his hat and hurried through the store. "I'll do that, ma'am. Thank you."

When he got outside, Luke couldn't see where Bickle had gone. Before picking what seemed to be the likeliest direction the other man might have chosen, he stood still and listened for a second. In that short stretch of time, he heard a few clumsy footsteps scraping against the dirt, followed by a wheezing voice and the thunk of something hitting the ground. Smiling since those noises came from the direction he would have chosen anyway, Luke ran to find the portly shop owner stooping down to pick up a candlestick from the box he'd dropped.

"No!" Bickle sputtered. "Nonononononoo!" He grabbed the candlestick, cocked it back as if he meant to throw it, but shoved it back into the box and kept running.

The back end of the row of shops was a crooked collection of small porches, outhouses, and sheds. Even the buildings themselves were irregularly shaped with some jutting out several feet past their neighbors and others tucked in so far that they hardly looked like anything at all. Compared to the side facing the street, which was flush with the boardwalk, the back end looked as if it had been cobbled together from spare parts.

Now that he'd cleared the end of the building next to the old woman's place, Luke could see most of the row that ended at a wide alleyway. Bickle was huddled against another short building and hidden from sight by anyone who emerged from the old woman's store. If he hadn't been so fidgety, Bickle might have been able to stay put and let Luke pass him by. Instead he raced for the alley and Luke had no trouble following him.

Somewhere along the way, Bickle stepped in a rut and turned his ankle too far in one direction. His entire body jerked to one side, causing the box of candlesticks to rattle noisily. Sheer desperation and panic kept him moving as breath churned in and out of him like steam through a piston. When Luke saw Red emerge from the alley ahead of the shop owner, he slowed to a stop.

Bickle saw Red as well and must have been completely overcome by fear because he finally parted with one of his candlesticks by throwing it at Red. His aim was dead-on because the piece of merchandise sailed straight for Red's face.

Reflexively, Red threw up both arms to cover his head. Although he blocked most of the impact, a corner of the candlestick struck through to scrape against his cheek. "Ow!" he hollered.

Blocked in on two sides with a building on another, Bickle rummaged in the crate to fish out another candlestick. "Don't come any closer!" he warned as he raised his makeshift weapon.

"You don't even know who we are," Luke said.

"I know who sent you!"

"We aren't here to hurt you."

"Speak for yourself!" Red said. "You ain't the one that got hit by a damn pipe or whatever that was!"

Luke held out both hands to show they were empty. "You never gave us a chance to explain ourselves. I gather you're Jordan Bickle?"

"You . . . you know who I am!"

"Just take it easy," Luke said. He made an effort to fight back the impulse to charge at the man he'd been chasing and hoped Red would keep his temper long enough to do the same. When Luke took a step forward, even though it was slow and easy, Bickle reacted as though he were facing a tribe of wild Apaches.

Lobbing a candlestick at Luke, Bickle started running in the only direction that wasn't blocked. That took him into a wide lot filled with the skeletal remains of at least half a dozen wagons and rusty carts. The ground was uneven and scarred, which meant Bickle had a difficult time taking one or two steps without stumbling. Every move brought a yelp of pain, but he kept on running.

Luke ran after the fleeing store owner until he felt a hand slap down onto his shoulder. Carlo's grip was just strong enough to pull him back. His other arm was already raised so he could take aim with the pistol in his hand. After sending a single shot through the air, Carlo lowered his gun and walked forward in a leisurely stroll.

Bickle let out a surprised shout, turned to look at the source of the gunshot, and promptly tripped over a wheel rim that was partially buried in the dirt. He hit the ground on both knees, dropping the crate in his hands and sending the remaining candlesticks rolling in several different directions.

"Sorry about all of this," Carlo said.

Scrambling to collect his prized items, Bickle shot back with, "No, you're not!"

Striding forward while allowing his gun arm to hang at his side, Carlo replied, "You're right. I could have watched you waddle around like a fat rooster with its head cut off all day long."

"Joke all you want, Procci. You can't just fire at a man without answering for it."

"Who will I answer to? You? The law?" Now that he was standing less than two paces away from him, Carlo looked down at the store owner as if he were doing so from the top of a mountain. "You wouldn't be foolish enough to lie to the law, now, would you?"

Clutching some of the candlesticks close to his chest, Bickle said, "I won't have to lie."

"You don't have to say anything at all," Red said as he approached with his Smith & Wesson in hand. The spot on his face where he'd been hit was red, and blood trickled from a small cut in the middle of it. "You try to make any trouble for us and it'll be the last thing you ever do."

"Shut up, kid," Carlo barked.

Luke knew that Red's instinct would be to do anything but remain quiet, so he stepped in before any mistakes were made. Holding out a hand, he met his friend's angry gaze and gave Red a look that told him to back down. Reluctantly Red complied.

"What do you want?" Although Bickle was trying to sound calm when he asked the question, he did a terrible job. He tried to cover the fact that his hands were shaking by keeping them busy placing the candlesticks back in the crate he'd been carrying.

"I just want to have a word with you," Carlo said.

"Is that why you brought a couple of gunmen along?"

Without even knowing it, Luke straightened a bit when he heard that.

"If you think these boys are gunmen," Carlo said, "then you've led a real sheltered life."

"Then who are they?" Bickle asked. "And why are they chasing me . . . while carrying *guns*?"

"They're chasing you because you ran away, you fool!" Carlo said. "You don't need to concern yourself with them. I'm the one talking."

Forming his mouth into a tight line, Bickle put some fire into his eyes as he defiantly said, "Fine. You want to talk? Say whatever you want to say. Just be quick about it. I've got a business to run." Once again, he did a terrible acting job.

Carlo took another step forward and then hunkered down so he was closer to Bickle's level. "You do have a business to run, don't you? That's something you didn't mention when we first met."

"We were meeting in regards to a different matter," Bickle replied. "My other affairs weren't important."

"See, now, that's where I disagree. You lied to me. You told me that you were in a different line of work altogether."

Bickle shrugged. "That's not necessarily a lie. A man can be in several different lines of work."

"What's any of this got to do with—" Red started to ask before he was cut short by a backhanded swat on the arm from his friend.

"I wanna hear this," Luke whispered. "Just keep watch for anyone trying to barge in on us."

"You don't tell me what to do," Red snarled.

"We're both keeping watch. Let's just make sure we don't let anyone sneak up on us."

Grumbling to himself, Red stepped outside Luke's reach and turned so he could watch the alley. Luke faced the stores in the other direction while also angling himself to watch Carlo and Bickle from the corner of his eye.

"I said not to worry about them," Carlo said in a tone that cut through the air like a knife. "Don't make me say it again."

Bickle moved the crate to one side as if he'd only just realized it wasn't his biggest concern at the moment. "I didn't tell you about my trading company," he said. "I didn't tell any of those men about it. I don't need those kinds of men knowing about something like that."

"Normally I would understand such a precaution," Carlo said. "I take plenty of precautions myself. This, for example," he added while lifting his gun so it was directly between his face and Bickle's. "I can use this for all kinds of things." Flipping it around to present its grip, he said, "I've even used this right here to knock in a few nails or crack a few skulls." With another snap of his wrist, the pistol turned around so it could be held properly again.

Every time that gun moved, Bickle jumped as if he were getting rapped on the nose with it.

"But mostly this is the business end," Carlo continued, obviously savoring every moment. "It's a great precaution against snakes and other vermin. You know all about snakes, right?"

Bickle shook his head. "I . . . I don't . . ."

"What's the matter? Now you can't talk so well? Seemed to me you were talking just fine when we met a few weeks ago."

"Whatever it is you think happened—"

"I don't have to think about anything that happened. I *know* what happened." Turning to Luke, Carlo asked, "How many wagons were parked outside the Eastern Trading Company?"

"I counted three," Luke replied.

"And I believe him," Carlo said as he shifted his attention back to Bickle. "He's a real bright kid."

The store owner put on a wide, shaky grin as he said, "And a fine-looking boy as well!"

"No need for the sweet talk," Carlo told him. "He's not mine. Although perhaps I should take him under my wing. I could sure teach him a few things about being able to spot a snake. See this right here, Luke?" he said while pointing his gun at Bickle. "This is a snake!"

"Wh-what are you talking about?" Bickle squeaked. "Why would you s-say such a thing?"

"How much inventory were you unloading today?" Carlo asked. "I've never seen one store getting so much at one time."

"Every store needs to keep its shelves full!"

"And where would you get the money for so much? It's not like this is the sort of town that can make a shop owner like you into a rich man!"

"It's just a matter of timing!" Bickle swore. "All my shipments decided to come in at once. That's all!"

Spinning his gun around to once more present the

handle first, Carlo raised it high and brought it down like a hammer to smash the top of Bickle's crate into splinters. "What's this?" he asked while reaching into the broken crate with his other hand to grab a candlestick. "This looks awful fancy for a general store in a town this size."

"I'm branching out."

"I'll just bet you are."

"What's the meaning of all this?" Luke asked.

"Yeah," Red added. "And what's this got to do with that money we're supposed to be getting?"

"The boys bring up a real good question," Carlo said. Keeping his intense gaze fixed on Bickle, he said, "That money I told you two about was meant to pay off an outstanding debt of mine."

"You already mentioned that," Luke said.

"It was a debt meant to be paid to someone who wasn't able to come and collect it himself," Carlo went on to say as if he hadn't heard anyone else. "Bickle here was sent to collect his money for him. I handed over the money and figured everything was fine. A week or so later, this man who I owe the money to sends word to me that he ain't been paid."

At this point in the story, Bickle got even more nervous. "I'm just a businessman," he said while shaking his head. "Ask anyone in town."

"You think them people I ask will know about you stepping in to barter a deal between an army captain and a gunman like me?"

"Probably not."

"That's right. You keep to yourself, don't you? What if it gets around that you have dealings with known killers and outlaws?" Carlo asked. "How many customers do you think you might lose then? Or the better question might be . . . what sort of customers do you think you might gain? Maybe a bunch of thieves and killers looking for another middleman to broker their deals? I doubt that'd last long when it gets out you can't even be trusted to do that much."

"You can't back up anything you're saying," Bickle insisted.

"I ain't no lawman," Carlo replied. "I don't need nothing more to go on than what I've already seen. And what I've seen is a man who took a whole lot of money from me that was supposed to be delivered on my behalf. That money never was delivered and then I see the man who took it rolling around like a pig in slop in a whole bunch of new stuff that must have cost a whole lot of *my* money!"

"It's merchandise for my store! Didn't you ever think that one of those other men who were there when that money changed hands might have taken it? They were desperadoes, you know! Killers and thieves."

Carlo shook his head. "They may be killers and thieves, but they know better than to double-cross a man like Captain Granger."

Although he'd been content to stand back and watch how things unfolded, Luke felt his composure unravel the instant he heard that name. This time, it was Red who reached out to stop him. When Luke looked over to try to shake loose of his friend's insistent hand, Red grabbed him by the front of his shirt to pull him aside.

"Let me go," Luke said. "They're talking about—"

"I know," Red said sharply once there was some distance between them and Carlo. "I heard him too. Now's not the time to get into all of that, though. Let's just straighten out one mess before gettin' into another."

Despite what his heart was telling him, Luke choked back the anger that had risen so quickly to his surface. Carlo and Bickle were still talking. By the looks of him, Bickle no longer had the strength to put up much of a fight or argue in any meaningful way.

"I don't know what you want me to do about it now," Bickle said. "What's done is done."

"No," Carlo told him. "You find a way to get that money to where it was supposed to go or *you're* done."

"Even if I did have the money anymore—but I don't—I—"

Carlo grabbed the shop owner's shirt and pulled him close enough to jam the barrel of his pistol into Bickle's chest as he asked, "What the hell do you mean you don't have the money anymore? You're telling me you spent every last dime of it on the garbage in them wagons?"

"First of all, it's not garbage. That's fine merchandise!"

"I swear, if you so much as look at those ugly candlesticks, I'll put an end to you right here and now."

Despite the fact that Carlo was obviously serious about that threat, it took some degree of willpower for Bickle to keep from reaching for the damaged crate. "Say what you will about the quality of what was purchased. The wagons are already here making the deliveries. It's too late to ask for a refund."

"Not if you pack it right up and send them wagons back."

"Even if I could, and I'm not guaranteeing anything, I don't know where to find Granger so I can deliver that money to him."

"I know where to find him," Carlo said. "How long will it take for you to get my money?"

Still staring down the barrel of Carlo's pistol, Bickle said, "I can . . . I can see what can be done about boxing up the merchandise that was delivered. Then I'll arrange for a way to ship it back and I'll have to have words with my suppliers in regards to a discount. That could take—"

"I don't care about that. How much can you get your hands on in the next day or two?"

Bickle's mouth opened and closed like a trout that had just been pulled onto a rowboat. Finally he managed to reply, "I don't . . . I . . . can't . . ."

Angling his pistol upward and placing it under Bickle's chin, Carlo spoke in a low, strained tone. "Those aren't the kinds of words I want to hear right now."

"If I had that kind of money . . . I wouldn't have needed to take what you gave to me."

When Carlo met Bickle's eyes once more, he was more ferocious than ever. "I don't care how, but you'll get my money and you'll get it to me quick. You hear me?"

"I hear you, but—"

"No buts! You'll scrape together what you can or I'll carve it out of your hide."

Bickle swallowed hard and nodded.

"I'm a reasonable man," Carlo continued. "I'll grant you some wiggle room, but that's only because I need to take Granger what I can as soon as I can get it there. And if you think today has been rough for you, just wait to see what's in store for you when Granger finds out how you kept money from going into his pocket. Even I wouldn't want to trade places with you for that."

"Please," Bickle whispered. "Let's just keep this between you and me. I'll make good on what I did. I promise."

"That's right. You will. Because if you don't, I'll come back and have another conversation that ends with me setting fire to your store with you in it. Got me?"

Bickle nodded. "I can get a good portion of the money to you soon. I swear."

Carlo glanced over his shoulder to where Luke and Red were standing. "What have you got in your till right now?"

"I'm not sure."

"You got five hundred dollars?"

"Probably."

"You'll hand that over to my young friends over there," Carlo demanded. "I'll be along for my payment tomorrow morning. It had better be good—you hear?"

"What's the five hundred dollars for?"

"It doesn't matter what it's for! Just get it as soon as I let you up and then start working on scrounging up the rest!"

"All right," Bickle said. "I will. I swear!"

Carlo backed away and holstered his pistol.

When he saw that Bickle was having trouble getting to his feet, Luke helped him up. He then escorted Bickle back to the Eastern Trading Company, where he received five hundred dollars in cash. It was the easiest money he would ever get.

Chapter 15

Later that night, after Luke and Red had stuffed their bellies with the finest cuts of beef prepared in Stormy's kitchen, they made their way back to the nameless stable across town. The man who answered the door when Luke knocked had a bit more meat on his bones than the skinny stable man from before, but not much.

"You two ain't them boys from earlier, are you?" the man asked.

"We are," Luke told him.

"Then you'll be on your way. I got a scattergun and I ain't afraid to put it to work!"

"We don't want any trouble. We're just here for Carlo Procci."

"I was told that's what started the trouble last time."

"Just a misunderstanding," Red said. "It's been sorted out."

"In case you people haven't noticed, this ain't a hotel me and my brother are runnin'," the man explained. "It's a stable. For horses."

Luke extended a hand with two silver dollars in it. "That's for your trouble. Go on and take it."

After taking the money and examining it, the man hooked a thumb toward the stable. "He's inside. Don't think you bought yourself any space in there unless you've got a horse to put up for the night."

"I know. Stable, not a hotel."

"You got that right."

Both of the young men entered the stable. As soon as the door was shut behind them, Red gave Luke a back-handed swat and said, "What'd you pay him any money for? He wasn't gonna be any trouble."

"It's to keep from making waves. Just take a breath and forget about it."

Carlo was in his stall, only he wasn't sleeping under a bunch of hay and a blanket. His horse stood next to its trough with its eyes closed and its head hanging low. "What are you two doing here?" he asked. He wore a fresh set of clothes and was in the process of folding the dirty ones up to put them into his saddlebags. "You got your money for Stormy."

"She's all paid up," Luke said. "And we appreciate the help in getting it."

"I'll take any chance to gouge that skinflint Bickle I can find. Still didn't answer my question, though. What are you doing here?"

"Tell me about Captain Granger."

Pausing just long enough to look over at them, Carlo said, "I was only fooling about taking you under my wing. Now move along before you get yourselves hurt."

"I just want to know if he's any relation to Bose Granger," Luke said.

Carlo's eyes narrowed and his gaze focused on Luke as if it had been drawn by a magnet. "Where'd you hear that name?" he asked.

"We're from a town called Maconville."

"Never heard of it."

"A man came through there and killed a bunch of

folks," Luke said in a voice that was cold and unfaltering. "He mentioned someone named Bose Granger was behind it."

"What was this man's name?" Carlo asked. "The one that passed through your town."

"Scott."

"Emory Scott?"

"All I heard anyone call him was Scott. He came to Maconville looking for something."

"What was he looking for?"

"I don't know that either."

After studying him for a few long seconds, Carlo got back to packing up his things. "Could be Emory, I suppose," he said. "Although I'm not sure if anyone's seen him lately. So why do you want to know about Captain Bose Granger?"

"That man he sent killed my family."

Once again, Carlo stopped what he was doing. "Sorry to hear about that. Sounds like Emory all right. That one's as cold as they come. If you know what's good for you, you'd count yourself lucky you didn't get in his way."

"Was Emory Scott a friend of yours?" Red asked.

Carlo chuckled and shook his head. "Men like Emory Scott don't have friends."

"Granger sent him to Maconville," Luke said. "And I'm hunting him down."

"Now, that," Carlo said, "is a foolish idea. Most folks don't even know where to find Captain Granger at any given time. He moves around a lot and has a knack for knowing when people are sniffing around after him. Those people aren't normally heard from again."

"I know where to find him."

Letting out another half chuckle, Carlo shook his head. "Whatever you heard, it's probably just some lie spread by Granger himself. Do yourself a favor and forget about finding him. Men like that will get what's coming to them."

"I don't think it's a lie," Luke said. "What I heard came from a good source."

"What source is that?"

"I heard it from Scott."

Having finished packing his saddlebag, Carlo cinched it shut and diverted all of his attention to Luke. "You spoke to Scott?"

"No. I heard him speaking to my stepfather before Scott gunned him and my mother down."

"And who was your stepfather?"

"Kyle Sobell. You know who he is?"

Carlo nodded slowly. "Yeah. I knew Kyle. I heard him mention some family he had in Kansas, but he never mentioned their names or what town they were in. He's dead?"

"Yeah."

"Why would Scott kill him and your mother?"

"Because he wanted to keep us all quiet," Luke said as if he no longer felt any attachment to the matter. "I got away. The rest of my family . . . didn't."

"Did Scott find what he was looking for?"

"I don't know," Luke said with a straight face. "All I recall from that night is blood and gunshots."

"So, where did he say Granger was at?" Carlo asked. When he didn't get an answer right away, he stormed toward Luke and grabbed hold of his shirt before either of the young men knew what was going on. "I asked you a question, kid! Where did he say Granger was at?" Carlo was interrupted by the unmistakable click of a pistol's hammer being thumbed back. When he looked in the direction from which the sound had come, he found Red standing there with Smith & Wesson in hand.

"Let him go," Red said. "I won't ask twice."

Carlo let him go. "The best thing I could do for you two is keep you from getting anywhere near Granger," he said. "Tell me where he's at and I can bring him down myself."

"So both Grangers we mentioned are the same man?" Luke asked.

"They are. Bose is a name he's called by some of the men under his command."

"He's really an army captain?" Red asked.

"Most definitely," Carlo told him.

"What's your business with him?" Luke asked.

Looking at both of them to make it clear he didn't care whether they were armed or not, Carlo said, "That's *my* business, which means it's none of yours."

Red started to inch forward to assert himself even more, but Luke stepped in and said, "All that matters is that we both have business with him. I imagine we can get everything squared away faster if we throw in together."

"You do, huh?" Carlo scoffed. "You want to know why you think that? Because you don't know any better. You were lucky to have gotten away from that little town of yours when Scott went on his tear. It's plain to see that you barely know your way around a gun. Hell, you two had your hands full in running down a fat shopkeeper."

"But we did it," Luke reminded him. "And we can do a whole lot better than that if we get the chance."

"It's not my duty to give boys like you chances to kill themselves. You'll tend to that well enough on your own."

"You don't know where to find Granger. I do."

"I'll be able to find him," Carlo said.

"Can you do that before he moves on again?"

"Yeah," Red added. "And can you do that before he sends more gunmen to hunt you down for swindling him outta his money?"

"I didn't swindle anyone!" Carlo said. "That fat man we chased down today spent it on candlesticks and . . . Lord knows what else."

"But does Granger know that?" Red asked. "And even if he did, do you think he'd care? You carry yourself like a gunfighter, but you're hiding out in a horse stall sleeping in a pile of hay. I reckon that means you need to find Granger even worse than we do."

"I'll find him."

"And then what?" Luke asked. "Put a gun to his head and convince him to forgive you? Whatever it is you paid Granger to do must have been important or you wouldn't be so interested in finding him at all."

"And it must be expensive too," Red said. "Judging by all the candlesticks and whatnot your money bought and paid for."

"Maybe you're right about us all having business with Granger," Carlo admitted. "But I also know I'm right when I say the both of you will get yourselves killed right quick if you keep trying to use those guns of yours."

"Then show me what I'm doing wrong," Luke said. "Tell me how I can better defend myself."

"No."

"Why not?"

"Because," Carlo said, "you're too eager for it. And you," he said while looking over to Red. "You've got just enough of a temper to be more dangerous to yourself than to anyone else. I've got nothing to gain by helping you boys. Nothing but a guilty conscience, that is."

"We're going to meet Granger whether you help or not," Luke said. "I say we've all got something to gain by making the ride together."

"Is that a fact?" Carlo asked.

"Yes, sir. How much money do you owe?"

"To Granger or everyone in general?"

"Granger."

Placing his hands on his hips and staring at Luke as if he were about to deliver a knockout punch, Carlo said, "Three thousand."

Red let out a low whistle.

"What if I could get that money for you?" Luke asked.

Shaking his head as if he already knew the answer to his own question, Carlo muttered, "How could you do something like that?"

"It doesn't matter how. What if I could? Would that be enough to convince you to ride with us to face Granger together?"

"That's the part I'm trying to keep you from, kid."

"Stop calling me that," Luke demanded. "I'm no kid."

"I don't know anything else to call you," Carlo said. "It ain't as if you properly introduced yourselves."

"I'm Luke Croft and that's Red."

"Pleased to meet you," Carlo said. "And now that we have that out of the way . . . we can part company. Nice meeting you both."

"I'm being serious."

"So am I. The two of you have been lucky so far. If you want to spit in the face of someone like Granger, you'll need more than luck on your side."

"That's right," Luke admitted. "Which is why the three of us stand a better chance."

"Look, as much as I'd like to keep going round and round about this, I'm pretty sure I'll have a busy day tomorrow tying to wrangle that shopkeeper again to get a portion of the money he stole. After that . . . well . . . you two don't need to concern yourselves with after that. Run along now."

Spitting a disgusted breath while turning his back to the stall, Red said, "I say we leave this vagrant where he is. We don't need the stink of him fouling our air anyhow."

Although Red was all too willing to leave the stable, Luke stayed behind.

"What are you waiting for?" Carlo asked. "Don't you have a tantrum of your own to throw?"

"I think if you were in our place, you'd be angry too."

"Could be."

"What sort of thing were you paying Granger for anyway?"

"Why do you want to know?"

"Because I'd like to know what I'm getting into when I face him."

"You're a smart fella," Carlo said. "The best thing for you to do is not face Granger at all. Even if you think you stand a chance against him, you wouldn't be facing him alone. And even if you think you could figure out a way to get to him when he is alone, you'd never make it back alive."

"I'm not worried about that last part," Luke said in an icy tone.

Carlo laughed under his breath while shaking his head. "I know you've probably heard this from plenty of others, but I know exactly what you're thinking. I used to think the same thing, you know."

"And what am I thinking?"

"Well, right at the moment you're thinking I'm just another sack of wind trying to sound like he knows what he's talking about."

Luke shrugged. "Good guess."

"You're also thinking you're immortal. Not right at this exact moment perhaps, but it's in there. Strangely enough, that goes hand in hand with thinking that you're all settled up with dying."

Although Luke had been doing a good job of keeping

his poker face intact this far, he couldn't help twitching when he heard that.

Carlo nodded to acknowledge that he knew he was on the right track. "Some big part of you thinks it's seen all there is to see or that you've seen so much that you don't want to see no more. A kid your age—and I'm sorry if that rubs you the wrong way but you are still a kid to me—he gets a notion in his head that he can walk right up to death and tell him to wait until he's ready. Me? I used to go around tellin' everyone I wouldn't live to be any older than my pappy was when he died. Know how old he was?"

Luke tried to look as though he didn't care.

"He was twenty-six," Carlo said. "I was certain I wouldn't see one day past that number. The part that makes no sense is that I also thought I was somehow safe until then. That's why I had no fear of God or man when I took up a knife and swung it at anyone that looked at me cross-eyed. When I was bested by someone who was better with a blade than me, I picked up a gun and put that to work."

"Seems like you handled yourself pretty well," Luke said. "You're alive and I'd wager you're older than twenty-six."

"Sure. I'm also on the run and sleeping in a horse stall. The only reason I've got that much is that I thought harder about another trail to follow because the one I was on led nowhere."

"I know what trail I'm on," Luke said. "Until I get to have a talk with this Captain Granger, there isn't another one for me."

"There's always another one, Luke."

"Do you want to ride with me and Red or not?"

"I can find Granger on my own," Carlo said.

"But you'll get there quicker if you know where he is."

"What sort of help do you think I can offer anyways?"

"You're good with a gun," Luke replied while ticking his answers off on his fingers. "You know Granger better than I do, so you know what we'll be up against when we get there. And if things take a turn for the worse, it can only help to have more guns on our side."

"Doesn't it bother you to drag your friend into this when you could both wind up dead?"

"I didn't drag him anywhere. He does what he pleases."

"He's a good friend. Don't treat him like he's got nowhere else to be other than where you need him."

"You're just plumb full of advice," Luke grumbled.

"I'll save my breath, then. To be honest, what I said wouldn't have made a dent in me either when I was your age. As far as your offer goes, I'll pass."

"You sure about that?"

"Yeah."

Luke started walking away. "If you change your mind, we'll be at Stormy's for another day."

"Don't worry, kid. I won't change a thing."

Chapter 16

Bright and early the next morning, Carlo was up and brushing the stray pieces of hay from his shoulders, legs, arms, chest, and head. His horse stood looking as unimpressed as ever with his saddle and bags waiting nearby. Everything was packed, and if the need arose, Carlo could be galloping away in a matter of minutes.

"Hey there, Old Man," Carlo said as he patted the horse's neck and sifted his fingers through his gray-black mane. "Hope you slept better than I did."

The horse glanced over to him, nudged Carlo with his nose, and stuck it into his trough for a drink.

"We're not heading out just yet, but I want you to be ready. Hope you don't mind."

When Carlo buckled the saddle and bags onto his back, the horse seemed to mind it as much as he minded anything else. Judging by the animal's lack of movement, he might not have been aware of the saddle or Carlo's presence whatsoever.

Once that was done, Carlo left the stable and crossed the street to have some breakfast at a little bakery that served its day-old biscuits and bread at a discounted price. The woman who worked there recognized him on sight and prepared a plate of biscuits along with a cup of honey.

"You're in luck," she said with a gap-toothed smile. "These are yesterday's day-old biscuits, so you can have 'em for free. It was either that or I'd be tossing them out."

"Three-day-old biscuits, huh? I suppose I'll take whatever luck I can scrape up. Much obliged."

"A good man like you shouldn't have to scrape for luck."

Carlo tipped his hat. "Thanks to the good graces of angels like yourself, I don't have to."

The old woman smiled and headed back into the kitchen to finish baking the day's fresh cakes. Carlo took his plate to one of the small tables in the front corner of the bakery. His backside didn't even get a chance to warm the seat before the honey and biscuits were gone. After spending the last several days surviving on scraps and handouts, his belly was in a constant state of discontent. Wolfing down the breakfast helped take the edge off his hunger but didn't come close to squashing it entirely. He got up, brought the plate to the counter, and leaned toward the kitchen door.

"Anything I can do for you, ma'am?" he shouted.

"There's a stack of wood outside that could be brought in for my stove," she replied.

Without another word, Carlo went out and circled around to the back of the bakery. Sure enough, there was a pile of wood there, which he carried inside and stacked next to the stove. It only took two trips, but the woman was so grateful that she offered him more to eat.

"No need for that," he said. "You've been plenty helpful since I've been in town."

"It's the least I can do for a fighting man like yourself," she said with a beaming smile.

"I honestly do appreciate it."

"I'll have something good for you tomorrow," she assured him. "Just you wait."

"I'm afraid I'll more than likely be leaving town today."

"Then stay put," she said as she started bustling about the kitchen to grab bread and cheese from a few different spots. She even went to her front counter to collect some bacon that she kept in short supply. "I'm making you something for lunch."

"No, ma'am. You've been more than helpful. I couldn't."

She reappeared with more speed than her little body seemed capable of producing. When she spoke to him, it was in a fierce whisper that could not be refused. "These are rough times for folks like us. Men like you need to do what you can to keep the spirit alive. You hear me?"

"Yes, but—"

"But nothing!" she interrupted. "It's your duty to fight and my duty to keep you fed and . . . well, that's about all I'm good for anymore, so just take what I give you along with my thanks for what you done."

Carlo didn't have to wait long for her to put together some sandwiches and wrap them up for him. When she handed them over, he gave her his thanks and she gave him a farewell hug. Outside, the town was bustling with folks getting their workday off to a running start. Carlo looked down the street toward Westminster and started walking along the straightest route to the Eastern Trading Company.

After rounding a corner and walking along the boardwalk, he caught sight of Bickle's store. Carlo stood in front of a smaller place so he could watch for any sign that Bickle might be up to something. There were a few people standing around near the front of the Eastern Trading Company, but nobody struck him as familiar.

The wagons from the day before were no longer parked in front of the place. Once he got inside, however,

Carlo had no trouble telling several large payloads had been dropped off. Every one of the store's shelves was full and there were even a few barrels situated near the front counter that bore large, freshly painted signs advertising new wares for sale at reasonable prices.

"These rugs are lovely!" declared a tall woman with flowing black hair. She wore a dress that seemed much too formal for that time of day and a hat that looked as if it might start flapping its wings to take off on its own.

Bickle stood behind the front counter, poking keys on his cash register and puffing his chest out like a peacock. "Why, thank you, Mrs. Havermeyer," he said. "They only just arrived yesterday."

"I hear there was a problem with your shipment when it arrived. Something about a robber?"

"Oh, I'd rather not discus that," Bickle replied. "Rest assured, nothing was taken. In fact, there are even more of those fine broaches you like so much in this case. Have a look for yourself."

"What about the candlesticks?" Carlo said as he approached the counter. "Don't forget about those candlesticks."

Mrs. Havermeyer turned to look at him and was clearly displeased with what she saw. "Thank you, no," she said as if she'd just taken a swig of lemon juice. "I'll just have a look at those broaches." Whether she was truly interested in jewelry or just wanted to get away from a man who looked as if he'd spent the night in a stable, the finely dressed woman couldn't get away from the front counter fast enough.

"What are you doing here?" Bickle asked in a fierce whisper.

"Did you forget already? I'll have that money you owe me."

"I told you I couldn't get all of it so quickly. Especially

after you made me hand over so much to those two thugs."

"Then I'll take whatever you've got," Carlo said.

"Come back tomorrow."

"That wasn't the proposition I offered. You were to pull together my money or as much as you could. Not spend your time painting signs and arranging broaches."

"Oh, so that was the proposition you offered?" Bickle asked in a mocking tone. "Well, I think about as highly of that proposition as I did of the first one where you put that money in my hands to begin with."

Carlo did not like the way Bickle was speaking or the confidence that grew with every smug word the shop owner threw at him. Although Bickle was a naturally grating man, the fact that he was suddenly brave enough to defy Carlo when he'd been a sniveling little toad the previous day meant something had changed. For some reason, Bickle thought he had an advantage. Carlo didn't have to wait long before that advantage showed itself.

"Get out of my store," Bickle said. "If I see you in here again, it'll be the worst day of your life."

Hearing footsteps knock against the floor behind him, Carlo turned to see two men emerge from a storeroom. He recognized them as workers who'd been unloading the wagons the day before. Today, however, the only thing they carried was shotguns.

"You really want to do this?" Carlo asked. "Looks like you just got everything straightened up and now you want to make another mess."

"I've got a broom," Bickle replied. "Now leave."

"I will . . . just as soon as I get my money."

Both armed men fanned out so they could take aim with their shotguns from two different angles.

"I heard from Granger," Bickle said. "He is upset by not getting his money, but he doesn't have the slightest notion where it went. He's convinced you took it, and considering who you are, that's what anyone would think. That means you're still the one that has to answer for that money, and since you can't take it from me," he added while motioning toward the two shotgunners, "you'd best put this town behind you and not look back."

"Why don't I worry about what's best for me?" Carlo said. "And I wouldn't be so certain that I can't take my money back right here and now."

Both of the other men were burly and thick with muscle. While they held their shotguns with confidence, neither had the look of anything but wagon drivers.

"I've got more hired guns guarding my money," Bickle warned. "You'll never get to it."

"We'll see about that."

The shotgunners shifted on their feet, tightening their grip on their weapons and slowly bringing them up to take aim. Before they could get settled into something close to a firing stance, Carlo walked toward Bickle. Almost immediately, the shop owner became the panicked ninny from the previous day and wailed, "Shoot him! Shoot him!"

In one smooth motion, Carlo dropped to one knee while drawing the pistol from his holster. When he hit the floor, thunder exploded from a shotgun to tear apart one of the rugs that Mrs. Havermeyer had been admiring. The rug was hanging from a wooden rod above a table stacked high with others of its kind, and it billowed like a flag in the wind as buckshot ripped through its woven fibers. The air filled with even more smoke when one of the second man's barrels erupted noisily. As Carlo had hoped, both shots were well off their mark after being taken in a rush.

Mrs. Havermeyer screamed and ran away from the display of broaches, waving her hands in the air. She looked even more birdlike as her hat flopped on top of her head and she scurried in one direction after another.

Squeezing his trigger, Carlo sent a round through a stack of dishes next to the closer shotgunner. When they exploded, the burly man hunkered down and fired his other barrel into the rugs piled beneath the one that had already been blown apart.

"Watch where you're shooting!" Bickle hollered.

Even as another shotgun blast tore through the shop to chew apart the inventory a few feet to his left, Carlo couldn't help smiling. Bickle would not stop shouting about the damage being done to his store. Carlo's only regret at that moment was that he couldn't see the other man's face when he stood up to fire his pistol from the hip.

Both shotgunners were in the middle of reloading their weapons as Carlo stuck his head up like a prairie dog from its hole. Aiming roughly in one shotgunner's direction, Carlo made certain to hit the most valuable merchandise he could find. He sent a pair of rounds through some drinking glasses, which popped better than fireworks on the Fourth of July. He then pivoted to fire another two shots at a long glass display case in the general vicinity of the other shotgunner.

"What are you doing?" Bickle screamed. "I just got that case!"

One of the shotgunners stopped reloading and looked over to the man who was paying him to be there. Apparently he didn't take kindly to being considered less valuable than some pieces of wood and a pane of glass.

"I'm just here to talk with the owner of this place," Carlo announced. "If he's the one that wants to be difficult, then he's the one that should get hurt. Anyone wants to clear a path for me, I'll give them this one chance."

Mrs. Havermeyer was the first to go. Hot on her heels was the offended shotgunner. As those two headed for the door, Carlo removed the cylinder from his pistol, replaced it with a loaded one, stood up to his full height, and cocked the hammer back before taking aim at the shotgunner who'd held his ground.

"Just so you know," Carlo said, "I've been missing you on purpose."

That was enough to make up the second man's mind. He placed his shotgun on the pile of rugs on his way out.

"All right, Jordan. Guess that leaves you and me."

"I don't have your money!" Bickle shouted from where he now hid behind a row of barrels filled with nails and other building materials.

"You've got to have some money in here. Just give me something to start making up for what you stole. Emptying Captain Granger's pockets wasn't a good idea. Dealing with me now will be a lot less painful than dealing with him later."

When he spoke again, Bickle had crawled into the corner of his store that was filled with blankets and linens. "I already told you, Procci. Granger is convinced you took his money and ran with it. What else would anyone expect from a traitor?"

That last word bit into Carlo like a hungry mosquito. He fought back the impulse to answer back right away so he could narrow down the direction that the shop owner was headed. Following the sounds of hands and knees scraping against the floor, he circled around to catch Bickle just as he was about to make it to a locked back room.

Towering over the other man, Carlo held his pistol in an easy grip and said, "The only reason you're alive right now after what you just said is that I need that money. Now . . . tell me one more time how you don't have it."

Bickle's mouth was open, but his brain was fast enough to keep anything from coming out of it. He got to his feet, slowly, and held his hands out where they could be seen. Pointing toward the unmarked door, he said, "What I've got is in there."

"Good. Open it."

With trembling hands, Bickle fished a key from his pocket, fit it into the door, and opened it. He walked inside and Carlo followed him. Since Bickle had been so liberal with his boasts and threats earlier, Carlo wasn't surprised to find another pair of burly men waiting in there for him. The first was the biggest one so far and he swung at Carlo's head as if he meant to knock it from his shoulders, through a wall, and out into the street. Carlo ducked while stepping to one side, allowing the thick fist to slam into the door's frame. Since the big fellow was leaning forward that way, Carlo pounded the side of his pistol into the man's stomach before grabbing his collar and pulling him face-first into the wall. The big man's chin thumped against solid wood and he slid down into a heap.

Carlo turned his attention to the second hired hand to find the man brandishing a hunting knife with a thick blade. Acting as though he'd been caught at a disadvantage, Carlo holstered his gun and raised his hands. The man with the knife was nervous and became even more so as Carlo moved toward him. Those first few steps were taken nice and easy, lulling the man with the knife into matching the slow pace. Then, without warning, Carlo lunged forward.

The other man swung his blade, but was obviously more accustomed to using it to skin deer. Carlo had no trouble jumping away from the attack and grabbing the man's hand at the wrist before he got a chance to take another wild swing. Twisting the knife against the man's thumb, Carlo pulled it away from him and brought the sharpened edge directly beneath the man's chin.

"Leave," Carlo said.

As soon as he had the room to move without cutting his own throat, the man left. He stepped over his unconscious partner and walked straight past Bickle.

"You," Carlo said to Bickle. "Get that money."

Now that the two bruisers were no longer trying to take his head off, Carlo had a chance to look at the rest of the room. There wasn't much to see apart from a square table covered in papers and ledgers, a chair, and a coatrack. A single lantern hung above the table but wasn't lit because a little window set in one wall provided enough light to fill the space. After being in there for less than a minute, Carlo felt as if he'd been sealed in a coffin.

Bickle went to the table and sat in the chair. "I already told you I don't have all of it."

"Then get what you do have and be quick about it."

"The law's probably gonna be coming," Bickle warned.

"And when they get here, I'll be sure and tell them what you were up to when you met with known killers to broker a deal with me and then hired four men to try to kill me when I came back for what's mine. After the beating they took for whatever pittance you were paying them, I'm sure those gunmen of yours will be more than willing to stand by you."

Reaching under the table for a lockbox, Bickle set it on his lap and opened it. There was barely enough cash inside to fill his grubby fist. "This is it," he said while handing it over.

Carlo snatched it away and examined it. "This barely looks like a hundred dollars."

"It's eighty-seven dollars. Give or take."

"You've got to do better than this!"

"You saw all the merchandise I bought," Bickle whined. "I have expenses, plus those men I hired weren't free."

"You're a real piece of work, Jordan."

There was a lot more that he wanted to say, but Carlo couldn't get any of it out before men stormed into the store through the main entrance.

"What's going on in here?" someone yelled.

Carlo stuffed the money into his pocket and walked out. Two men stood at the front of the store, surveying the damage that had been done in the fight. Both men wore tin stars on their chest.

"Who are you?" asked the man with the larger star pinned to his shirt. "Was anyone hurt?"

"I was just caught in this mess," Carlo said. "I can see my own way out."

"You'll need to stay and answer some questions, mister," the lawman said.

Hooking a thumb back toward the small room, Carlo said, "The owner of the place is in there. He can answer your questions."

The younger one, a deputy, stepped forward with one hand outstretched and the other resting on the grip of his holstered gun. Carlo could tell by the unbroken leather of the holster and the hesitance in the deputy's eyes that he was much more familiar with displaying the pistol than pulling its trigger. Even so, Carlo halted as if he were intimidated by either man's presence.

"Hello there, Sheriff!" Bickle said as he emerged from the back room. "We did seem to have had a bit of a scuffle here."

"A bit of a scuffle?" the sheriff asked. "Is that what you call all of this?"

Bickle laughed and swiped at his brow. "There's an explanation, I assure you."

"Mind if I leave?" Carlo asked.

Both lawmen looked to the store owner.

Twitching nervously, Bickle eventually nodded. "He's just a customer I found hiding in the back. He didn't see much of anything."

"Is that right?" the sheriff asked.

Carlo nodded. "I heard a commotion and found a place to hole up."

"Go ahead and go, but let me know where to find you if I have need to."

"Of course. I'm staying at the Briar," Carlo said, rattling off the name of a hotel he'd passed when entering town.

"Go on, then."

Carlo left with eighty-seven dollars in his pocket, give or take, and a knot in his stomach. Bickle was spouting off about some fabricated explanation for the shots that were fired and the mess that was made, but Carlo didn't stay in the Eastern Trading Company long enough to hear it.

Chapter 17

“Three of a kind,” Red said as he placed his cards on the table to show a king and the three of clubs along with his trio of eights. Grinning from ear to ear, he reached out to scoop in the pot that had accumulated in the middle of the table. Although there was less than ten dollars there, the man who grabbed hold of Red’s wrist did so as if he were protecting a fortune in gold.

“No so fast, boy,” the protective fellow said. He had a long face and an even longer mustache that hung over his mouth and drooped almost an inch below his chin. Although his clothes were more expensive than what could be found on the other players at the table, they were just as rumpled as everyone else’s. Anyone who’d been inside Stormy’s for any time at all tended to get more than a little rumpled.

“Think you can beat my hand, Collin?” Red asked. “You’ll have to prove it.”

Keeping Red’s hand pinned to the table, Collin fanned his cards to show them all. “Straight to the nine.”

“You took my other eight!”

Before Red could get too riled up, the woman in his lap rubbed his chest until she could slip her hand beneath his shirt. "Simmer down, sweetie," Rose purred. "Straight beats three of a kind."

"I guess," Red groaned as if he was conceding the point just to be polite. "Go on and take your money. I'll just win it back anyway."

"That's the spirit," Carlo said as he wound his way through the parlor that took up a good portion of Stormy's lower floor. "There's always more where that came from, right?"

Carlo might have just arrived, but he already had two young women hanging on him to compete for his attention. "That's more than I can say," he added with a grin to both girls. "I'm flat broke."

Hearing that, the women bade their farewells to him and cast their lines into another pond.

"What're you doing here?" Red asked. "If you want to be dealt in, you'll have to come up with something to use for an ante."

"You just learn about that?" Carlo said.

"I know plenty about poker!"

"Guess you just don't know much about the men you're playing against. This one here," Carlo said while pointing at the man who'd just won with a straight, "will fleece you faster than a sheep."

"You callin' me a cheater?" that man asked.

"Nope. Just giving my friend fair warning."

"I don't got to be insulted like that," the man said. "There's plenty of friendlier games around here."

"Hey!" Red snapped. "You chased him away before I could get my money back."

"That money's gone," Carlo told him. "Make peace with it."

Rose's arm had been draped around the back of Red's neck and shoulders for most of the afternoon. It was early evening and she had yet to move from her spot. Not that Red was about to discourage her. "Don't fret about it," she cooed into his ear. "I can think of some friendlier games as well."

Red turned so his face was brushing against hers. "I like the sound of that."

"Before you two get preoccupied," Carlo interrupted, "tell me where I can find Luke."

"What do you want him for?" Red asked without taking his eyes away from the woman in his lap.

"It's about that bit of business we were talking about. Do you recall or has all the blood rushed out of your head?"

"I recall."

"Then tell me where to find him." Since he wasn't getting an answer and it looked as if he wasn't going to get one anytime soon, Carlo snapped his fingers less than an inch from the younger man's face.

When Red turned away from Rose's eyes, he found Carlo as well as the remaining players glaring back at him.

"You wanna tell him what he needs to know?" asked a ranch hand who'd come into town to spend his pay at the table and on the busty brunette who stood behind him. "I wanna get back to the game!"

Suddenly Red was interested only in grabbing the cards, shuffling them, and dealing them out. "He's with Emma. I don't know where."

"Upstairs," Rose said. "Second room on the right. Be sure to knock first. They're probably busy."

"Yeah," Carlo said. "I gathered as much." Before he took two steps away from the table, the cards were being dealt and bets were being made. The whole place was coming to life and it wasn't even suppertime. Carlo figured if he had even a portion of what Stormy would rake in that night, he wouldn't be in so much trouble.

Carlo hadn't been inside Stormy's very often, but it struck him as similar to plenty of other similar places in plenty of other towns. He followed the directions he'd been given and knocked on the door he'd been told about. It was so quiet inside that room that Carlo thought he might have the wrong one. Just as he was about to knock again, however, the door was opened a crack.

He couldn't see much more than a sliver of blond hair and smooth skin of the young lady who answered. "I'm busy," she said.

"Not here to see you. Is there someone in there by the name of Luke?"

"Yes."

"I need to speak to him."

"Wait here," she said before closing the door and locking it.

A few seconds later, the door opened again. This time, Carlo could see the sliver of a different face through the crack. The door opened wider and Luke stood there wearing only his pants with suspenders dangling from the waist. He carried a gun in one hand and made sure Carlo could see it. "What do you want?" he asked.

"I'd like to have a word with you . . . regarding what we talked about before."

"Yeah?"

"Should I say everything out here in this hall or can I come in?"

Luke looked over his shoulder before stepping aside. Emma was still pulling on a wool wrap as she padded from the room on small, bare feet. "You two have your talk," she said. "I'll fix something to eat."

"This place serves food?" Carlo asked.

Holding the door open, Luke said, "Come in and speak your piece."

Carlo stepped inside and took a deep breath. The

room smelled like a woman's skin. Not the scent one might expect in a cathouse, but the true scent of warmth, comfort, and peace. "She's not like the others, is she?"

"No," Luke said as he walked over to the bed and sat upon its edge. The old Colt rested on his knee, pointing in Carlo's direction.

Nodding toward the pistol, Carlo asked, "What's with the gun? You're the one who wanted me to ride with you to Wichita. Now you want to shoot me? It's not as if I have anything to steal."

"No, but I do. And since you know as much, maybe you came here to take what I've got so you can pay the debts you owe."

Laughing to himself, Carlo made his way over to a chair and sat down. "I actually hadn't thought of that. Not a bad idea."

"Actually it's a terrible idea," Luke said while thumbing back the Colt's hammer. "For you."

"Settle down, kid. I'm not here to steal anything. I don't even know where your money is at or even if you truly have any money for that matter."

"Of course I do. I told you so, didn't I?"

"Sure," Carlo replied, "but since we're tossing suspicions back and forth, I could have a few of my own. Maybe you're looking to fast-talk someone into coming with you to act as cannon fodder against Captain Granger. Or maybe you mean to hand me over to him for some sort of reward."

Luke's eyebrows went up. "Reward? Now, there's something I hadn't thought about."

"Because you're not stupid."

"So what brings you here?"

"I still need that money."

"I heard there was some sort of commotion over at the Eastern Trading Company," Luke said. "Was that you?"

"Yeah. That sniveling shopkeeper didn't have my money. I didn't really expect all of it or even most of it, but there wasn't even enough for me to get anything from Granger apart from a belly laugh and a bullet through the skull if I were to present it to him."

"So now you want to ride with us?"

"I don't have any choice. And don't look so offended," Carlo added. "This is a business arrangement. You not being my first choice is nothing to get bent out of shape about."

"I'm not bent out of shape. I'm thinking."

"There's not much to think about. You made an offer and I'm here to take you up on it. What else is there?"

"Why didn't you come over here sooner?" Luke asked. "That commotion at the Trading Company was earlier this morning."

"If you need to know, I saddled up my horse and started riding on my own. I turned back around and headed here because I didn't have money or anything else. It was just pride that made me want to make the ride alone. Also, I knew you'd still be headed to Wichita as well. Didn't make sense to pass on that offer of yours for no good reason."

"You don't like taking payment from a kid," Luke pointed out.

"I don't like taking payment from much of anyone. Truth be told, you're also right. A man with any sort of pride shouldn't be quick to take money from someone as young as you. Now, if you still want to make the ride to Wichita together, say so. If you've changed your mind, then say that. Just don't try to make me crawl for the payment you're offering, because you'll need my help a lot more than I need yours. There's other ways for me to get my hands on money."

"And there are other gunmen for hire," Luke replied.

"All right," Carlo said as he stood up. "If that's the way it is, I guess I misjudged you. Riding to Wichita with a couple moody kids will only get the three of us killed."

"The offer still stands."

Having made it halfway to the door, Carlo stopped and turned around. "The deal is . . . we're partners. All three of us."

"I'm the one putting up the money," Luke said.

"But you're not buying me. We work together, and when lead starts to fly, you take orders from me. I can see that makes you bristle, but that's just the way it is. You want me along for my experience with a gun? You'll have to let me put that experience to good use. Questioning me not only makes you look like a kid, but it wastes time and puts us at a disadvantage."

"All right. We'll be partners."

"First things first. Partners don't point guns at each other for no good reason."

Luke put the Colt in his lap where it was no longer pointed at Carlo.

"Second," Carlo said, "I need to see the money."

"I've got it. Don't you worry about that."

Carlo shook his head. "That ain't good enough. If you were in my position, you'd say the same thing."

Luke's eyes darted more than once toward the bed. That was all Carlo needed to see to figure that if the money was anywhere at all, it would be tucked under the mattress or the bed itself. Even so, he stayed put and let the younger man arrive at his own conclusion.

"I can prove I've got the money," Luke said before too much longer. "Come back in a few minutes."

"I've wasted enough time. Just get it now. I'm sure you wouldn't let it too far out of your sight." Seeing the hesitance in Luke's eyes, Carlo added, "If we're going to be trusting each other with our lives, this is hardly anything."

"We haven't earned that kind of trust yet."

"True, but if we'll be riding together, that money will be with us anyway. If I aimed to steal it, I could do that at any time."

"And I can gun you down at any time."

"Yep. So let's cut through all the dancing around and get to business. There're better ways for a man to spend his time in this place than talking."

For the first time, Luke grinned at Carlo. "You've got that right." He stood up and carried the Colt with him to the bed. Reaching down while holding the gun at hip level, he dragged a dusty valise from under the bed and got back to his feet. "Here," he said while tossing the bag across the room. "See it for yourself."

Carlo was almost surprised enough to let the bag hit him in the chest and drop to the floor. Managing to wrap one arm around it before it fell, he took it by the handle and opened it. Inside, there was more money than he'd ever seen in one place. "I've got to admit, this is a whole lot more than I thought. Where'd you come by this much cash?"

"Doesn't matter."

"Oh, I disagree. If this came from where I think it came from, then it matters a whole lot."

"Where do you think it came from?" Luke asked.

"Was your family wealthy?"

"No."

"Then I think this is the money Emory Scott was after," Carlo said. "Granger liked sending him out to make collections because he never came back empty-handed. From what you told me before about what happened with your family, I'd say your stepfather was sitting on a whole mess of money. And this," he said while angling the valise so Luke could see its contents, "is what I call a mess of money."

Luke weighed his options in a short amount of time. "You're right," he said. "That's the money Scott was after. Does that change things?"

"Depends on how much is in here. Have you counted it?"

"No," Luke said. "I've just been taking from it as we need it. Considering where it came from . . ."

"I understand. Considering what this money did to your kin, I wouldn't want to get my hands dirty with it if I was in your place. I still need to know if there's enough to cover my debt. Looks like it to me, but let's make sure." Carlo turned the bag over and dumped the money onto the bed. It formed a pile on the rumpled blanket before spilling onto the floor.

Luke stood there with his mouth agape. Finally he whispered, "I knew it was a lot of money, but. . . .that's a *lot* of money!"

"Yes, it is."

Carlo was able to count out the money he needed to settle his debt and there was still some left over. He didn't bother counting the remainder, but his three thousand wasn't even half of it. Looking down at all of that cash, he shook his head and started to laugh.

"What's so funny?" Luke asked.

"Between the money I owe and what you kept from getting to him, Captain Granger's pockets are mighty light. I've never known him to be a forgiving man, but he must be spitting nails right about now. You sure you want to cross paths with him now?"

"The sooner, the better. He's got a lot to answer for."

"It might not be a bad idea to wait a spell," Carlo suggested. "I wouldn't ask you to forget about what happened to your family, but men like Granger value their money more than they do anyone's life. Taking this much away from him is like walking up and kicking him right in the . . . well . . . where it hurts a man the most."

"Yeah, well, I feel real bad about that," Luke sneered.

"If the three of us were experienced gunmen, I might say we could put something together to give us the element of surprise. A man in Granger's spot doesn't exactly fear much from a few solitary souls like us. From what I've seen of you and Red . . . it might serve you well to get some more experience under your belts and let this particular storm pass."

"This is how it was meant to be."

Finally taking his eyes away from the pile of money on the bed, Carlo said, "You've got a peculiar notion of destiny, kid."

"Destiny? Seems more like luck to me. Me and Red on our way to Wichita and we find you, who needs to go that way too. Pretty lucky that both of us have business with Captain Granger."

"I wouldn't say that much," Carlo told him. "Granger's got his hand in all the dirty business in this state as well as a few others. Just about every third or fourth trail leads back to him somehow. What I'm saying is that we might not want to be anywhere near him until he comes to terms with missing so much of his money."

Luke studied him carefully. "There's one thing I don't understand."

"Just one? You truly are sharper than most."

"If you want to pay Granger for . . . whatever you were buying from him . . . why do you also want to come along with me and Red? We're not exactly gonna leave him in any condition to do much of anything for anyone."

"What I'm getting from Granger is use of certain resources that are at his disposal," Carlo explained. "If I can get my hands on those resources, I don't exactly need him. The money is just the grease that will make the wheels turn."

"Well, there's what you owe," Luke said while waving at the stacks that Carlo had separated from the rest. "I suppose it doesn't matter if you tell me about your business or not. I'm paying you for a job and you'll be getting something out of it as well. Just tell me one more thing." Luke tightened his grip on the Colt. "Now that you have your money, why should I believe you'll come with us all the way to Wichita?"

"Let's just say my days of having a bunch of gunmen riding along with me are over. Granger moves around too much for me to sit idly by and wait for another chance. If you know where to find him, we need to hit him now. If he's not in Wichita when we get there, I'll be on my way. If he is, you and your friend are the best partners I'm likely to cobble together under the circumstances. You want some advice where that partner is concerned? Keep a close eye on your money. I'm not the one you should be worried about where spending it is concerned."

"What's that supposed to mean?"

"I suppose Red just now decided to take up playing poker? I sure hope so because he ain't very good at it."

Luke shrugged. "At least he's learning a trade."

"Poker's a trade? Blacksmithing is a trade. Being a tailor . . . that's a trade too. Poker is tossing your money away, hoping your luck holds, and being able to lie when it doesn't. And that's the good days when you don't need to shoot or stab some drunk accusing you of being a cheat."

"Sounds better than being a tailor."

Carlo started putting the money back into the bag.

"Guess you might as well live it up. We all should, I suppose. Since we're riding to spit in the face of a man like Captain Granger and using his money to pay for everything along the way, we shouldn't count on having many days left to enjoy."

"You think we have a chance of pulling this off?" Luke asked.

"By my calculations, I should've been dead a few times already, so what do I know? Between all three of us, we may have just enough crazy to get the job done."

Chapter 18

The sun was just a shimmering promise in the early-morning sky when Carlo buckled his saddle once more onto his horse. He'd only just taken it off the animal's back the day before, but he went through the familiar motions without the slightest hint of impatience or anxiousness. On the contrary, every move was as precise as ever as he took a moment to brush a few tangled spots on its gray coat.

"Today we're really going to get you some exercise, Old Man," he said. "I know you got anxious to stretch your legs yesterday, but it didn't quite work out the way I thought it would. Come to think of it, I was partway convinced that I might be dragged in by the sheriff before last night was through. I guess that shopkeeper must have done some fast talking in our favor, huh? Imagine that."

"When's the last time we've been to Wichita?" he asked while putting the saddlebags in place. Although the horse only seemed interested in lapping up a few more sips of water, Carlo said, "Well, we're headed back that way again. Should be eventful."

"You always talk to your horse?" Luke asked as he walked into the stable.

"Mostly when I don't think anyone's around," Carlo

replied. "But since we'll be riding together, I imagine you'll be hearing it plenty."

"Red's waiting outside."

"He's probably not too happy about leaving town."

"He's not happy about leaving Stormy's," Luke corrected. "Probably wouldn't matter what town it's in."

"Makes sense. A place like that is right close to heaven when you've got a bag full of money. That girl you were favoring. Emma, was it?"

"Yeah."

"Did you tell her about that money?"

Luke bristled as he said, "What does that matter?"

"It matters because the fewer people that know about it, the better."

"She didn't steal anything, if that's what you mean."

"You don't know that," Carlo said as he calmly prepared his horse for the day's ride. "You told me you never even counted it."

"You got your money just like I promised. The rest isn't your concern."

Carlo turned to face the younger man. "I'm not questioning her loyalty, but you just met her. You don't have any notion of where her loyalties lie. She may be sweet and all, but you've got to keep your eyes open. She's a whore, and whores—"

Without hesitation, Luke pounced at Carlo. His right fist flew straight at Carlo's head and slapped against a callused palm before strong fingers closed to trap him. Luke tried to pull his hand free but couldn't break the other man's grip. The moment he moved his other hand to take a swing, Carlo warned, "Don't do it, kid."

"Don't call her a whore!"

"It's not meant as an insult. That's just the job she picked. If you intend to ride this path you're on, you've got to start seeing things simpler. A woman in her line of work, call it whatever you like, steals from the men she entertains. That's just the nature of the beast. And stealing wasn't even what I was concerned about. Just telling her about that money did enough damage."

"Yeah?" Luke grunted as he kept trying to reclaim his trapped fist.

Carlo relaxed his grip to let Luke yank his hand away. "That much money coming from a known killer . . . do you really think nobody else will come looking for it?"

"I . . . meant to keep moving."

"That's a good idea," Carlo said. "But all someone has to do is keep asking around before they eventually find someone who talked to some girl who talked to your Emma to find out where that money was headed."

Luke shrugged. "I bet Emma or any of those girls could get a man to believe anything they want. They could send a man off to New York City looking for me, just to get them away from here."

Where Carlo had been calm and near tranquil before, he suddenly became something else. His expression darkened and his eyes turned cold as he knocked Luke back with a quick shove. "Right there is why you've got no business making the ride into Wichita! You don't know anything about how this world works."

"I've seen plenty of this world!"

"You've seen some blood and felt some pain, but I'm talking about the world where killers live. Killers who don't forget when they're slighted and they don't get sweet-talked by some little thing with a pretty face. They have no qualms with taking a knife to those pretty faces or a hammer to their soft little hands just to make them talk. And no matter how good their intentions are, even if that girl you fancy truly thinks highly of you, there ain't no one who will stand up under that kind of misery. That's the world I'm talking about and that's where you're fixing to go!"

"Maybe I know about that too," Luke said. "I didn't just take that money away from the man that killed my family. I killed him to get it. I shot him dead and left him to rot on the floor."

Without so much as a flinch, Carlo shook his head and said, "That doesn't mean a damn thing. Getting lucky and firing a few scared shots into someone isn't the same as being the one who walks into a quiet place on a quiet day knowing full well that he'll be spilling blood before he leaves. It takes a certain kind of man to do a thing like that, and that man ain't you. Not yet."

"I can do what needs to be done where Granger or his men are concerned."

"That might be true," Carlo replied. "And that's why I keep trying to talk sense into you. I've seen plenty of men who've done their share of killing. I've waded through more blood than you can imagine, and the ones who ride into hell of their own accord aren't the same as normal folk. They got no spark in their eyes. Your friend may have a big mouth and is quick to anger, but his spark is still there. Yours is dwindling, kid. That's what worries me."

"You don't even know me."

"I know enough." Slowly, the darkness in Carlo's features receded and he appeared to be more human than he'd been a second ago. "It may not be my place to change you or even to try. At least I can help you stay alive."

Doing his best to salvage some of the dignity he'd lost by being so easily stopped when he'd tried to punch Carlo, Luke turned his back to him and waved him off. "Eh, what do you even care? You'll be getting what you want out of this."

Carlo reached out to place his hand on his horse's neck and kept it there. "When a man has been broken down to a certain point, he tends to grab on to any chance at all to do some good. For some of us, those chances don't come along too often. I don't expect you to understand, but you probably will before too much longer."

"You did your part and preached to me about being a good person," Luke spat. "Are you coming with us to Wichita or not?"

"I suppose I am. I still need what Granger has."

"Yeah," Luke grunted. "That's what I thought. Get your horse ready and meet us outside."

Waiting until Luke was almost out the door, Carlo said, "One more thing."

Luke stopped and turned toward Carlo without looking directly at him. "What now?"

"Don't mistake kindness for weakness. You talk to me again like I'm some dog you're telling to sit or fetch, and I'll hit you so hard you'll forget your own name. Got that?"

This time, Luke was so rattled he didn't think to hide it. When he turned away, it wasn't out of disrespect or youthful smugness. It was to keep his face from being seen directly. "I got it." He then went outside where Red was waiting.

Carlo rubbed his horse's ear. "You want another drink before we go? Take your time and have a drink. We're in no hurry."

Chapter 19

As the crisp autumn winds blew across the plains, they brought with them scents of burning leaves, cooking fires, and the chilly promise of the approaching winter. Luke, Red, and Carlo had been riding for two days without stopping unless it was absolutely necessary. The first day had been used to put Wendt Cross behind them and settle in as a group.

The second day was quiet.

On the third day, the riders had grown accustomed to one another and became more focused on the task at hand. Wichita wasn't much farther down the trail. As they drew closer, Luke and Red became anxious while Carlo fell into a calmness that wrapped around him like a shroud. Once his breakfast of bacon and oatmeal had settled into the pit of his stomach, Red looked over to him and asked, "So, what's that money for anyway?"

Carlo and the others were riding at a smooth pace that allowed them to make progress without unduly taxing the horses. Glancing over to Red, Carlo asked, "What money?"

"What money do you think?" Red said. "The three thousand you took from us."

"You mean the three thousand I took from what was taken from someone else?"

"Well . . . yeah. What's it for?"

"Captain Granger was supposed to provide a service for me," Carlo said. "It's a service I need done, so I needed to pay for it. If the wheels have already been set into motion for what I need done, I'll need that money to keep 'em turning."

"This fella sure knows how to dance around something, doesn't he, Luke? All them words and not one answer among 'em."

Luke laughed at that but didn't have anything to say.

"Captain Granger is the man to see to get things done," Carlo explained. "Folks from Kansas and as far out as the Dakota Territories come to him for guns, ammunition, hired killers, or anything else they can think of. The Captain before Granger's name isn't just decoration, which means he's got the army behind him."

"So the army is in the business of selling guns?" Red asked.

"The army knows what Granger tells 'em. As long as he protects enough settlers against Indians or throws enough grief at any Rebs that come through, he gets to do whatever he wants. With the war on, there's plenty of profit to be made by supplying either side."

"So he's a traitor," Luke said.

"Depends on how you come at it," Carlo told him. "He probably sees himself as a businessman. Folks with that kind of stain on their soul tend to find a simple way of looking at things. Granger is what you'd call a profiteer. He looks for other people's misery and finds a way to use it to line his pockets. Gotten real rich doing it too. After all, there's plenty of misery to be had nowadays."

"Still more dancin'," Red chuckled.

Luke looked over to Carlo and said, "He's right. You've said plenty without saying a thing about what he asked. I'm guessing you weren't trying to buy guns or such from Granger. So what kind of misery was he banking on in your case?"

"I wanted to disappear," Carlo said. "Still do."

"We found you half-buried in a horse stall," Red said. "Seems to me like you were doing a pretty good job of disappearing on your own."

Carlo smiled as he swayed to the plodding rhythm of his horse's steps.

"You're running from the law," Luke said. "That it?"

Red snapped his fingers. "He killed a man! I bet that's it. Maybe he killed a whole bunch of men. He's a gunfighter! We seen that much by how he handles a pistol."

"You're real smart," Carlo said.

Red sat proudly in his saddle. "You hear that, Luke?" he said. "Book learnin' ain't the only kind of smarts there is."

"He was stringing you along," Luke told him. "There's no reason to pay someone like Granger that much money if he just killed someone. He could've used that cash to go to Canada or something."

"That's not a bad idea," Carlo said. "Why don't we take that cash so we can all go to Canada? I hear it's real pretty this time of year."

"He's still stringing us along, right?" Red grunted.

"And dancing better than ever," Luke added. "He still hasn't given a straight answer."

"That's right! What are you h—"

"Quiet!" Carlo snapped. When he sat upright in his saddle, the caution he displayed spread quickly through the other two riding with him. Red went so far as to draw his pistol and hold it at the ready.

"What is it?" Luke asked.

"Someone's up ahead," Carlo told him.

Leaning forward in his saddle, Red squinted at the

horizon to find two men on horseback cresting a rise less than a mile away. "What are you so worked up about?" he asked. "They could be anyone."

"They're circling around to get behind us," Carlo warned.

"They could be goin' anywhere!"

"They were ahead of us before and then they turned to go up them hills like their tails were on fire." Carlo reached into a saddlebag to retrieve a set of field glasses encased in a dented metal housing that looked as if it had seen more action than both of the younger men combined. He put the glasses to his eyes and studied the distant figures in front of him for a few seconds before twisting around in his saddle to look behind.

"You gonna tell us there's someone already behind us too?" Red asked.

"Yep," Carlo replied. "That's exactly what I was gonna say."

Both Red and Luke turned to survey the trail at their backs. "There's nobody there!" Red said. "You're just ribbing us again."

"No, he's not," Luke said. "There's another two back there."

"Where? I don't . . . Ohhhh yeah," Red said. "I see 'em now. Doesn't mean they're following us."

"There's one good way to find out," Carlo said. He dropped his field glasses back into the saddlebag from which they'd come and then snapped his reins. "Let's give them a race."

"Now, there's something I like to hear!" Red said with a wide grin. With all the enthusiasm he'd show to a friendly challenge from his best friend, he flicked his reins and tapped his heels against his horse's sides to get the brown gelding off and running.

Allowing Red to take the lead, Luke urged his horse

to catch up to Carlo. Since Missy was a whole lot younger than Carlo's Old Man, he pulled alongside him and kept even. Without taking his eyes from the trail ahead of them, Luke shouted to be heard over the thunder of hooves, "Where are we going?"

"Doesn't matter just yet," Carlo replied. "If those men aren't who I think they are, they'll let us pass 'em by."

"Who do you think they are?"

"Men who won't let us pass them by." With that, Carlo snapped his reins to get his horse moving even faster. Old Man might have been lackadaisical most of the time, but he'd saved up enough steam to answer the call to speed right now. His hooves pounded against the dirt, building momentum until he was at a full gallop.

Luke could have overtaken him, but he kept just a pace or two behind so he could follow Carlo's lead.

"Red!" Carlo shouted.

For the moment, it seemed Red was too engrossed in stretching his horse's legs to worry about anything else. Carlo urged his horse to go a little faster, and somehow Old Man found the strength to meet the challenge. When he got closer, Carlo shouted to the younger man again. This time, Red turned around to look back at him and shout, "What?"

"If anyone shoots at us, you break right and I'll break left."

"Who's shooting at us?" Red asked.

"Nobody yet," Carlo replied. "Just do what I say if anyone does take a shot at us."

Before Red could ask yet another question, a rifle shot cracked through the air to send a round hissing over their heads.

"Go!" Carlo shouted.

Red pulled his reins to the right and peeled away from the other two.

"You," Carlo said to Luke, who was still keeping pace with him. "Follow Red and I'll meet these men head-on."

"But there's four of them!" Luke protested.

"Do as I say, damn it!"

"Fine!"

As soon as Luke steered away from the trail to thunder across the stretch of flat, open land to the right, Carlo reached for the boot in his saddle to draw a Sharps rifle and lever in a round. Allowing the lower half of his body to move along with the motion of his horse, he steadied his upper half and brought the rifle to his shoulder. He fired twice, not worrying about hitting anything. His only intention was to let the other riders know they had a fight on their hands if they wanted to keep after him. The message was delivered well enough for the closer pair to split apart and close in on the trail from separate directions.

The firing stopped for a moment, but Carlo knew better than to take any comfort from that. Both of the riders that had split off were going to try to close him in, and he'd completely lost sight of the other two. Rather than try to push his horse any harder, he pulled back on the reins to slow him down.

"Easy, boy," Carlo said as he fished in his pocket for some spare rifle rounds. When he found them, his hands went through the well-practiced motions of replacing the ones he'd fired. Still riding at a good pace, Carlo wasn't able to take exact aim, but he could get a lot closer than he'd been able to before. More shots cracked in the distance, coming from the right side of the trail. Apparently the other two riders had gone after Red and Luke instead of surrounding the easiest target. It had been a gamble that he could draw all of the riders to him, and Carlo was satisfied that he'd at least convinced half of them to come his way. The even larger gamble was that there weren't any more riders he hadn't yet seen.

Carlo's instinct and training were to take aim with his rifle and bring down as many targets as he could. However, he fought that back and lowered the Sharps on the off chance that the riders might just be responding to some mistaken threat. If they saw someone ready to take another shot at them, there was no reason why they wouldn't fire on him. If this was just some case of mistaken identity, they might retreat before anyone got hurt.

Hope truly did spring eternal. Unfortunately Carlo had found that drinking from that spring too deeply could get a man killed. The next shot that was fired burned through the air much too close for Carlo's liking. "Should've known better," he grumbled as he gave his reins a snap and steered Old Man in another direction entirely.

A few more rounds blazed through the space where Carlo would have been if he'd kept his old course. He charged toward the trail, turned sharply, and came around so the two riders firing at him were once again in his line of sight. Without hesitation, he brought his rifle up, fired a round, and then fired again. He knew those shots would be wide and high, but they were mainly a way for him to adjust to his awkward position and the movement of both him and his targets. Old Man had been with him long enough that he didn't get rattled by gunfire and responded to the touches of Carlo's knees against his sides since his hands were too busy to use the reins to steer.

Ignoring an incoming bullet, Carlo fired at one of the riders to convince him to break off from the offensive until he could steer back to come in at a better angle. Harder to ignore were the shots still coming from Red and Luke's side of the trail.

Carlo forced his ears to shut out everything he heard so he could concentrate on what he could see. His mind filled with angles, estimations, and calculations required to make a shot that most would consider to be too difficult to attempt. It had been a while since he'd flexed those particular muscles, but Carlo found they came back to him nicely when needed. When he was at the height of the arc of Old Man's stride, he let out the breath he'd taken and squeezed his trigger. The Sharps bucked against his shoulder to send a bullet into the center of his target.

One of the riders grunted and flopped back in his saddle. He somehow managed to keep from falling long enough to slow his horse and fire a few wild shots that thumped harmlessly into the ground between him and Carlo. As soon as he saw the rider lose his balance and drop from his horse, Carlo shifted his aim toward the next one.

That man was taking some extra time to line up a shot as well, which gave Carlo a chance to do the same. Two shots burned through the air. The first exploded from Carlo's Sharps, and the second was taken by the rider who was hastily trying to avoid being dropped. Recognizing panic when he saw it, Carlo levered in another round and fired in the rider's general direction. As expected, the rider's sense of self-preservation took over and he steered sharply away from the fight to gallop out of harm's way.

"Whoa," Carlo said as he shifted the rifle to one hand so he could better control his reins. After bringing his horse to a stop, Carlo sighted along the top of the Sharps while searching for Red and Luke. The remaining horses weren't difficult to find on such flat terrain, but he was having some difficulty distinguishing friend from foe.

"Come on, boys," Carlo said under his breath. "Bring them in closer."

There was no way for him to expect Red and Luke to

follow a plan that had never been formally made, but he repeated the order again and again while waiting for at least one rider to strike a familiar chord. Finally the sunlight hit one of them at just the right angle for Carlo to spot the fiery red hair sprouting from his head. When another rider fired a shot at that one, Carlo shifted his aim away from Red and started thinking through the angles required to make the long-distance shot.

Carlo pulled in a breath to steady his aim. As he let it out, he slowly tightened his finger around the trigger. Before the Sharps could send its round through the air, a puff of smoke spewed from Red's hand and the rider that had fired at him reeled before falling from his saddle. Without wasting another moment, Carlo shifted his aim at the other two riders on that side of the trail.

From what he could see, there were no surprises over there and no additional men had come along to lend a hand with the ambush. Both of the remaining riders looked identical from a distance, so Carlo focused instead on their horses. He was just about to give up and ride in closer when he reminded himself that Luke's horse had brown patches along its side and rump. He picked out that one without much trouble, but kept his aim slightly high just to be on the safe side. Squeezing his trigger, he fired and immediately lowered his rifle so he could reload.

That wasn't the only round that was fired since both Luke and Red were now pulling their triggers to unleash a firestorm at the last attacker. Rather than try his luck with two gunmen and a third that was shooting at him from afar, the last ambusher peeled away while firing his remaining pistol rounds behind him to cover his retreat.

Carlo hadn't replaced all of his spent rounds but snapped his reins anyway and rode across the trail. As soon as he thought he was close enough to be heard by the other two, he yelled, "Let him go!"

The younger men didn't stop shooting, so Carlo continued to ride up to them while shouting for them to back off. Red was all too happy to charge after the retreating rider with his pistol blazing away, but Luke turned to acknowledge Carlo with a wave. He then rode after Red to pass Carlo's request along.

Once it was clear that both remaining attackers had no intention of doubling back, Carlo turned around to find the man he'd knocked from his saddle. That one's horse was standing dutifully over its fallen rider, which made Carlo's task that much easier.

Coming to a stop several yards away from the wounded man, Carlo dismounted and drew his pistol. He kept his steps slow and quiet as he approached the spot where the stranger's horse was grazing. The rider lay nearby. He wasn't moving.

"Danny?" the rider called out. "Is that you?"

Carlo stepped closer without responding. He wanted to make sure the rider wasn't holding a gun, but the man's hand was obscured by grass and weeds. After a few more steps, he could see the glint of iron buried amid the swaying green blades.

The rider tried to crane his neck enough to get a look at who was coming. When he moved too far in one direction, he let out a strained grunt and slumped into a heap once again. "Danny?"

Approaching from the rider's blind side, Carlo strode close enough to drop one boot upon the fallen man's wrist to pin it to the ground. Now that the rider couldn't lift his pistol, Carlo stared down at him and asked, "Who's Danny?"

"You probably killed him, didn't you?"

"There wouldn't have been any trouble at all if you men hadn't started it."

"Yeah," the rider said in a tired voice. "You must've killed him."

"Who are you?"

"You're dead anyway," the rider said. "Doesn't matter anymore."

Hunkering down to take the rider's pistol away, Carlo asked, "Why did you shoot at us?"

When the rider looked up at him, he hacked up a cough that turned his teeth red with foamy blood. "We . . . know who you are. Captain Granger . . . put the word out. The army . . . is paying for you and your company . . . dead."

"You picked us out from a distance. You fired on us before you got a good enough look to see who you might hit."

The rider clutched his chest where his shirt and jacket were slick with a growing crimson stain. His face was already pale and his eyes were losing their focus. "We were . . . told you'd left . . . Wendt. . . ."

"Someone told you we left town?" Carlo asked. When it was clear that the rider didn't have much time or breath left, he reached down to turn his face toward him so he could see when he asked, "Who told you where I was or what I was doing?"

"Trader."

"A traitor?"

"No," the rider said with renewed vigor. "Trading company."

"Was his name Bickle?"

The rider smiled. "That's the one. You don't have any friends in Kansas. Ain't no one gonna harbor. . . . one of . . . one of his men. I'm just glad I could . . . see the look on your face when . . ." He swallowed and his eyes drifted in another direction as if they could no longer find anything to see.

Carlo closed the rider's eyes before he started searching the dead man's pockets. All he could find there was a few dollars and a couple of clay poker chips with a buffalo's head painted on their face. He took those items and then stood up to find the rider's horse watching him with large brown eyes.

"Did you round them all up?" Luke asked as he rode toward him.

"One of the men who came for me got away. From what I saw, so did one of yours."

"Yeah, and they're not coming back."

"We shouldn't be too certain of that."

"That's right," Luke said. "Especially since they seemed to know all about us and what we'd be doing."

"Is the one that Red shot still alive?"

"No, but he had a few words to say before he gave up the ghost. Seems nobody around here is very happy with you or anyone riding with you. I'm starting to wonder if it was a good idea to bring you along."

"I was trying to tell you that from the start," Carlo said.

Surprisingly, Luke laughed. It was a weary sound that shook him a bit more than it should, but it was a laugh all the same. "I was just fooling. You rode at those men like a demon and still had time to send a few shots at the ones me and Red were supposed to get."

"You were supposed to lead them away," Carlo reminded him. "Not shoot them. You and Red are lucky to be alive."

"Red's the lucky one. He'll be boasting about the man he shot for a while, I'm guessing, but I saw what happened. He was firing all over creation and managed to put one round where it was supposed to go."

"Did either of you get hurt?" Carlo asked.

"I caught a scratch, but it's nothing worth crying about," Luke said as he raised his left arm to show a spot where his jacket had been ripped by a passing round. The material looked to have been clawed by a wild animal and was stained with only a small amount of blood.

"And Red?"

"I'll have to ask him once he sits still long enough to answer. Should we go after them two that got away?"

"No," Carlo replied. "Whoever they are, we'll be seeing them again soon enough."

Chapter 20

Wichita

The day they intended to ride into Wichita was a quiet one. Not only was it uneventful, but none of the three men making the trip seemed very interested in talking. Even though they could have made it into town the previous day, Carlo insisted on making camp early so they could scout the area. He didn't receive any arguments. Luke gathered firewood while Red hunted for something to roast for supper. Carlo rode off to do his scouting a few hours before sundown and had yet to be seen when the sky was pitch-black and the stars were scattered overhead.

Having shot a few rabbits, Red turned them on their spits over a fire while staring into the flames. "Could be he ain't coming back," he said to break the silence that had shrouded most of the day.

"He'll be back," Luke replied.

"How do you know?" Picking up a stick to poke a large piece of wood into the fire, Red added, "If we had any sense, we'd find somewhere else to be as well."

"You really think that?"

"Ain't I been sayin' it most of the time?"

Luke sat with his back against a tree stump, keeping

his hands busy by disassembling the pistols he'd taken from Scott, cleaning the barrels, and fitting them back together again. "You want to turn back, you go right ahead. That's what *I've* been saying this whole time."

"What if Carlo did decide to leave us behind?" Red asked. "You still goin' into Wichita after Granger? Even after hearing about who he is, being a captain and all?"

"I don't care if he's a general or president. He sent the man that killed my family. If I don't at least take a shot at him, I won't be able to live with myself."

"Figured you'd say as much," Red sighed. "I'm not too worried about Carlo comin' back myself. He didn't have to come with us in the first place. Seeing how he can handle a gun, if he wanted to take his money and be on his way he could have done it at any time."

"If he was of a mind to do that," Luke added, "he could have taken all the money and been on his way."

"I wouldn't go that far. I been watching that money pretty close."

"I have too, but that doesn't change the facts. That's the reason why I showed him all the cash in the first place."

Red looked over at his friend while starting to laugh. Seeing the expression on Luke's face, however, erased the burgeoning grin. "You're not kidding, are you?"

"Nope."

"You put all that money in front of him just to see if he'd take it?"

Luke nodded. "If he's any sort of gunfighter, we wouldn't be able to stop him anyway. Best to know what his intentions are before we get too far along. If I make it easy for him, he'd take it and have no reason to turn on us directly."

Testing the meat that he was cooking for tenderness, Red put enough muscle behind the stick in his hand to skewer the skinned rabbit nearly clean through. "I ain't afraid of him."

"It's not about being afraid or not. It's about knowing whether we can trust someone."

"But that's our money! What would have happened if he stole it?"

"That's not our money," Luke said vehemently. "It's what Scott was after and it's what Granger wants. It's why my ma is in a hole six feet under instead of . . ." Luke couldn't find the strength to finish that sentence. When he opened his eyes again, they were too cold for tears to come anywhere near them. "I'd toss that money onto this fire if we needed it to stay warm."

"Well, there's plenty of wood around here, so get that notion out of your head," Red protested. "If you're so fired up to be rid of that sack of money, I'd be more than happy to—" Suddenly his head perked up and he snapped his eyes to the south. "Did you hear that?"

Luke's head had come up as well, but he wasn't just looking in the direction Red was concerned about. Something had broken a twig or rustled through a bush over there. "Someone's coming," Luke whispered. "Sounds like one but could be more."

"Could be Carlo."

"Or," Carlo said as he approached the camp, "it could be a whole mess of gunmen surrounding your camp. Didn't I tell you to keep the fire small?"

"I rustled up some rabbits," Red announced. "Can't exactly cook 'em over a candle flame."

Carlo could barely be seen until he got close enough for the light from the fire to find the outline of his head and shoulders. He walked slowly with Old Man's reins in his hands. Despite the step or two that had announced their presence, the horse was doing a fairly good job of walking lightly. "It's a good thing I came along on this ride," Carlo said. "You two are so reckless that it would only be a matter of time before you got yourselves shot if you were on your own."

"Where did you get off to?" Luke asked.

"Scouting. Just like I told you."

"You were supposed to be back before dark."

"Did a bit of asking around in town," Carlo said as he tied his horse to a tree where the other two animals were tethered. "Seems that Captain Granger isn't exactly hiding. His men set up a camp a mile or two northwest of town. Had a look at it, but needed to be careful. There's patrols on the perimeter and guards posted on high ground."

"Sounds like a fort," Red said.

"Apart from the lack of walls and a barracks, it could be," Carlo told him.

"How many men are with him?" Luke asked.

Taking a seat by the fire, Carlo removed his riding gloves and held his hands close enough to soak up some of the warmth from the crackling flames. "Less than a dozen. Could be less than ten, but they're soldiers. Fighting men. Not to be taken lightly. That's why I needed to wait until sundown before I could sneak away without being seen. Is that rabbit? I'm starving."

"Fire don't look too big now, does it?" Red scoffed.

"Anyone looking for it would've seen it by now," Carlo replied. "Damage is done, so I might as well have something to eat. We have any of them taters left?"

"I want to go back with you," Luke announced.

Both of the other two stopped what they were doing so they could take a good look at him. Carlo was the one to ask, "You mean back to Wendt Cross or Maconville?"

"Back to Granger's camp."

Slumping his shoulders in disappointment, Red took one of the rabbits off the fire so he could start cutting meat from bone.

"That was the plan," Carlo said. "I'll be taking both of you back there tomorrow to get a look for yourselves."

"No. I mean tonight. I want to go there tonight."

"Riding in the dark is never a good idea," Carlo said. "Anyone knows that."

"You made it back just fine," Luke pointed out.

"That's because I took my sweet time. Also, I've done enough riding at night to keep from breaking my neck out there. Dragging someone else along makes it a whole lot tougher."

"Is it close enough to walk?"

Carlo let out a prolonged sigh. Staring at the fire, he said, "I just got here. I'm hungry. I'm cold. We're all tired."

"You said yourself that going at night makes it easier to slip past them soldiers."

"Right. So we can go back tomorrow night."

"I didn't come all this way to dawdle about," Luke said. "We're less than a mile away from Wichita, so I know we could walk into town from here. You said that camp was only about another mile and a half more from there, right?"

"Yeah," Carlo groaned.

"Then what's the problem? We walk."

"It's been a hard ride just getting this far," Carlo said. "You want to throw all that away at the last second because you got impatient?" After staring at the younger man for a few seconds, Carlo asked, "I didn't even make a dent, did I?"

"No."

"How about meeting me halfway? Let's eat these here rabbits and sleep for a spell and then we can take our walk. It'll be mighty late, but that only means the sentries will probably be about ready to drift off also. How's that sound?"

"I suppose that'd work."

They spent the next hour or so fixing the meal, eating it, and cleaning up afterward. Once that was done and the fire was brought down to something that was just big enough to provide a hint of warmth, Carlo spread out his bedroll and lay down. He was snoring loudly within seconds after his head hit the ground and Red was dead to the world soon after. Luke sat quietly and continued familiarizing himself with the guns he'd taken from Scott. His eyes were sharper than they'd been since he'd left Maconville.

"Get up," Luke said while nudging Carlo's shoulder.

Carlo lifted his head and peeled his eyes open. "I was hoping you'd forget about taking that walk of yours."

"I didn't. Let's go."

"You're a bossy kid—you know that?"

"Just keeping us on schedule," Luke replied.

"What time is it?" Even though Luke didn't attempt to answer him, Carlo said, "Never mind. It feels late and that's all that matters. Knowing the hour won't make me want to start walking anyhow."

So far, Red hadn't moved. On his way past him, Luke gave him a kick that was just hard enough to rattle him out of whatever dream he'd been having. "We're going to that camp," Luke said.

"Huh?"

"Me and Carlo are walking to that camp."

"Yeah," Red said without fully opening his eyes. "Don't get shot."

"We won't. Watch the horses and make sure nobody comes around looking for us."

"Yeah." Even before the other two had gotten more than twenty paces away, Red was out cold once again.

Luke and Carlo started off slow. The first couple of

minutes were spent picking their way across flatland on the outskirts of Wichita. Once their eyes had grown accustomed to the darkness, they were able to see a dim outline of the town itself. Carlo was right when he'd said it felt late. There was a stillness in the air that only came after a certain hour had passed. Luke didn't bother checking the time. All he had to do was look up at the inky black sky and pull in a lungful of the bitingly cold air to know why folks called this the dead of night.

Now that they had something to set their eyes on, the two of them picked up their pace. Luke pointed himself toward the middle of town, but Carlo tapped his arm and pointed toward the northwestern edge. "No need to go all the way into town," Carlo said. "We can get close enough for you to see what you need to see. This ground is so flat we can see for miles in just about any direction so long as nothing is too tall to get in our way."

"No need to worry about that," Luke said. "I grew up in Kansas. Ground's so flat you can roll a ball from one end of the state to the other."

"I've seen just enough of it to know you're right about that. See those trees over there?"

Luke had to squint, but eventually he could make out the shapes of bare branches reaching to the sky like skeletal fingers trying to scratch the top of the world. "I see them."

"That's about as far as I got before I started running into those sentries I told you about. We get there and we should be able to get a look at that camp. We should stay quiet from here on out. Keep your steps light and your eyes open. I'll signal to you if we need to lie low."

"Were those guards on horseback?"

"The ones I saw were," Carlo replied. "But that doesn't mean there can't be more out here. Just do as I say and stick close to me." With that, Carlo moved toward those trees at a slow run.

They kept going for a good, long while. Luke wasn't able to keep track of how long exactly, but by the time they got close enough to hear the wind whistling through the branches of those trees, his lungs were burning and his legs were aching. Carlo's pace never faltered and his breath was as steady as if it came from a set of steadily pumped bellows creating the occasional bit of steam from his mouth.

From a distance, there seemed to be more trees than there actually were. Now that he was closer, Luke could see there were barely a handful of them sprouting from the flat ground, but they were spread out enough to represent a much larger area. He and Carlo hunched over and wound between the trees as their feet crunched upon a blanket of dead leaves.

Every step they took was announced by a loud rustle.

Every breath expelled from his lungs made Luke think he was marking his presence to anyone looking in his general direction from any number of vantage points.

No matter how intently he paid attention to his surroundings or the noises he made, Luke still didn't see the mounted guard until Carlo motioned for them to stop and pointed him out.

"Don't move a muscle," Carlo said in a voice that could barely be heard above the howl of a passing wind.

"He'll see us," Luke insisted. After being stopped in midstride, he was hunched slightly but not nearly low enough for his liking.

Sensing Luke's urgency to drop to the ground, Carlo hissed, "Stay right where you are. Even if he can see us, it's too dark for him to think we're anything other than more trees. If you move like a man, he'll know that's what you are."

Every one of Luke's muscles tensed. His stooped back was alight with fiery pain shooting up and down his spine. Now that he'd stopped moving, the heat his body had generated on the long walk from camp quickly bled off and allowed the autumn night's icy fingers to wrap around him.

As he stood there, rock still and trying not to breathe too hard, Luke was able to see the sentry clearer and clearer. His eyes remained focused upon the mounted guard and were able to pick out more details with every second that passed. The man had a rifle in his hand. Its stock was propped against his hip so the barrel was pointed up and away from his head. As his horse moved slowly along, the rider turned his head from side to side as if looking specifically for two intruders approaching Granger's camp.

Light from that camp was also becoming clearer and brighter. Luke knew that was just a trick of his eyes, but his stomach clenched all the same. He shifted his eyes without moving his head to look in the direction of the camp. As he stared at the dimly glowing light cast by several distant fires, he could make out the shadows of figures walking back and forth in front of the flames. He was too far away to catch any details, but could sense he was close to his reason for leaving Maconville in the first place.

"Easy," Carlo whispered. "Looks like he's about to move on."

"What if he comes this way?"

"He won't."

Although Luke wanted to ask how Carlo could know such a thing, he held his tongue and trusted that the other man wanted to avoid getting caught as much as he did.

"His back is to us," Carlo said. "Drop down nice and slow."

The air's chill had become so biting that Luke swore

his knees would creak when he eased himself to the ground. He barely felt the cold dirt when his fingers finally touched it and didn't stop moving until he lay like a snake with his belly pressed against the earth.

Carlo lay prone as well, keeping his legs and torso still while reaching behind him to slip one hand into a pouch that was strapped across his body like a bandolier. He quickly found his field glasses and brought them to his eyes so he could take a better look at the horseman.

"He's heading away all right, but not to the camp," Carlo said.

"Where's he going?"

"Probably making his rounds, circling the perimeter."

"Any more of them?" Luke asked.

Twisting to look in the opposite direction, Carlo said, "Probably at least one more. Odds are that another sentry will be more or less on the other side of the camp than this one. If we want to get in closer, now's the time to do it."

"All right, then. Let's go."

"Now, just to be clear, we're only scouting here."

"Right," Luke snapped. "I heard you the first couple of times you told me that."

"And somehow I still don't think you've heard me." When Luke started to climb to his feet, Carlo grabbed the shoulder of Luke's jacket to give one quick tug that was strong enough to take the younger man off his balance. "If you go off half-cocked," Carlo said as Luke glared at him defiantly, "you're on your own. Don't be stupid."

"I won't."

"We need to get a look at what we're up against. That way we can put together something of a plan before riding in to face Granger."

"All we've been doing is planning," Luke said. "Them

four that came after us knew we were on our way, so that means Granger knows too. Since two of them bush-whackers got away, I'd say we're lucky this whole county isn't swarming with Granger's men."

"Granger may be an army captain, but he doesn't have his pick of the litter where soldiers are concerned. He needs to be careful when making a move, and so do we. The last thing we want is to make things easy for him."

Luke pulled free of Carlo's grip and stood up. "I'm paying you to do a job. Let's go and do it."

As Carlo led Luke toward the camp, he felt more like a rat wandering into a bear's den.

Chapter 21

The sky was shifting to a dark purple hue by the time Luke and Carlo were close enough to see their horses tethered near their camp. Neither said a word to each other, but not out of any malice between them. They'd had two long walks in the frigid night air with a whole lot of crawling in between. They were so tired and intent on getting back to camp that neither one of them noticed the armed man creeping up on them until it was almost too late to do anything about it.

Luke pivoted toward the approaching footsteps. Carlo did the same while dropping to one knee and drawing his pistol.

Red walked up to them with Smith & Wesson in hand. "Where have you two been?" he asked while looking at them over the top of his pistol's barrel. He was so angry that he didn't even lower his weapon once he'd seen who was nearing the camp.

"Put the gun down, Red," Luke sighed.

"Him first!"

Carlo holstered his pistol and stomped toward the crackling fire. "If you want to shoot me, go right ahead. After the night I've had, you'd be doing me a favor."

Shifting his aim between both of the other two, Red let out a frustrated grunt and jammed his revolver under his belt. "You two just wander off in the middle of the night and then stroll back without a word of explanation?"

"We explained it to you before we left," Luke said. "You were half-asleep and probably don't recall."

At the moment, Carlo didn't recall either, but he wasn't about to join the conversation before helping himself to some of the coffee brewing over the sputtering flames.

"No, you . . . Oh, wait . . . ," Red said as some of the fury left his voice and face. "I do recall you two chattering on about something when I was trying to get some shut-eye."

"Well, that's what we were chattering on about," Luke grunted as he moved past his friend. "Did you make any breakfast?"

"I made coffee."

"How about fixing some breakfast? I can hardly move."

Red furrowed his brow in a way that made him look every bit the angry kid that had taken a swing at Luke when they'd first gotten to know each other outside their schoolhouse. "You think you can just order me around to do your cooking?"

Turning to face him, Luke asked, "Why haven't *you* had any breakfast yet?"

"Um . . . well . . ."

"Go on."

"I just got up," Red admitted.

"And we've been walking all night, crawling on the cold, hard ground, and trying not to get our heads blown off while getting a look at Granger's camp. That," Luke said with unmistakable finality, "is why you're gonna stop complaining and fix the breakfast."

When Red turned toward Carlo, all he got was an

amused shrug from the older man. "Okay. I'll make breakfast," Red said. "But not because you told me to. Because I'm hungry and you two can't cook to save your souls."

"Perfect," Carlo said. "I'll have griddle cakes and bacon."

"Don't push it," Red growled. "You'll have what I give ya. Now tell me what you two saw when you were sneaking about."

"It's not a very big camp," Carlo said as he poured some coffee from the tin pot and swirled it within his cup. "About half a dozen tents and most of those are just big enough to shelter an infantryman or two. Two officers' tents and two wagons. One of them's probably for the cook, and the other must carry supplies. Horses are corralled in one spot. Some men riding the perimeter. Nothing special there."

Red looked over to Luke, who shrugged and said, "That about sums it up."

"Sounds like what my brother said when he wrote home about the camps he lived in while marching into Virginia," Red said. "Only a lot smaller."

"Granger may be working outside of any law," Carlo said, "but he's still an army captain, and the habits that come along with that uniform are hard to shake."

Luke nodded. "That's good. If his habits are that predictable, it'll make it that much easier for us to get to him."

"Hold on, now," Carlo told him. "We've made it this far by keeping our wits about us. No need to lose them now."

"We did our scouting and I held up my end. I didn't go off on my own doing anything stupid."

"So let's keep it that way. Another few days of scouting and we should be ready to—"

"A few days?" Luke roared. "What's gonna be different in a few days? That is, apart from Granger and his men having more time to do some scouting of their own. Maybe they get lucky and find us!"

"If you would've let me finish, I was gonna suggest we break camp today and ride into Wichita. A town that size, we can rent a room and go unnoticed for a good while."

"And what do we do in that time?"

"I've got some ideas," Carlo said. "While I see to them, you two just need to sit tight."

"Sit tight while you ride off on your own?" Red asked. "I don't know if I like the sound of that."

Fixing a stern glare on Red, Carlo said, "Then it's good that it don't matter one bit if you like it or not."

Luke stepped up to the fire and placed his hand on the grip of one of his holstered guns. "I want to know what that money is for."

"What?" Carlo asked.

"I want to know why you were paying Granger."

"It's not important."

"I didn't think so at first," Luke said. "But things are different now. Perhaps we've just made it farther than I thought we would, but we're putting our lives into each other's hands, and one slip can make a difference between seeing the next day or not."

"We may be riding together, but that don't mean I have to answer to you for every step I take. I'll be relieving myself after this coffee runs through me," Carlo said while holding up his cup. "You want me to ask permission for that too or can I just tend to my own business?"

"That isn't all," Luke said. "You seem to know an awful lot about Granger and how he conducts himself. If you're closer to him than you let on, that could turn out real bad for me and Red."

Red took a reflexive step back. "How close? What did he do? What does he know?"

"Calm down," Carlo said. "Both of you."

"We will," Luke told him without moving his hand away from his holstered gun. "Just as soon as you give us some answers."

"You don't need them. All that matters is that we're here and we've both got things to settle with Captain Granger."

"That was enough before," Red said as he walked around the fire to stand at his friend's side. "But not anymore. Tell him what he wants to know."

Carlo set his coffee down and slowly climbed to his feet. Although he still looked every bit as tired as he'd claimed to be, there was nothing in his posture that made his gun hand seem impaired in the slightest. And there was nothing in his eyes to hint that he might be starting to feel the first lick of fear at facing both men in front of him. "I haven't done a thing to deserve this," he told them.

"We're trusting each other with our lives," Red said. "I know I can trust Luke here. Give me a reason why I should trust you."

"Because I've already fought to keep both of you breathing back when we were ambushed," Carlo said.

"All we're asking is for you to put your cards on the table," Luke said. "I've told you everything about what I did to get here. You do the same."

Carlo's eyes narrowed into slits. When he moved again, both of the younger men flinched. Instead of making a move to the gun at his side, however, Carlo's only move was to sit back down and pick up his coffee. Staring down at the little fire, he said, "I was a soldier."

"Figured as much," Luke said. "Keep talking."

"I'd been in the army since I was your age. Then the

war broke out and things changed. Everything changed." Slowly shaking his head, Carlo said, "You can't even know what war's like until you're hip deep in good men's blood, seeing the dead piled up in one place and the survivors screaming as the doctors . . ." He closed his eyes and steeled himself before opening them again. "Well, let's just say I'd rather die on the battlefield than let them butchers get a hold of me with their saws."

"Where did you fight?" Red asked.

"South Carolina at first. Then I was attached to another commander who led a smaller group of men. We headed north. I . . . scarcely recall where we were at any given time. It was just one fight after another. We'd meet the enemy and move on. Fight and ride. Fight and ride. That's what my life became."

"You're not in a uniform," Luke said quietly. "You weren't living like a soldier when we found you. So that means you deserted?"

"The man who led me and my friends into battle," Carlo said as if he were speaking about a ghost, "he lost sight of why we were fighting. He didn't need a reason no more. He was blinded by blood, spurred on by the gunfire that never let up, crazed from lack of sleep . . . I don't pretend to know what demons were in his head, but I do know he was leading us all to our graves.

"Every soldier knows any day could be his last. That don't mean he's about to throw his life away on another man's whim." Grinding his teeth together, Carlo gripped his coffee cup as if he was about to crush it into a ball and throw it into the woods. "What we were doing . . . it wasn't fighting anymore. It was just destruction for the sake of destruction."

"That's what war is," Red said with fire in his tone. "A soldier goes where he's supposed to go and does what he's supposed to do."

"That's what I thought too," Carlo said. "That's why I followed my orders for as long as I did until there was a day when I just couldn't stomach it anymore. Once a fighting man loses that edge, he's no longer useful. Even worse . . . he's dangerous to himself and those around him."

Scowling with disgust, Red said, "So you ran away. What's any of this got to do with Granger?"

"Captain Granger provides a lot of services," Carlo explained. "Services that are valuable with the war on. One of them is to take people away from where they don't want to be so they can start fresh somewhere else."

"Like those folks who help slaves come north?" Luke asked.

"Something like that, I suppose."

"Only instead of helping people get their freedom," Red said, "he's helping traitors run away from their duty. Ain't that right, traitor?"

Carlo stood up and walked over to Red. The younger man met him and puffed out his chest when he stood toe-to-toe with him. Even though Red was obviously welcoming a fight, he wasn't prepared for the speed in which Carlo snapped his hand up to clamp it around his throat.

"I know you've got a brother in the army," Carlo said in a fierce voice. "And I know you want to enlist as soon as you get the chance. I respect that, which is why I've allowed you to get away with what you've already said to me."

Red bared his teeth as he tried to speak, but his words were trapped beneath Carlo's grip and could not escape. His face reddened, both with frustration and a lack of air getting through to his lungs.

"I've got to pay for what I've done," Carlo continued. "I've got to answer for my sins . . . but I don't have to answer to some strutting, selfish kid who barely knows a thing about how the world works."

Carlo's fingers loosened as quickly as they'd snapped shut, allowing Red to fill his lungs with a couple of gulping breaths. Red created some distance between himself and Carlo with a powerful two-handed shove. "Don't put your hands on me again, tr—"

Red's insult was nipped in the bud by a slap across the face that was even quicker than when Carlo had grabbed his throat. The impact of Carlo's palm echoed in Luke's ears like a crack of thunder. He'd seen his friend display a violent fit of rage over much less, so he didn't know what to expect after this. One thing he knew for certain was that he didn't want to get in between the other two.

For a moment, Red was too stunned to do anything. Before he could get his wits about him, Carlo said, "That's a whole lot less than what you deserve, boy. If you doubt me, just think about what your brother would do to any man that looked him in the face and called him a traitor more than once."

"My brother wouldn't have to worry about that," Red told him. "Because he'd never do anything to deserve that name."

"As far as you know, I didn't either. You march through a street covered in blood and then tell me I'm wrong for not wanting to be a part of it any longer. Until then, keep your insults to yourself and show some damn respect."

Much to Luke's surprise, Red nodded. "All right. I guess you've got a point. I still owe you something, though." Without a second's hesitation or a hint of warning, he balled up a fist and delivered a sharp, snapping left cross to Carlo's face. Carlo recoiled at the impact but brought his head straight back around to look at Red.

Brushing the side of his hand against the spot where he'd been stricken, Carlo said, "You done?"

"For now."

"Good." Carlo then looked over to Luke and started talking as if the only interruption he'd had to endure was a loud sneeze. "Captain Granger was to provide me a safe passage on a cargo ship bound for the Caribbean."

"You couldn't do that yourself?" Luke asked.

"Not if I wanted to avoid dodging all the men that would be looking for me. In case you didn't know, there's a lot of ground to cover between Kansas and a seaport. Plenty of soldiers to be found at stations and such, not to mention the ones marching from one engagement to another. Makes it a whole lot easier if someone who knows about troop movements can tell you which way to ride and when to lie low."

"Surely the army's got better things to do than hunt down one deserter," Luke said.

Although he turned on him with the same venom in his glare that he'd directed at Red, Carlo knew the name Luke had just called him wasn't meant as an insult. Having earned that title, Carlo couldn't see his way clear to punishing the one who'd thrown it back at him. "They may have some bigger fish to fry, but the men who rode under my commander's flag are every bit as infamous as the man himself."

"Still seems like you'd be able to find your way on your own," Luke continued. "You've done pretty well this far."

"I found a town hardly anyone knows about in the middle of Kansas," Carlo said with a humorless chuckle. "That's a long ways from freedom. Besides, what I meant to buy from Granger was more than a ticket on a boat. It was a clean slate. He's got dirt on men who have the means to wipe a man's name from official records. Once that's done, there's not much reason left for anyone to hunt me down. Trust me when I tell you that's worth the price I meant to pay."

Dropping himself down next to the fire, Red sat hunched forward and said, "Could've come clean with this earlier."

"Yes," Carlo replied as he turned to look at him, "but something made me think it wouldn't go over so well."

"He's come clean now, Red," Luke told him. "That's the important thing. He didn't have good reason to trust us before just like we didn't have much reason to trust him. All that matters is that we're on level ground now. Ain't that right?"

"I suppose," Red grunted.

"And we are on level ground?"

Red took his time to prod the fire beneath the coffeepot with a charred stick. He was still muttering to himself when Luke came over to take that stick away from him and swat him across the shoulder with it hard enough to snap the stick in two.

"Ow!" Red howled.

"Are we on level ground?" Luke repeated.

"Fine! Whatever you say!"

Turning to Carlo, Luke tossed his half of the stick and said, "I think that's about the best we're going to get for now."

"I appreciate the effort," Carlo said.

"So, we've done our scouting," Luke said. "We've seen the men Granger has with him and it's a far cry from a typical army post. The captain is probably banking on his rank and station to protect him more than surrounding himself with a bunch of hired guns."

"I'd say you're partially right," Carlo admitted. "But those men we saw are more than just hired guns. They're professional soldiers, and if Granger has them with him, they must be real good at their job."

"There still ain't very many of 'em," Red chimed in. "Least, that's what you two said you saw when you snuck off."

"Don't take this the wrong way," Carlo said, "but one seasoned soldier is worth ten men who just have a gun in their hands and fire in their eyes. I've seen sharpshooters that could hold off a dozen riders for days just so long as he had bullets for his rifle and a good spot to fire from."

"He's right," Luke said. "We go in there thinking it'll be easy and we could be setting ourselves up for a fall."

Carlo turned to him and said, "Good to see you've gotten some of your sense back."

"I still don't see why you want to wait so long to do anything, though."

"Let's just take some time to think it over," Carlo requested. "We've been riding for a while and sleeping on the ground. If I have to eat more oatmeal and jerked beef, I'm liable to lose my mind. There's much better food to be had in Wichita and softer beds as well."

Red's head snapped up. "And saloons."

"Yep. Probably them too."

Luke studied Carlo as he asked, "Are you just suggesting that to buy the time you're after?"

"Every fighting man performs better when he's rested and well fed. Right now we're none of those things."

"I agree with that!" Red said.

"There's more scouting to be done," Carlo continued. "In town, there's bound to be plenty of folks who have something to say about Captain Granger and his men. Every little scrap we can find out about them will help when the time comes to make our play."

"And when will that be?" Luke asked.

"Are you really that anxious to put your neck on the chopping block?"

"It's not my neck with the ax hanging over it," Luke said before turning and walking away from the fire.

Chapter 22

It hadn't been long since Carlo had last been to Wichita. Although he hadn't let on to either of his young companions on this ride, he knew his way around town fairly well. Fortunately Luke's eye was drawn to a gunsmith's shop they found on their way to put up the horses for the night, and Red was drawn to almost every saloon he saw. The last he'd seen of that one, Red had been grinning back at a girl dressed in a filmy skirt and a bodice that was laced up tight enough to put her finest assets on prominent display. There had been a few words exchanged between Red and Luke, but Luke was willing to part with some more of Scott's money if only to stop being pestered for it.

"You need any?" Luke asked as if he were handing out drinks of water instead of crumpled cash.

"I suppose for expenses and such," Carlo replied.

Only when he caught a few passing locals taking more than a casual interest in the bag he carried did Luke bother to cover what he was doing. He handed over some money without making a show of it and said, "We should arrange a time and place to meet up to figure out what to do next."

"We know what to do," Carlo told him. "Take a look around town and listen to what folks have to say about Granger and the men posted in that camp. Just don't be too obvious about it or you'll draw them soldiers straight to you. Understand?"

"Yeah, I understand," Luke replied skeptically.

"I'd go with you, but it's best if we split up. That way, if word gets back to Granger that someone's been asking about him, it's only one or two men doing the asking. They won't be looking for all three of us if things go from bad to worse."

Although Luke nodded, he did so reluctantly. "Remember that hotel we passed on our way into town?"

"Which one?"

"The one that was across from that saloon Red was all worked up about."

"That doesn't help narrow it down very much," Carlo said.

"It was a big place hosting a poker tournament," Luke explained.

"Now I remember. I think that hotel was called . . . something about a horse. I know which one you mean."

"Meet up with us tonight at that hotel sometime around midnight. That should give Red enough time to burn off some of the steam he's been building up."

"I don't know," Carlo said. "That kid can hold a lot of steam."

"You don't have to tell me. I grew up with him. We'll meet up and go over what we found out when scouting."

"Just remember what I told you. Keep your ears and eyes open for whatever you can find about Granger, but don't draw attention to yourselves while doing it. And be wary of men wearing an army uniform. They don't need much of a reason to drag you into a jail cell, and if they're one of Granger's, they'll need no reason at all."

"Where are you going?" Luke asked.

"Other end of town. I figure you and Red have the saloon district covered well enough."

Luke nodded and they parted ways. Carlo could tell the younger man still had his suspicions, but was biding his time before acting on them.

For the next hour or so, Carlo kept moving from one spot to another without paying much attention to where he was going. Instead he was more concerned with anyone else that might be tagging along from a distance. He knew Luke had it in him to try to follow him through town to make sure Carlo was doing what he said he'd be doing. There was also the chance that one of Granger's men was on his trail after having lost two of their number in the ambush just before Carlo, Luke, and Red had made it to Wichita. Carlo kept alert as he wandered the streets and didn't find anything to make him believe he was being followed. That made him feel a little better, but not much.

One of the places he stopped was a corner saloon that seemed inviting enough from what Carlo could see through doors that were propped open by an old milk jug. Of course, with all the trail dust collecting in the back of his throat, any place serving beer would have been inviting. He went inside, stepped up to the bar, and knocked on the wooden surface to attract the attention of a mouse of a man wearing a dented bowler hat.

"What can I get you?" the man asked.

Carlo asked for a beer and when it was given to him, he picked up the mug and drained half of it in one swig. Before he could lift his arm again, he felt a frail hand take hold of his wrist.

"Not so fast, mister," the barkeep said. "You need to pay first. And if you're thinking of trying to get one over on me on account of my size, you should know I'm plenty strong enough to pull the trigger of the shotgun I keep within easy reach."

Carlo set the mug down. "No need for threats. I'm just thirsty, not a thief. I got every intention of paying."

"Good. Then I'll have the money for this drink."

"This right here should cover it and the next few rounds," Carlo said as he laid down the clay chip he'd taken from one of the dead bushwhackers outside town.

The barkeep looked down at the chip as if it had dropped from the back end of a mule. "That's not one of mine," he said.

"It ain't?"

"You see anything around here to make you think I'd honor that?"

Carlo looked around at the sparse amount of decoration in the place, which mainly consisted of a few grainy photographs on the walls and signs spelling out the house rules for everything from gambling to spitting on the floor. "Well, where would I go to cash this in?" he asked.

"The Red Bison! It's a billiard room across town."

"Just billiards?" Carlo asked.

Scowling, the barkeep said, "I ain't about to sing the praises of some other place. You gonna pay for that beer you drank or do I have to take what you owe out of yer hide?"

Digging into another pocket, Carlo took out enough money to pay for the beer he'd been given and one more. After he handed that over, the barkeep became a bit friendlier. When he was finished, Carlo stepped outside and looked up and down the street for any familiar faces. He found none and even as he made his way down the boardwalk, nobody seemed to take notice of him in the slightest.

Now that he was fairly certain he was alone, Carlo had some business that needed tending. This wasn't the first time he'd been to Wichita, but he wasn't exactly looking for street names or landmarks. Instead he took his horse from one stable to another, asking about prices and rates for different kinds of feed. The first place he went to was clean and had plenty of open stalls.

"These the best rates in town?" he asked the burly stable man.

"Damn straight."

"Is it worth it?"

"We're the best in Wichita. Ask anybody."

Carlo moved on.

The next place he found was a few streets over. It was a bit smaller than the first, and when he asked about prices for feed, he noticed the old man speaking to him losing interest by the second.

"There's a bigger place near here who offered some good rates," Carlo said as a way to test the waters.

The old man shrugged. "Go where you please, mister."

"A friend of mine put his horse up in a stable that was a lot worse than this one. Little place. What was the name of it?"

"Probably the Bar T Corral on the corner."

"Could be it. Is that the smallest stable in town?"

"Only three stalls," the old man said after spitting onto the ground between them. "Any smaller than that ain't hardly a stable."

"All right, then. I'll be back."

The old man hardly seemed to care when Carlo walked away.

It took some doing, but Carlo eventually found the Bar T wedged in between a butcher shop and a tobacco store. His horse was far from fussy, but even he began to fret when he got in the midst of those competing scents. Carlo stroked the horse's gray and black mane and coaxed him into the run-down structure that barely passed for a stable. As promised, there were only three stalls inside. Two were fit to host a horse, and the other was roped off where a gate should have been. Its back wall had been kicked out by an unhappy customer some time ago and was never repaired.

"What are your rates?" Carlo asked the man tending the place.

Rail thin and looking like death warmed over, the keeper chewed on a piece of straw and replied, "How much you got?"

"You serve quality greens?"

"No."

"I've got fifty cents for the rest of the day."

Shrugging, the sickly man said, "That'll do, I suppose."

"I may be using the stall myself if I can't find a room."

The keeper held out a filthy hand. "You pay yer money, you do what you please. Just like everyone else."

"You get a lot of folks wanting to sleep in your stalls?"

"Just drunks and vagrants," the keeper said while wandering off. "Any of you come around asking for breakfast and I'll toss you out on your ears."

Before Carlo could ask about that, the keeper had shuffled out of earshot. He was either going to an outhouse or just finding someplace that didn't smell like dead pigs and cheap cigars.

Carlo had been able to see everything the stable had to offer by looking in through the front doors. Actually he could only look through one of the doors because the other was nailed in place and refused to budge. Despite his low expectations, the inside of the stable wasn't too bad. Most of the straw had been recently changed and the horse that was occupying one of the functional stalls seemed friendly enough. Carlo opened the gate to the second stall and led Old Man into it.

"Real good system you came up with," said a gruff voice from the next stall.

Placing his hand on his holstered pistol, Carlo turned

toward the man who'd spoken up and said, "I don't know what you mean."

The man who stood up and brushed himself off was tall and slender with a narrow chin and scraggly mustache. His face was smeared with dirt and his clothes looked as if they might have been lying at the bottom of that stall longer than the man wearing them. He showed Carlo half a smirk and said, "The hell you don't know what I mean. It was your idea. Find the sorriest excuse for a stable in whatever town we were meeting in and wait there like a vagabond."

"Only when we're on the run," Carlo replied.

"And when aren't we on the run?"

"Lately . . . not too often." Carlo extended a hand across the low wall separating the two stalls. "Good to see you, Frank."

"Where you been, Carlo? I waited for you in Topeka for three days and you never showed."

"I was headed that way but got sidetracked."

"Marshals?"

Carlo shook his head. "Bounty hunters. Five of 'em."

Frank let out a low whistle. "They're stepping up their game. Most I ever had on my tail at once was three."

"That's just because my head's more valuable than yours," Carlo said with a grin. "Always will be."

"If they're in the market for the smelliest scalp in Kansas, maybe," Frank was quick to reply. "Haven't seen you for the better part of a month! What kind of trouble have you been getting into?"

"Same as the rest of you, I reckon. How many of us are here?"

"Just me for now, but a few stragglers are on their way."

"How'd you know to come here?" Carlo asked. "I tried sending word to you to meet me here, but never got a reply."

"Where'd you send it from?"

"Some little hole in the wall called Wendt Cross. It's a few days' ride from here."

Frank's eyes were sharp as an oiled blade. They studied Carlo intently as he said, "Last we heard, you'd be found in that town near the Missouri border if things took a turn for the worse. How come you never showed? More bounty hunters?"

"Same ones I already mentioned. They ran me so far from where I was supposed to go that I couldn't exactly double back and risk leading them to the rest of you."

"I suppose that was a good notion," Frank said.

Carlo slapped Frank on the shoulder and laughed. "Unless you and the rest enjoy fending off a bunch of bloodthirsty killers who'd stab you in your sleep just as soon as they'd look at you, it was a good notion indeed. I'm just glad you tracked me down. How'd you manage that?"

Although Carlo was still smiling, Frank didn't appear to be in such high spirits. "We crossed paths with a pack of bounty hunters that had been tracking us since we left Missouri," he said. "Had a word with them over a long couple of nights. Well, long for them anyhow."

"Yeah. I bet it was."

"Worked them over the whole time. Some of the others hurt them real bad. Once two of them died, the others were willing to talk." Narrowing his eyes until his gaze became as focused as sunlight through a magnifying glass, Frank said, "None of them mentioned seeing you."

Carlo knew better than to make a move toward his gun, but the muscles in his arm and hand flexed in preparation for a quick draw. Frank was a good man and a loyal partner, but he was also smart and deadly with any shooting iron he carried. "There's prices on our heads,

Frank. All of our heads. That's a lot of money, which means plenty of men looking to collect."

"Sure," Frank said in a cool, detached tone. "But what are the odds that anyone, even someone as stupid as most of the bounty hunters we find, would forget an ugly cuss like you riding a horse that's older than the dirt beneath its shoes?"

Finally allowing his gun arm to relax, Carlo balled up his fists and put them up to stand in a sloppy fighting pose. "I told you to never say a bad word about my horse! Don't make me beat the tar out of you like I did back in Leavenworth."

Frank defended himself against Carlo's halfhearted attacks while cracking a smile of his own. "You got in a few lucky shots in Leavenworth only because I was drunk."

"So, was that true, what you said about those bounty hunters?"

Now that the friendly assault had abated, Frank placed his hands on top of the low wooden wall separating the two stalls. "Sure enough. After what the bunch of us have been up to in these parts, we've got plenty of men looking to bring us in."

"And it doesn't look like it'll let up anytime soon."

"That isn't up to us."

"If those men you caught never even heard of me," Carlo said, "that means I've either been doing something real wrong or very right."

"Probably a mix of both," Frank told him. "Those men I told you about hadn't heard anything about you, but the pair we caught a few days later had tracked you almost all the way to Wendt Cross. That's how I finally caught up to you."

"Someone in Wendt Cross knew who I was?"

"The fella running the shoddiest stable in town remembered you. Actually he remembered Old Man over there," Frank said while giving the gray horse a friendly pat.

"Folks tend to remember the more handsome one between the two of us."

"I was gonna say something along those lines, except it was which one of you two smelled better than the other."

"I like my version better," Carlo said.

"There was a shop owner by the name of Bickle who told us you'd left town, probably heading to Wichita. So," Frank said while still patting the horse, "what brings you here when the rest of us were gathered in another part of the state? And don't go on about bounty hunters, because I didn't see many of them in these parts."

Carlo felt his muscles twitch again. Several times in the last few seconds, his stomach had clenched at his tenuous position much as it would if he was leaning back in a chair and teetering on the precipice of falling over. Any shift of his weight in that chair had to be done quickly or it was all over. "I had some business to conduct," he said.

"Did you, now?"

"That's right."

"What sort of business?" Frank asked.

The man in front of Carlo was several years younger, but had been chiseled into a formidable presence by the hardships of war and a life on the run. The bloody days of brother fighting against brother had a similar effect on many men, leaving every family member scarred and stronger for the experience.

"You remember that double-dealing captain that hunted us down just to make us pay a toll for crossing into this state?" Carlo asked.

"The one selling the guns that were stripped from some of his own dead soldiers?"

"That's him. He's the one who sent some of those bounty hunters after me. After all of us, really, but they found me first."

"Makes sense," Frank said. "He'd only be doing his job by hunting us. Doesn't make the rest of what he does any easier to swallow, but at least he's doing some of his duty."

Carlo spat on the ground as if it were someone's face. "When those bounty hunters came for me, the first thing they did was try to recruit all of us. I was to pass along a message to Anderson that if we joined up with his bunch and took orders from Granger, our days of being hunted by troops and bounty hunters alike were over."

"I would have liked to pass that along to the others. We've all been holed up for so long we could use a good laugh."

"That's what I thought any of you would say," Carlo told him. "Which is why I decided to take the opportunity I was given."

"What opportunity would that be?" Frank asked.

Carlo reached into his pocket for the poker chip he'd acquired outside town and tossed it through the air. Frank caught it in one hand, turned it over, and studied the picture drawn on it.

"That came from a place called the Red Bison Billiard Room," Carlo explained. "Obviously there's more than just billiards being played there."

"This isn't exactly the only billiards room in Kansas."

"Maybe not, but it seemed important to some of Granger's men. After what he pulled when we first rode into this state, I've been wanting to get my hands on that strutting bastard so bad I could taste it."

"You're not the only one. Without him making things difficult for us, we could have free rein in this state and a good part of Missouri, besides. That captain is dug in worse than a tick. Even if he ran his men by the book, he'd be enough of a problem. Him being crooked only makes things worse." Turning the poker chip over by rolling it across his knuckles, Frank asked, "You think he can be found at this billiard hall?"

"I've got reason to believe so," Carlo replied. "I need to have a look-see for myself before doing anything that might scare him off."

Frank shook his head and sighed. "You and your scouting. Enough to test the patience of a saint."

"I go in alone and I should be able to keep from being noticed. If more than one of us goes anywhere near Granger, we'll be spotted for sure. That happens and he moves to some other place he's got staked out."

"Or he tucks himself into a fort or some other armed camp," Frank said.

"Which makes things messy."

Although only in his early twenties, Frank wore his scars with the weariness of someone twice his age. When he grinned, he looked more like the young man he truly was. "We like messy," he said. "Messy is what we're here to be."

"Messy, yes," Carlo said. "Not dead. If the rest of the men were all here, I'd say we burn that billiard hall to the ground with Granger and as many of his soldiers in it as we could fit. We could even flush him out and hunt him like the mangy dog he is. But the rest of the men aren't here." Studying Frank a little closer, Carlo asked, "Are they?"

Frank let the question hang in the air for a few moments before saying, "Not yet. It's just like I said before. Most were in the northeastern part of the state. Anderson and the rest are pretty well scattered for now. Given some time, I'm sure I could round up a few reinforcements."

"Given enough time, I'd like to round up all of them. Lord knows they all deserve to carve off a piece of Granger for themselves. That captain is slippery, though, and he could be moving along any day. If he's here, I'd like to make the most of the opportunity to nail him to a wall."

"And I'd like to help in any way I can."

"Much obliged, Frank. Let me do some more scouting and I'll let you know what I find. After that, we can put something together that will shut Granger down for good."

"I like the sound of that," Frank said as he once again offered his hand.

Carlo shook it firmly.

"Now that I found you," Frank continued, "I ain't about to spend another night in this stall. There's a hotel not too far from here called the Horse Tether. I'll stay close to there all day tomorrow. That give you enough time to see whatever it is you'll be out to see?"

"More than enough."

"Good. I'll look forward to hearing from you. Sure you don't need any help before then?"

"I appreciate that," Carlo replied, "but I'll need to move swiftly to keep from being seen. That's best done when I'm alone."

"Figured that's what you'd say. Of course, the last time you went off to scout on your own, we didn't see you again until . . . well . . . now."

"There's a war on," Carlo said with a weary shake of his head. "Things tend to derail awfully quickly sometimes."

Frank's eyes narrowed in a way that Carlo found particularly troubling. “Yeah,” he said. “They do. Think you’ll know something by noon tomorrow?”

“Without a doubt.”

Frank nodded. “That’s good to hear. Try not to get sidetracked again. If you’re too late, I’ll have to come looking for you.”

Carlo did a good job of hiding it, but he did not like the sound of that.

Chapter 23

Carlo and Frank parted ways amicably. When they left the stable, Carlo said he had to pick up some supplies and walked in the opposite direction from Frank. Every step of the way, Carlo was expecting to see another familiar face look out from a nearby store. Fortunately he saw nobody of concern. Even more fortunate was the fact that Frank didn't walk in the direction of the hotel that both he and Luke had mentioned. After rounding a corner, Carlo broke into a run.

He didn't head to the Horse Tether straightaway. Instead he took the cautious route in the event that someone had accompanied Frank and simply hadn't been spotted yet. Carlo cut down alleys, crossed through empty lots and used any shortcut he could find to take a crooked route to the hotel in hopes of beating Frank there.

The Horse Tether wasn't a large hotel but was prominently displayed at a corner that received a good amount of traffic from newcomers to town. Carlo was panting like a tired dog when he stepped inside and looked around.

"Can I help you?" asked a cheerful woman behind a long desk adjacent to the door.

Carlo was about to ask where the restaurant was but

spotted it on his own through a doorway to his right. Leaving the clerk without saying another word, he stepped into the dining room to find about a dozen tables. Three of them were occupied. One of those occupants was Red.

Approaching the table, Carlo said, "We need to get out of here."

Red had his face buried in a bowl of stew. Startled by Carlo's entrance, he looked up and asked, "Where did you come from?"

"Listen to me. We need to go. Where's Luke?"

"He's out scouting like we agreed. He told me to stay here in case you showed up."

"Come on," Carlo said as he looked out a large window with a good view of the street.

Red stood up and took his time wiping his face with a rumpled napkin. "I didn't think you'd come back so soon. Fact is, I thought you'd probably take some time to yourself and not be back until tomorrow. That's why I took some time and had something to eat."

"You're always eating, Red. Now just come outside with me before I knock you over the head and drag you out."

Red followed Carlo to the front door. As soon as they stepped outside, Carlo cursed under his breath for not trying to find another way from the hotel that didn't put them in plain sight to anyone on the busy street. Since they were already through the door, Carlo kept his head down and hurried toward the front of a nearby steak house.

"What is wrong with you?" Red snapped once they finally stopped moving.

"Which way did Luke go?"

"Answer my damn question!"

Facing Red, Carlo replied, "Someone else is coming for Granger."

"That ain't too big of a surprise, considering what kind of business he gets up to."

"They're not the sort of men we want to cross."

"How do you know?" Red asked. "What are they to you?"

"I met up with one of them while I was on my own—"

"I knew it!" Red exclaimed. "There was always something shady about you, and I figured you had your own plan running."

Carlo tried his best to watch the street while also watching Red. "Just let me finish what I was saying."

The younger man's teeth were clamped together and his breath was making his chest swell. "The way you snuck around in Wendt Cross. The way you did all that talkin' without hardly saying much of anything at all. I knew there was something wrong, but Luke wanted you along to help when the lead started to fly and I should've put my foot down."

"Red, stop talking for a second!"

Although he did stop talking, Red made a quick reach for the gun tucked under his belt.

Carlo was even faster as he plucked the Smith & Wesson from Red's grasp. "We need to find Luke, and we need to find him fast."

Still shocked that his weapon had been so easily taken from him, Red blinked and sputtered for a second before asking, "Why? What's going on?"

"There are other men coming after Granger and they'll be meeting up at that hotel. When was Luke going to come back?"

"Probably around noon like we agreed."

"Do you know which way he headed?" Carlo asked.

Red had composed himself once again after being taken away from his meal less than a minute ago. "Who are these other men you're talking about?"

"They're dangerous. That's all you need to know right now."

"The hell it is. Gimme back my gun."

"You just need to trust me," Carlo insisted.

"I don't even trust that there are any other men at all. After all you've been spouting on about since me and Luke first laid eyes on you, it's hard to say when you're not just talking to hear your own voice."

Carlo was about to defend himself when a rumble rolled through the air as well as the ground beneath their feet. Both he and Red turned toward the sound to find a trio of horses thundering down the street, kicking up dust and scattering people in front of them. As the horses raced past, Carlo shoved Red into the shadow provided by an awning and turned so his back was to the street and he could watch the horses by glancing over one shoulder. He only caught a fleeting glimpse of the riders' faces, but that was enough to draw a curse from the back of his throat.

"What?" Red asked. "What's wrong?"

"Here," Carlo said as he slapped the Smith & Wesson into Red's open hand. "Take this. You might need it."

"I will? Why?"

Carlo had already started running along the boardwalk in the wake of the thundering horses. Shoving past several locals who were still rattled after nearly being trampled while crossing the street, Red caught up to Carlo with a few long, powerful strides.

"Tell me what's goin' on right now or I swear I'll shoot you in the leg!" Red shouted.

"Those are men I used to ride with," Carlo said without slowing down. "I thought I'd left them behind, but they caught up to me. They must've been following me."

"For how long?"

"Hard to say. I thought I was free and clear, but someone must have picked up my scent somewhere along the way."

Red matched Carlo's pace step for step, even as they cut across small sections of town to try to catch up to the group of horses. It wasn't difficult following them. All they had to do was listen for the beating of hooves against packed dirt and the surprised voices of those who were pushed aside.

They'd emerged from between two buildings to come out onto one of the narrower streets that cut through Wichita. Although the horses weren't in sight, the dust they'd kicked up still hung in the air. Carlo got his bearings and ran across the street to head for another alley.

Red remained at his side, dodging an elderly couple out for a stroll and leaping over a water trough instead of taking the time to go around. "What difference does that make to us? If they want to talk to the captain, we just wait, and if they kill him, we can head home and be done with it."

"Because," Carlo told him, "it could also be that they want to burn Granger's camp to the ground along with the town he chose to build it near."

"Why the hell would they do something like that?"

"Because that's what they do."

When he made it to the next street, Carlo recognized several storefronts from when he'd passed them earlier. He and Red had managed to get ahead of the horses, but not by much. The riders thundered past the next corner and moved on.

"I know where they're headed," Carlo said. "I just

thought we'd have a bit more time before they went there. Looks like the schedule's been changed around a bit."

Carlo was on the move again and Red was still with him. This time, however, the younger man got a step ahead of him so he could ask, "Where are they headed?"

"To a billiard hall called the Red Bison."

"That's where that poker chip came from," Red replied.

"You know about that?"

Red nodded. "Luke asked around and found out right before he left the hotel." Bolting ahead another couple of steps, Red planted his feet and stood in front of Carlo like a wall. He stopped the other man before they could cross the next street. "What do you and those riders have to do with Granger?"

"Buying guns from him, mostly," Carlo said. "Sometimes dynamite or powder. We always knew Granger was playing both sides of the fence, but we figured we'd just burn him down if he decided to try to hurt us. Granger made his play by sending bounty hunters after us in droves and cutting us off from the supplies we bought from him. Doing all of that and then sitting back like nothing is wrong is like spitting in a man's face. The men I rode with don't take kindly to that sort of thing."

"Is Granger working with the Rebs?" Red asked in a harsh whisper.

"He's working for himself. He doesn't care about blue or gray. His only concern is the color of a man's money or the weight of his gold. I thought I'd be able to trade with him for one last deal."

"Your ticket onto that boat."

"That's right." Carlo looked down the street, but the horses were long gone. "I thought if I could get what I needed before I was missed from the men I'd left behind,

I'd be long gone before they started looking. If I got far enough away and stayed there for a long enough time, they'd eventually stop looking. The way they were going, odds are they wouldn't last much longer anyhow. That's a big reason why I wanted to break away from them in the first place."

"And the rest of what you told us before?"

"Is true."

Now Red looked in the direction the horses had gone. "You think those men will set fire to Wichita just to get to Granger?"

"That's the least of what they'll do."

"Then what are we waiting for?" Red asked before leading the way across the street so they could continue to cut across town.

Carlo caught up to him and said, "Don't go rushing in. We're to hang back and watch until we see an opening. Otherwise, we'll only be giving those men more targets to shoot at and everything from there will only get worse."

"Sounds to me like you think you're already on their bad side."

"I'm not sure what side I'm on with them, to be honest."

Thanks to them being able to bypass streets to take the most direct route possible, they were within sight of the Red Bison just as the mounted gunmen were reining their horses to a stop. Standing in the shadow of an alley, Carlo watched the three men dismount. He recognized all of them. Frank was among them, speaking to the others in a rush. Most likely, he was talking about strategy for storming into the billiard hall and flushing out their target.

Carlo was wound so tight that he reacted to the sound of approaching footsteps by drawing his pistol and pivoting to meet whoever was coming. Luke had his gun drawn as well and kept walking toward him and Red without being deterred by the weapon currently aimed at him.

"What are you two doing here?" Luke asked.

Carlo lowered his pistol without holstering it. "I was just about to ask you the same question."

"I'm scouting, just like I said I was."

"Told you," Red scolded.

"You find anything?" Carlo asked.

When Frank and the other two men finished tying their horses to a post near the front of the Red Bison and started walking toward the billiard hall's front entrance, Luke had the good sense to turn his back to them so they didn't see him standing there with a gun in his hand. "There's a bunch of soldiers in that billiard hall," Luke said.

Fixing a hard glare on the young man, Carlo asked, "You went inside?"

"How could I scout the place unless I went inside?"

Carlo shook his head while looking back across the street.

"There were at least eight or nine soldiers inside," Luke continued. "Didn't seem like they were too worried about answering to anyone, though. Their uniforms were a sloppy mess and they strutted around like they owned the place."

"It's possible Granger does own that place," Carlo said. "I know he's made enough money to buy an interest in several businesses throughout Kansas. Only makes sense that he'd own a piece of at least one place here in Wichita."

The three men who'd ridden to the Red Bison were slowly approaching the place with their hands resting on their holstered guns. Another three rode in from the opposite end of the street to meet up with the ones Carlo had followed. At Frank's direction, three of them split off to go around to the back of the building while he and the other two headed for the front.

"Who are they?" Luke asked.

"Friends of his," Red said while hooking a thumb at Carlo.

When Luke looked over at him, Carlo said, "I used to ride with them."

"Are you all still friendly?"

"Nope."

"If Granger is in there," Luke said, "what will those men do to him?"

"Considering the trouble Granger has caused, they'll most likely kill him. The only question is whether they do it there or they drag him away to do it somewhere else after having some fun with him first."

"So let's ride out to that camp."

"If the fight is here, then why go all the way out there?" Red asked.

Luke looked at his friend and spoke as if they were once again back in their old schoolhouse. "Because if Granger's in that billiard hall, he's already got a fight on his hands. I'm guessing those six men can handle the soldiers inside. Is that right, Carlo?"

"More than likely."

"If that's the case, then Granger will be put down like he should. But if Granger isn't inside that building, he's probably at his camp. And since I saw a good number of soldiers in there," Luke said while pointing to the Red Bison, "then that means there's that many fewer protecting the camp. Sounds to me like the best time for us to head out there."

Red grinned and slapped his friend on the shoulder. "He always was the smart one."

"What do you say, Carlo?" Luke asked. "I'd rather not

walk into a shooting gallery inside that billiard hall. You see any reason why we shouldn't try our luck at that camp while fortune is smiling on us?"

More than anything, Carlo wanted to shoot that plan down with an argument that nobody could dispute. Unfortunately he couldn't come up with a single one.

Chapter 24

As they collected their horses and rode away from town, Carlo told Luke everything he'd told Red while they'd been running through the Wichita streets. There wasn't as much time to talk as he would have expected since they were moving as if their tails were on fire. It wasn't long before the echo of gunfire rolled in from the direction of the Red Bison. Once they were outside town, it was clear that a vicious fight had commenced and would spill out of that one building sooner rather than later.

Making the ride in daylight was a whole different story than when he and Luke had approached the camp at night. Apart from simply being able to see where they were going, Carlo felt more exposed and vulnerable to a marksman's bullet. Even from a distance, he could see movement near the camp. Horses were heading toward another section of town. One rider, most likely a sentry, took a sharp turn to head toward the three unexpected arrivals. Luke and Red barely seemed concerned with any of this. Carlo took no comfort from that. After all, there was rarely solace to be found in ignorance.

Now that he could see more than what was illuminated by firelight, Carlo could tell the camp was more spread out than he'd originally thought. There were small watchtowers, constructed near clusters of trees and barely large enough for one man, at three different locations. If he and Luke had gotten much closer when they'd done their previous scouting, they could very well have been picked off by anyone posted in one of those towers. He signaled for the other two to stop and they reluctantly complied.

"What are we waiting for?" Luke asked. "If we got a chance to take a run at that camp, it's right now!"

"Don't you see those towers?" Carlo asked while digging in his saddlebag for his field glasses. "They might already have spotted us."

Luke squinted at the camp and picked out the towers.

Studying each one through the field glasses, Carlo grunted under his breath.

"What is it?" Red asked.

"Looks like only one of those towers is manned," Carlo said.

"Ain't that a good thing?"

"Could be. Or it could be a trap."

Luke shook his head. "There's no reason for an army captain to try and trap us."

"It may not be us he's after."

"Then we should be able to keep ridin'!" Red said. "If anyone tries to stop us, we shoot 'em."

Carlo looked over to Red and scrutinized every harsh line scrawled across the young man's face. "Since when did you become so eager to shoot anyone?"

"Since we got so close to putting this whole matter to rest and goin' home."

Luke lowered his eyes. "I can do this on my own from here. We won't get a better chance than this."

"You're so sure about that, huh?" Carlo asked.

"It just makes sense."

"Well . . . I happen to agree with you." Carlo put the field glasses away and pointed to one side of the camp between the two empty watchtowers. "We'll ride in right there where it's open. We leave the horses in the trees and go in on foot. Now, are you two sure you still want to do this? This isn't a game. We could get killed in a dozen ways. There's a chance none of us makes it out of there alive."

"I know," Luke said. "So if you want to turn back now, I understand."

There was no changing Luke's mind or convincing him to wait. There was no pointing him in another direction. His mind was set and he would take a run at Granger now or later, with help or on his own. Ever since they'd left Wendt Cross, Carlo had been watching the kid to see just how serious he was. If there'd been any glimmer of hope in ending this mission of vengeance, it was gone as of this very moment.

"I'm not turning back," Carlo said. "I've got business with Granger as well, remember?"

Luke nodded. "So . . . do you have any ideas about the best way to get close enough to take our shot at him?"

"You're actually asking for advice?"

"That's why we brought you along." Smirking, Luke added, "Sure wasn't for your cooking."

"Well, as a matter of fact, I do have an idea or two."

After a brief discussion about strategy, the three of them rode toward the closest thing the camp had to a blind spot. If they were in more rugged terrain or someplace that had more hills to offer, Carlo would have felt a lot more comfortable with making his approach. Since relocating the camp wasn't an option, they made do with what they had.

Before they even reached the trees, a pair of riders had circled around to meet up with them. Luke and Red dismounted and were tethering their horses when the uniformed soldiers spread out to cover them with rifles and reined to a stop. The soldiers were positioned so if any shooting started, they would have the three unannounced guests in a cross fire.

"Who goes there?" one of the soldiers asked. He was a burly fellow with a thick beard partially covering a scarred face. The other soldier looked to be around the same age as Red and had a minimum of insignias or markings of rank on his dark blue coat. While both of them wore the trappings of Union soldiers, they were far from polished. Their buttons were tarnished. Their collars weren't starched. Compared to the soldiers Carlo had seen before, these men were more like vagabonds.

"We're from town," Luke said in a rush. His eyes darted back and forth between the two soldiers and he froze while reaching toward Carlo's horse.

Carlo was still in his saddle, head down and body slouching forward.

"Who sent you?" the bearded soldier asked.

"One of the men from the Red Bison. There's trouble."

Although the bearded soldier kept a stoic expression, the younger man was quick to ask, "What kind of trouble?"

"A fight. Some men rode up and started shooting up the place."

"Was anyone hurt?"

Before Luke could answer, the bearded soldier asked, "Why were you sent out here? Why didn't one of them come with you?"

"They had their hands full, sir," Red said. "Whoever attacked that place did it in a hurry. Just started shooting through the windows without caring who was hit."

"And you happened to see all of this?"

"It was a shooting right out in the open," Luke replied. "Everyone saw it."

The soldiers looked at each other, but the rifles in their hands didn't waver. Finally the bearded one said, "You were to find someone for help."

"That's right, sir," Red answered.

"Why didn't you fetch the law?"

Pointing to Carlo's slouching frame barely staying atop his horse, Luke said, "Because he told us not to. He said to bring him straight back here as quick as we could."

"And who is that, exactly?"

Carlo groaned as he tried to lift his head, managing only to reveal his chin and the bottom portion of his mouth beneath the brim of his hat.

The two soldiers closed in for a better look and when they were straining to see his face, Carlo brought both hands up to point a gun at each one of them. The pistols in his hands went off in a quick staccato beat, knocking both soldiers from their saddles.

"What are you doing?" Luke asked.

Keeping both smoking pistols in hand, Carlo swung a leg over Old Man's back so he could slide off and hit the ground with both feet. "This is the job you signed on for, kid. Too late to turn back now."

"We don't know if these men had anything to do with the man that came to Maconville," Luke protested. "We were supposed to take them prisoner. Tie them up and keep them out of our way."

"If they're Granger's men, they had enough to do with what happened to your family. Besides, we don't get to pick and choose who we fight in a war."

"This isn't war," Red said.

Carlo was standing over the bearded soldier when he looked up to fix a fierce glare on Red that caused the younger man to retreat half a step. "If you believe that, then you never should've left your mama's side. Now help me search these two before— "

The younger of the two soldiers barely moved before Carlo was on him. Both Red and Luke were shocked by how quickly he covered the patch of ground to stand over the man he'd shot. The soldier's chest was bloody and his face was already losing its color as he opened his mouth to speak.

"How many of you are here?" Carlo asked before the soldier could get out a word.

"Who. . . .who are . . . ," the soldier grunted.

"Never mind who we are. Just answer my question and you'll get to a doctor."

"F-five. Or six of us. Some went to town . . . heard the shooting."

"Is Granger here?"

"In . . . his . . . in his tent."

Without taking a moment to think or address the soldier's pleading eyes, Carlo stomped his boot into the young man's face to knock him out cold.

Jumping at the dull impact, Luke said, "You've lost your mind. This wasn't how the plan was supposed to go."

"You wouldn't have gone along with this if I told you how I was going to play it, but this is the only way we stand a chance. You came here to kill a man, didn't you? That ain't no time to be squeamish."

"We were supposed to sneak in," Luke protested.

"You saw the look in that one's eye," Carlo said while pointing back to the spot where the bearded soldier lay. "He wasn't going to let us go anywhere. The only way for us to gain any surprise here is to do the one thing they don't expect and that's to burn a path right to their front porch when they're at their weakest."

"They're after us now," Luke whispered. "Someone must've heard those shots!"

"They would have been after us anyway. Best for us to get through them now than give them time to form ranks and come at us stronger while we deal with Granger."

"What kind of fool plan is that? Weren't you the one telling me not to go off half-cocked?"

"It's all a matter of timing, kid," Carlo said. "I'm telling you now's the time to charge."

Luke looked over to his friend for support and got only a wary shake of the head from him. "He's right," Red told him. "It's now or never. Too late to switch tracks anyways."

Without waiting for the boys to come to a consensus, Carlo took the rifle from the nearest unconscious soldier's hands and roughly pulled at the uniform's tarnished buttons. "One of you take that one's coat," he said while nodding toward the bearded soldier. In a matter of seconds, Carlo had the younger one's coat on and Luke was shrugging into the other one. "This won't do much, but it might buy us a second or two," Carlo said.

Not far from their position, men shouted orders to one another while drawing closer. Carlo hunkered down and set his sights on the camp. "Follow my lead and stay close," he said. Then, without any further warning, he shouted, "There's only two of them, coming in from the east!" Carlo tossed his hat away, held the rifle in both hands, and lowered his head while rushing into the camp.

Luke hurried to catch up, but Carlo was weaving between the trees and moving so erratically that it was hard to keep eyes on him. Fortunately the two other soldiers that came along had the same problem. When they did spot Carlo, they paused to get a look at the face of the man in the uniform. It wasn't much of a pause, but more than enough for Carlo to fire a shot at them. The first went down with a wound to the chest and the second was hobbled by a shot from the pistol Carlo pulled from his holster.

"Take care of him!" Carlo said as he moved on.

Luke's mind was swimming with confusion, fear, and trepidation. He was grateful for the chance to slow down for a second and collect himself as he ran past the dead soldier and pointed his gun at the wounded one. That man's leg was bleeding profusely from a messy wound in his thigh. He lifted a pistol that was a similar, albeit newer, make and model to the Colt Luke had fixed up back home. Upon seeing the gun being pointed at him, Luke brought up his own weapon and pulled its trigger. His senses were flooded with so many sights, sounds, and smells that they bled together like a sloppy watercolor on a greasy canvas. The shot he'd fired did nothing to slow the soldier down. In fact, the wounded man took an additional second to take aim.

That second was the clearest thing in Luke's world.

It dragged by, ingraining itself upon him, assuring him it would be the last thing he would see on this earth.

A shot was fired.

A bullet hissed through the air, impacting upon flesh with a hard, wet slap.

The wounded man was knocked flat onto his back, his arm flopping to one side as his finger clamped around his trigger to send a shot into the dirt.

Luke blinked several times and shook himself out of the stupor that had befallen him. That's when he realized he hadn't been the one to put that soldier down. That shot had come from the rifle in Red's hand, who walked forward while still sighting along the top of his weapon.

"This is the fight you wanted, ain't it?" Red asked. "Try not to get yourself killed."

Anger flared within Luke's chest, which also ignited a fire that burned away all of the haze that had been settling inside him like a fog. It would be the last time in Luke's life that he would ever be filled with so much doubt again. Now that it had passed, everything was clearer than it had ever been. He and Red charged forward, ready to burn to the end of the trail that had brought them all the way to Wichita from the small town where their childhoods had been laid to rest.

But there was nobody left for him to shoot. Even the gunshots that had cracked through the air in front of him had been silenced somehow, leaving only echoes and a ringing in his ears. The silence that had enveloped the camp was peculiar and out of place. It was soon broken by a sharp command.

"Drop your weapons and raise your hands!"

The camp lay several paces ahead of Luke and Red, just past a thinning row of trees. He could see tents and a few horses tied to a wooden rail. Gritty smoke hung in the air from the last barrage of gunfire. It stung Luke's eyes and made it difficult to discern shapes in the thick of it. One of those shapes stepped forward, dressed in dark blue and covered in polished brass. In one hand, he carried a pistol and in the other was a gleaming saber.

A wind cleared away some more of the smoke, allowing Luke to see Carlo kneeling with his hands pressed against the top of his head in front of two other soldiers who had him at gunpoint. Luke looked around for more soldiers and only found a few scattered here and there. Judging by the looks on their faces, those uniformed men were almost as rattled as Luke had been not too long ago. They were standing their ground now, however, just as Luke was holding his.

Red was beside him as always, breathing hard and itching for a fight. Although Luke could only see his friend from the corner of his eye, he knew he was ready to throw himself through the gates of hell if it came down to that. As Red grew more agitated, Luke felt the calm that had taken hold of him sink its teeth in even deeper.

Chapter 25

Whatever pain Luke had been spared before came rushing back to him along with a wave of cold that grabbed hold of him and yanked him suddenly up from the depths of unconsciousness. Not only did one side of his head feel as if it had been cracked open like an eggshell, but every breath pulled water into his lungs. Luke fell forward and hacked up as much as he could. The heavy slaps against his back helped him spit some water out, but didn't help the sense of dizziness that had filled his head.

"There you go," a man said from behind him. "Cough it up now."

Luke drew another breath, which was free of water. Using his hands to clear his eyes, he quickly realized that he hadn't been drowning. The water had been splashed on him from a bucket in the hands of a soldier standing directly in front of him. Before he could take in any more than that, Luke's hands were pulled behind his back and bound with a length of rope.

The floor beneath him was dirt. The walls surrounding him were canvas. It came back to Luke in a rush. He was still in the camp.

There was light coming through the tent, so it was either just a bit later that same day or a whole new one.

Red was tied to a support post. His head lolled forward and his body was being held up by the ropes.

"You haven't been out for long," the man behind him said as if listening to Luke's racing thoughts. "You would've been out for quite a while if we hadn't given you that bath. Took a few buckets of water to bring you around. That knock to the head must've been a good one." He came around to stand in front of Luke. Although his pistol was holstered, the saber was still in his hand. With a snap of his wrist, he placed the blade to Red's throat. "Thought I'd have a word with you before wasting any more water on him."

The man looked taller than before, but that was only because Luke was forced to look up at him. In truth, the man was average height with a stocky build and a slight paunch. His face was rough from the pockmarks on one side and the coarse stubble on his chin. A thick mustache covered his upper lip and a smaller patch of whiskers was centered on his chin. He wore his hair slightly longer than what someone might expect on an officer and it fell just short of his shoulders in dark, unruly curls. His uniform was well kept and his boots freshly polished. He looked down at Luke with mild curiosity and said, "You're not one of the boys I've seen riding with Mr. Procci before. Must be new."

"He's not one of my men," Carlo said. Luke twisted around to find Carlo tied to another post.

"What about this one?" the man with the saber asked as he nudged Red's chin with the tip of his blade. "You gonna tell me he isn't one of yours either?"

"That's right," Carlo said.

"Then you won't mind if I take care of him right now. I'm sure you know that many officers don't bother sharpening their blades since they're used while on horseback. With that much power behind it, an edge doesn't make much difference. This one's plenty sharp, though. I'm not like most officers, just like the man you take orders from, Procci."

Luke watched until his head was clear enough for him to form words. "You. You're Captain Granger."

The man with the saber looked over at Luke and nodded. "That's right. I suppose Mr. Procci told you all about me."

"He told me some. I heard about you before I ever met him, though."

"Did you, now?"

"From the man you sent to Maconville," Luke said.

Granger squinted and scowled until he finally said, "Maconville! That's right. I have some associates out that way. Last man I sent to Maconville never reported back."

"His name was Scott. I killed him."

Even though Granger still had his saber at Red's throat, he no longer seemed interested in using it. "You expect me to believe you killed Emory Scott? How'd you manage that?"

"I was there when he killed my family."

Granger narrowed his eyes as if to look all the way through Luke's body. "You're Kyle Sobell's boy?"

Anytime up to a few weeks ago, Luke would have made a point to correct that statement by pointing out he was Kyle's stepson. Now he merely nodded and felt a pang in his heart as he thought of all the times he'd refused such a simple concession when Kyle had been alive.

"Well, now," Granger said. "Doesn't that just beat all? Sorry about how things turned out between me and your old man. He didn't exactly leave me much choice."

"What did he do for you?" Luke asked.

"We worked together for a good number of years. He

was one of the best trackers in the business. Could hunt a man through rain or shine, across land and water, night or day. Got his start handling explosives, though. Bet you didn't know that, did you?"

Luke shook his head. All he really knew about Kyle's profession was that it took him out of Maconville for long stretches of time and provided money for the family in drips and drabs. Other than that, he hadn't really cared. Looking back on himself now, Luke felt like a spoiled, ignorant child.

Granger, on the other hand, wore a fondly wistful expression on his face. The tone in his voice made it sound as if he was looking back on sweet, rose-colored memories. "That man could do things with dynamite and black powder . . . even kerosene . . . that were damn close to magic. Had the makings of a real artist. Lost his taste for it when we robbed a train bound for Rock Island, Illinois. We were set to blow a bridge to hell and pick through the wreckage for enough gold to make us all rich men. Kyle decided he didn't want a part of that kind of destruction and it was all I could do to get him to set a smaller charge that derailed the train just across the Iowa state line." Granger shook his head. "I was just starting out in the army in those days. If I'd retired along with the rest of the boys back then, I suppose I wouldn't be the officer I am today. Bet you never knew your pappy was so influential."

"He wasn't a killer," Luke said. "That's why he stopped working with explosives like you wanted him to."

Granger's smile was cold and reptilian. "Kyle was a killer all right. No question about that. He just didn't want to kill so many at one time. Sorry to tarnish his memory, but you asked me what he did for me and I feel obliged to tell you. After helping us derail that train, he met a woman that convinced him to live a quieter life. I'm assuming that was your mama. When we needed someone tracked down or if there was a safe that needed blown or some small bit of demolition to be done, we'd send for Kyle. Toward the end, he wasn't good for much more than being the hen to sit on a nest egg collected by me, him, Emory Scott, and a few others all them years ago. Turned out he couldn't even do that very well."

"He did his job," Luke said. "The money was there and my ma and I never knew about it."

"That's just the thing. The money wasn't supposed to be *there*. It was supposed to be here. He was supposed to send it along and he didn't. Since he'd gone soft on that wife of his, I thought he might have gotten stupid and decided to claim our nest egg for his own. So I sent Emory out there to get it with orders to make things right if there was one dollar missing or if anyone knew it was there." Granger shrugged halfheartedly. "I'm certain Kyle was spending that money for years to pay for whatever dusty piece of land he and that wife of his settled on."

Luke hated to hear Granger spit his words out as if the subject of his mother and stepfather were profane in and of themselves. It angered him even more to see the uniformed man start to laugh as he looked directly into his eyes.

"The funny thing is how you ended up," Granger said. "Kyle retired because the woman who'd put him on such a short leash didn't like him associating with such disreputable company. And here you are, riding with someone that makes me look like a saint by comparison!"

Granger was looking at Carlo now, stalking toward him and bringing his saber around to point it at the middle of Carlo's chest. Carlo's mouth was tightly shut and an intense fire burned in his eyes. He glared up at Granger as if nothing else on the face of the earth mattered to him anymore.

"Carlo may be an outlaw," Luke said, "but at least he's no traitor to his country. You're a disgrace, Granger! You wear that uniform and you take part in robbing trains and killing innocent folks just to get your hands on a bag of money. You want your money so bad? It's with my horse. Take what's left of it and choke on it!"

"You've been waiting awhile to say those words to me, haven't you, boy?" Granger snarled.

Luke nodded once. "Yes, sir, I have."

"It's been eating away at you, that's plain to see. I already got my money . . . or what's left of it. Smart move bringing it back to me. That's why you woke up to a splash of water instead of a bullet through the eye." Granger stepped away from Carlo so he could pick up a glass that had been sitting on a folding table. Rather than sheathe the saber, he laid it on the table and eased himself down onto a small round stool. "You ever hear of something called firing with your blinders on?"

"No."

"It's something I've heard sharpshooters say that means getting your sights set on one target and keeping them locked there no matter what." Granger held out a hand, keeping it turned sideways and flat so he could look along the edge of his index finger as if he were sighting down the barrel of a rifle. His fingers were pointed directly at Luke when he said, "Usually it happens when a target is being particularly tricky. Moving around, ducking in and out of cover, that kind of thing. What happens is that the man behind the rifle gets so wrapped up in that one target that he misses everything else going on around him. Other targets pop up, more dangerous ones, even easier ones, and the man with the rifle doesn't even know they're there because his eyes are so set on that first man."

As he was speaking, Granger moved his flattened

hand around as if he were tracking a hopping jackrabbit. When he allowed his hand to come to a stop again, it was pointed directly at Carlo. "You truly think this man here is just an outlaw?" Granger asked.

"I don't care what he is," Luke replied. "He's proven himself a couple of times. He proved himself by getting me this far. He also proved himself when he helped take care of them riders you sent to ambush us outside town."

"Those riders I sent. Yes. And because you're young and full of yourself, you assume that those riders were sent after you. I did send them, but you've seen what I've got to work with here. Even if you just saw whatever you could take in when you approached this camp today, you must see I have a limited supply of men. Why would I send one or two of them to deal with the likes of you? It is the arrogance of youth to believe I would send *four*!"

"So you sent them after Carlo," Luke said.

"In a matter of speaking." Clearly relishing the moment, Granger let it drag for another couple of seconds before he turned to Carlo and asked, "Do you want to tell him or shall I?"

Carlo's head hung low and his eyes were partially shut. In some ways, he now seemed even less invested in the conversation than Red, who was still unconscious and slumped against his post.

"It's no surprise that Procci doesn't want to speak on the matter," Granger said. "It's in his best interest to keep his identity as well as that of his friends a closely guarded secret. After what he and the rest of those bloodthirsty animals did in Lawrence and Centralia, I'm surprised they've got the fortitude to remain in this state at all."

"Lawrence and Centralia?" Luke asked.

"You know what happened in those places, don't you?

They were pillaged, the good people who lived there slaughtered like sheep by Quantrill and his murderous raiders. I may not be a prime example of a Union soldier, but at least I have a soul. Quantrill and his men are devils of the worst sort."

Anyone who lived in Kansas and didn't have their heads buried in an anthill knew about Quantrill. The Confederate raiders had burned a trail through that state in a way that brought the war sharply to the front porches of regular folks who were too far away to hear the cannon fire from battlefields where entire armies shed their blood. Like monsters who came in the night, Quantrill's men were rarely spoken of as if mentioning their names would make the killers appear.

"I wager he didn't mention any of this to you," Granger said mockingly. "If you doubt me, why don't you ask him now for yourself?" He then stepped aside to make sure Luke had a clear line of sight to the other prisoner.

Carlo sat with his hands bound behind him and his head hanging forward, which was how he'd been when Luke had first regained consciousness. There had always been suspicions about who Carlo was, which was no secret among the three men as they'd ridden the trail into Wichita. In many ways, what Granger said made perfect sense. As silence filled the tent, Luke decided against breaking it. A confrontation with Carlo was exactly what the smug army captain was hoping to witness. And so, Luke allowed his own head to droop quietly forward. In times when he'd been plagued by the trivial burdens of a child, Luke's mother had advised him to either find a way to cut through his troubles or simply keep a level head and allow things to run their course. He felt a warmth spread through his heart when he was rewarded in a matter of seconds for his patience.

A horse galloped toward the tent, its hooves beating a thunderous rhythm against the dirt that could be felt as a tremor rippling beneath the ground. The animal's pace was such that even Granger tensed in case he would need to jump aside before being trampled. The horse's rider dismounted amid the rustle of leather and the jangle of spurs before a smaller set of steps hurried closer.

The man who burst into the tent wore Federal blues that were even more rumpled than those of the men who stood guard at the camp. His face was flushed and his eyes were so panicked that they barely seemed to notice anyone inside the tent other than Granger himself.

"They hit the billiard parlor!" the rider said amid a series of panting breaths.

Granger's hand was still resting on his holstered Colt. "The Red Bison? *My* Red Bison?"

"Yes, sir!"

"Who hit it?"

"It was a contingent of Quantrill's men. Maybe half a dozen of them or more."

"You're certain they're Quantrill's?" Granger asked.

The rider nodded. "Henderschott recognized one of them from the Centralia massacre. Busted in with guns blazing and shot three of our troops before anyone had a chance to bat an eye. They started shooting and never let up, not even when one of them put a torch to the place. You can see the smoke from here!"

Granger cursed loudly while storming past the soldier and out of the tent. He cursed again, even louder this time, when he was able to verify the rider's story with his own eyes. When he came back inside, the captain threw open the tent's flap with enough force to shake the entire canvas structure. "Assemble all of the men and ride out to meet those murderous savages!" he roared. "I want to send half of them around the eastern perimeter of town and the other half around the west. We'll flank them on either side and cut them off from making an escape. You said there were only six of them?"

"Yes, sir, but there could have been more," the rider admitted. "I had to get out of there awfully quick."

"Who else is with you? Maybe he has more actionable intelligence."

"There isn't anyone with me, sir. I was the only one that made it out of there."

That stopped Granger in his tracks. "What was that, soldier?"

The rider shook his head solemnly. "None of our men in that billiard hall made it out with me. I stayed as long as I could, but the place was burning down. Those Quantrill men . . . they filled that whole building full of holes. Anyone inside was cut down where they stood. Our men . . . even a few locals who were in there just to have a game—"

"Get a hold of yourself," Granger snarled. Looking over to one of the uniformed men who'd captured Luke and Red, he said, "My orders still stand. Muster every man here and get them on a damn horse!"

"All due respect, Captain, but we don't have enough men to flank anyone," that soldier replied.

"Don't question my strategy!"

The soldier looked confused and even glanced over to Luke as if waiting for him to say something to back him up. Finally the soldier said, "These three killed four men before we could get to them. That only leaves—"

"I can count!" Granger roared. "I know how many that leaves! You men," he said while pointing to all but one of the soldiers within the tent, "come with me and I'll show you how to deal with a bunch of murderous Rebs." Looking to the one soldier that remained, he added, "You stay with these three. If even one of them makes a move you don't like, shoot them all." With that, Granger took the men he'd selected outside where they gathered up their horses.

Carlo lifted his head to watch them go . . . and smiled.

Chapter 26

Luke listened to the sounds of orders being shouted and horses racing through camp. Strangely enough, his blood had been pumping faster through his veins when things had been much quieter and the only sound that presided over all the others was that of Granger's gravelly voice. Red was still slumped in the same position as he'd been when Luke had first opened his eyes. Since his friend wasn't the sort to play possum, that meant Red was still out cold.

"Hey, you yellow-bellied dog."

Both Luke and the guard turned toward the source of that insult.

Carlo stared up at the remaining soldier with tired eyes set within a face stained with blood that had been spilled when he was cracked in the head. "You heard me. I bet you're mighty glad to be in here and out of sight while all your friends ride off to their death."

"Shut your mouth, you Reb bastard."

The single laugh Carlo spat back at him seemed to sap most of his strength. "Yeah, you're scared all right. That's plain enough for everyone to see."

"I told you to shut your mouth."

Carlo barely had the strength to turn his head so he could look over at Luke. "You can see it too, right, kid?

I know I just took a knock to the head, but I'd swear he's shaking in his boots. Not just how folks say that, but I believe he is truly shaking."

The soldier took a step toward Carlo and glared down at him while staring down the sights of his rifle. "I told you to keep quiet."

Without seeming to mind that he was at gunpoint, Carlo kept his weary eyes fixed on Luke. "Am I seeing things? Isn't he trembling like a frightened woman?"

Outside, the horses were galloping away and Granger was still barking orders at his men. Those sounds didn't concern Luke as much as what was happening right in front of him. "Maybe you should ease up on him, Carlo," he said cautiously.

Carlo's head drooped once more and he expelled a breath that left him shrunken and deflated. "You hear that, Union man? The kid wants me to take it easy on you. He doesn't want me to get too rough with my harsh words. You know," he added as he strained to lift his head. "Kind of how someone might look out for a sweet little girl."

At first, the soldier had been angry. Then he was taken aback by what was being said to him. Now he grinned and stalked closer to Carlo like a hungry dog that had finally been let off its chain. "I know you heard what the captain said about me being able to kill you. So all I can think of is that you're needling me just to get it over with before the captain figures out a torturous way for you to die. Either that," he said as he reached for the bayonet hanging from his belt in a leather sheath, "or you're just delirious and—"

Carlo snapped awake as if someone had flipped a switch. The guard was so intent on glaring down into his eyes that he didn't see Carlo's leg moving until it was too late to do anything about it. His foot came around like the end of a whip to knock the guard's legs out from under him in one powerful sweep. As soon as the guard's back hit the ground, Carlo brought that same foot up and slammed it down again into the middle of the guard's chest. That stunned the uniformed man just long enough for Carlo to drop his boot again. This time, his heel pounded into the guard's neck with a muffled crunch.

"Can you get loose?" Carlo asked.

Luke was almost as stunned as the guard had been with the sudden turn of events. "Get loose? How?"

"Never mind." With one powerful effort, Carlo pulled the wooden pole out from the ground so he could slip the ropes between his wrists underneath it. Next, he lay on the ground and slid his arms down past his boots and around so they were in front of him. Although the dislodged pole allowed a portion of the tent's roof to sag, the structure remained more or less intact.

"How did you do that?" Luke asked.

"This ain't my first time being captured," Carlo replied as he took the fallen guard's bayonet from its scabbard. "Been working on loosening that post since I woke up. What about him?" he asked while nodding toward Red. "He going to wake up anytime soon?"

"Probably not on his own. I could splash some water on his face. That worked well enough on me."

Carlo held the bayonet between his feet to keep it still as he hunkered down and scraped the ropes back and forth against the blade. After only a few desperate passes, he'd cut through enough of the rope for him to snap them apart using pure muscle and will. "Don't bother," he said. "This is all gonna be over before he'd have a chance to get his wits about him. All we need to do is try to survive long enough to reap the rewards."

"Rewards?" Luke asked as Carlo approached him

and went around to cut his ropes with the bayonet. "What rewards?"

"The reasons we all came to Wichita in the first place. Just stick close to me and don't lose your head."

Until now, most of the sounds outside had come from Granger issuing orders while he and his men rode through camp. By the time both Luke and Carlo were free, the first shots within the camp were fired.

"What was that?" Luke asked.

"If you don't recognize the sound of gunfire by now," Carlo replied with half a grin, "then you haven't been paying attention."

"What's going on out there? Who are they shooting at?"

"Remember what Granger was talking about in regards to me riding with a contingent of Quantrill's men?" Carlo asked.

"Yeah."

"Well, he wasn't lying. Granger moves his base of operations around quite a bit, and those men storming this camp right now have been trying to nail down exactly where he was for some time. They hit that billiard hall and now they aim to clean out this here camp."

More gunshots cracked through the air as Union soldiers returned fire. It wasn't long before a stray bullet or two punched holes through one side of the tent all the way through to the other. "We can't stay in here," Carlo said. "Things are bound to get worse before they get better. Shots will go wild. There may even be a horse trampling through here. We need to be out where we can see what's going on."

"But that means we'll be out where the shots are being fired!" Luke protested.

"Take my word on this, kid. I've been on enough raids to know. This ain't a proper battle where ranks are formed and orders are given. This is directed chaos and if you can't see which way the tide is flowing, it'll sweep right over you. Now pick your friend up," Carlo said as he sliced through the rope binding Red's wrists in one chop, "and follow me."

Of the two friends, Red had always been the stronger one. He just came from heartier stock and never missed an opportunity to remind Luke which of them could beat the other when it came to fisticuffs. But this was no test of strength or bare-knuckle brawl. When Luke reached down to take hold of Red beneath the arms, he didn't consider what might happen if he couldn't lift him. He simply did what needed to be done and didn't question where he found the strength to carry Red away from that tent. He moved quickly because Carlo had already charged outside. And he moved even quicker when he got a look at the hell that had been unleashed upon Granger's base of operations.

Most of the horses he could see belonged to Granger and the Union soldiers. They were concentrated at the opposite end of camp, firing toward the outer perimeters as bullets whipped through the air from the trees. From those trees, like the very sound of the chaos Carlo had mentioned, came the cries of several unseen men. Some of them hollered as if it were the Fourth of July while others simply emptied their lungs in a rending battle cry. As Luke watched one soldier wave frantically toward a spot where the trees thinned out, no fewer than three bullets ripped through the uniformed man to send him flying from his horse.

Granger was nearby and he pointed to that same spot while shouting, "Here they come!"

Sure enough, four horses exploded from the tree line. Two riders fired pistols while the other two carried torches, which were thrown at the nearest tents. Those canvas tarps caught fire and smoke started to fill the air.

"Here!" another soldier cried before he was cut down by a volley of gunfire. Three men charged past him, two of whom carried torches. Instead of tossing their fiery cargo, they wove between the tents and touched the lit end of their torches to each in turn to set them alight one by one. Although only one of those riders was shooting back at the remaining Union soldiers, he was doing the work of at least two men.

That rider caught Luke's eye because, if he was older than him, it was only by a year or maybe two. He had a slender build and smooth features, but his eyes were intense and filled with cruel purpose. He sat in his saddle as if he was the master of everything around him, reins clamped in his teeth and a pistol in each fist. Even with the leather straps gripped in that manner, he still managed to let out a battle cry that sounded just as loud as the rest.

There were only a few soldiers remaining with Granger doing his best to lead them. The captain bared his teeth and fired a shot that dropped one of the marauders before he holstered his pistol and drew his saber. "None of these men leaves this ground!" he shouted. "We end Quantrill's rampage here and now!"

Even though they were outnumbered by rampaging attackers and their camp was in blazes around them, the Union men took strength from Granger's words and rallied to fight back against the other men. One soldier's horse took a bullet in the flank that caused it to rear up and turn away from the fight. Its rider allowed the animal to carry him through the middle of camp, which also pointed him directly at Luke and Red.

Although Luke was able to carry his friend some distance, he knew he wouldn't be able to get Red to safety before the rider got to them. Dropping him would only expose Red to the possibility of being trampled, and in the short amount of time left to him, Luke couldn't come up with any other choices. Before he was forced to pick from his unsavory options, Luke heard another shot fired from behind him.

Carlo had gotten his hands on a long rifle carried by Union infantry. His bullet caused the oncoming rider to drop down low over his horse's neck, but it did not convince him to steer away from his targets. Without missing a beat, Carlo gripped the rifle in both hands and charged. The bayonet he'd taken from the soldier in the tent might or might not have been the same one fixed to the end of that rifle. All that mattered was that the blade was sharp enough to drive deep into the mounted soldier's torso. Straining with both arms, Carlo pulled the rider from his saddle and drove the bayonet into him once more after he hit the ground.

Luke's only thought after that was to take his friend as far from danger as possible. Since Carlo was holding his own well enough, he found the clearest path between the burning tents and dragged Red along with him toward the trees.

"You!"

Turning toward that savage voice, Luke found Granger riding toward him with his saber held high.

"You brought this upon us!" the captain shouted. "You'll die right along with these good men!"

Luke saw the saber coming at him as if the entire world had started turning slower. Since jumping in any direction would require more strength to lift Red with him, he allowed his legs to go limp so both he and his unconscious friend could drop straight to the ground. Granger's blade sliced through the air directly over Luke's head as horse's hooves pounded against the dirt inches away from where he and Red landed.

Almost immediately, Granger pulled his reins to bring

his horse around for another pass. There was blood on his coat from wounds that were his own as well as from a few that weren't. His eyes were wide and his nostrils flared while drawing in a breath tainted by smoke from the burning tents and the barrels of roaring guns. As several of the invading riders fired at him, Granger ducked low, leaned from side to side, and steered his horse in a pattern so erratic that none of the gunmen could draw a bead on him.

The saber in Granger's hand rose high above his head and Luke knew he would taste that blade when it came down again. Only now did he remember Carlo tossing a pistol over to him, but it was too late to put it to use. His hands were busy carrying Red, which meant there was nothing left to do besides pray for Granger to miss.

Riding forward with his eyes locked on Luke, Granger brought his saber down in a smooth motion that hadn't missed a target in several years. Even when a shot cracked through the air to catch him through the upper region of his chest, Granger looked as if he fully expected to spill Luke's blood. The bullet had caught him squarely, however, and the impact of its passing kicked like a mule to send him toppling from his saddle.

Now that Granger had fallen, the battle raging through the entire camp died down. Flames roared and swelled to consume whatever they could as the remaining soldiers were chased into the woods by screaming young men on horseback. Luke still couldn't believe that someone had managed to hit Granger so precisely while he was not only riding a horse at full gallop, but ducking and weaving to make himself the most inconvenient target possible.

The Union captain scraped his boots against the ground while turning to look up at Luke. "Kyle," he said in a croaking voice. "He . . . owes me . . . owes me that money. It's . . . mine."

Chapter 27

Plumes of smoke drifted up from two separate spots on the horizon as a third fire crackled behind Luke's back. The sky was dark, but clear enough for him to see the vague, misty remnants of the fires that had consumed Granger's camp as well as the Red Bison. Along with the crackling of the nearby campfire, several young men's voices could be heard as they excitedly swapped stories regarding the day's events. Luke had been told about the raid on the Red Bison before he'd wandered off to be on his own. All that mattered to him now was that Granger and his men were truly gone. All of them.

Before long, Red was escorted by Carlo and another man to the spot where Luke sat. "They're tellin' me I missed everything," Red said while rubbing the spot where he'd been knocked. "That really true?"

"I wish it weren't," Luke replied. "Because that way I wouldn't have had to drag your sorry carcass through all those fires."

"I recall running," Red said. "Was that just a dream?"

"No, I suppose not. You were shuffling your feet for a while, but it wasn't anything close to running."

"Yeah, well, I suppose I should thank you." Rather than make it official, Red nudged his friend and called it a day. Both knew they owed each other so much. Saying it out loud was just beating a dead horse.

"Here," Carlo said as he handed over the Colt. "You never took this back."

"Keep it," Luke said.

"You're through with guns?"

"I didn't say that. I just want you to have that one. It should serve you pretty well."

"Thanks," Carlo said as he holstered the Colt at his side. "It already has. Tomorrow most of us are heading west through the state. New orders. Frank here will see that you get home safely."

"We know the way back to Maconville on our own," Luke told him.

Frank shook his head. "You'll need someone to watch out for Union troops or lawmen. After you've been seen in our company, folks will be out to hang you. Besides, we've got some personal matters to attend in Missouri, so we'll be riding within a stone's throw of Maconville."

Looking over to Red, Luke asked, "How many will be riding with us?"

"Just me and my brother." Turning toward the fire, Frank motioned to one of the other raiders. The young man who joined them was the one with the clean-shaven face and piercing gaze who'd charged through the camp firing two guns with his horse's reins gripped in his teeth. When Frank draped an arm over his shoulder, the young man lost some of the intensity that had been burning within him. Handling the raider in the roughshod manner of one brother to another, Frank shoved him around as if the other man were nothing but a rambunctious kid.

"This here is Frank and Jesse James," Carlo said. "Frank, Jesse, this is Luke Croft and Red Connover."

"Hell of a ride you made through that camp," Luke said.

Jesse nodded once. "We been trying to hunt down Captain Granger for months. Thanks to you, we could finally put him six feet under where he belongs. You handled yourself pretty well. Maybe you should forget about Maconville and ride with us."

"I don't know about that," Luke replied.

"Well, any friend of Carlo's is a friend of ours," Frank said. "My stomach feels like it's got a hole in the bottom of it, so I'm going to get some more of that venison before it gets eaten up."

Frank and Jesse both made their way back to the fire.

"Think I'll join 'em," Red said. "I'm famished."

"Yeah," Luke said. "Sleeping all day while the world burns down around you will do that."

Red deflected that barbed comment with a grunting wave and hurried off to claim his share of venison.

After a few seconds without hearing any more steps, Luke asked, "You were telling the truth before about wanting to get out of the country, weren't you?"

"You think too much. That keeps getting you into trouble."

Shaking his head, Luke said, "No. I'm right. You wanted out, and Granger was the one who was going to get you away from here."

"That's just what I told you so you would help me find Granger," Carlo said. "Sorry about the lie, but it was necessary."

"I think that was the truth and you had to change plans once the rest of those Quantrill men caught up to you."

"What makes you think I was trying to get away from them?"

"Because you were hiding when I found you."

"That's just a system me and Frank use," Carlo explained. "We're on the run from law and soldiers alike, so if we're in a new town we hole up in the dirtiest stable we can find like a vagrant and wait for the other to come along."

"That may be, but if you were waiting for someone, you wouldn't have left with me and Red to go to Wichita."

"I was hunting Granger. You want proof? Just look back to what's left of that camp."

"You were more concerned about paying him for your ticket onto that boat," Luke said with absolute certainty. "Once I told you I knew where Granger was, you could have just ridden off, met up with your friends, and gone to see him yourself. You didn't need me unless you truly were on your own. And before you try to say you just needed my money, I'm sure these men have plenty of it to spare after all the looting they've done."

"You're not going to let this drop, are you?"

"Nope." Looking over to Carlo, Luke added, "Not until you admit that I'm right."

Carlo looked straight back at him. "You're not right . . . about everything. But as far as me wanting out of this contingent goes, yeah. I suppose you are."

"Can't you just ride away?" Luke asked in a whisper. "Does Quantrill keep you men prisoner?"

"No. We're not prisoners. We are wanted, though. And these men aren't the kind who take it lightly when someone cuts and runs. I had a chance to split off on my own and I did my best to make certain I wasn't being followed. That's why I was staying in those stables. If Frank or any of these others were on my tail, they'd find me and I'd know I couldn't just do what I pleased."

"Best to look like you're going along with them right until you can split off for good," Luke said. "Makes sense."

"You're not the only one who thinks things through, kid," Carlo said while nudging him with his elbow.

"You could still get away from all of this. You're smart enough to figure something out."

"I wanted to say the same to you. Only I was hoping you were smart enough to recognize when you had a perfect opportunity to leave and when it was too late to do so."

Luke gazed up at the stars. "There isn't much of anything for me to go back to in Maconville. Red wanted to enlist with the Union army, but after what we've seen here I'd say we've both got a bad taste in our mouths from them blue uniforms."

"This is war, kid. There's plenty of ugliness on both sides of the fence. Believe me," Carlo said while glancing quickly toward the fire to make sure they were still alone. "I've seen more ugliness than I can stomach."

"I say take your chances in getting out."

"I will, but I need to wait for another opportunity. Any of us who rode under Quantrill's flag will be hunted long after this war is over, I reckon. You also got a choice to make."

"I think, with a bit more experience under my belt, I could make a good gunman. I was rattled now and again, but that's only because it was all so strange. That'll pass in time."

"Why would you want it to pass?" Carlo asked. "You've been through a tough stretch and you saw justice done to the men who hurt your family. This is over. You can go back to a quiet life. Some of us fight awfully hard for that same chance."

"I've been safe my whole life. Well," Luke added with a laugh, "until lately. I don't want to go back to a life in a quiet town with nothing happening. I like the notion of riding out, taking what I want, and fighting for what I need. I know I can survive out there, and I think Red is thinking along the same lines."

"I know all that too. That's what scares me." Drawing a deep breath, Carlo let it out amid wisps of steam from the chilly night air. "I can't sway you right now. The blood's still racing after all that shooting and things are still twisted around from what happened. Maybe you need to wander around and fend for yourself for a bit, but do me a favor and think twice before you decide to live your life by the gun. While you're at it, think three times." Carlo stuck out his hand and asked, "We got a deal?"

Luke reached for the hand being offered, but he didn't shake it just yet. "I'll think things over, but I'm not going back to Maconville for a while."

Carlo started to say something else but stopped short when he heard footsteps approaching. Jesse walked over to them carrying a tin plate of food in one hand and a fork in the other. "Did I hear something about you not going to Maconville?" he asked.

"Yeah," Luke replied. "But I'd still like to ride with you men for a while."

"Red was saying the same thing," Jesse replied in between scooping food from his plate into his mouth.

Carlo stuck his hand out a bit farther. "Just promise me you'll think things over like I asked."

Luke shook his hand. "I promise."

"Don't worry none," Jesse said through a gravy-stained smirk. "Me and Frank will keep an eye on him. Take both of 'em under our wings nice and proper just like Bill Anderson did to me when I first signed up with this contingent."

Carlo put on a tired smile and let go of Luke's hand. He'd done all he could for now and things had turned out better than they could have. Still, he had an uneasy feeling when he thought about where Luke's and Red's trails might lead. Then again, he'd also seen the two young men push through a whole lot of strife and come out the other side better for the journey. In the end, every man, young or old, rode his own trail. However hard that trail became depended on circumstance as well as that man's character. Carlo could only wish Luke and Red luck with their circumstances and have faith in their character.

Read on for an excerpt
from the Spur Award–winning

Tucker's Reckoning

A Ralph Compton Novel
by Matthew P. Mayo

Available now in paperback and e-book.

Despite the creeping cold of the autumn afternoon in high country, and the feeling in his gut as if an irate lion cub were trying to claw its way out, Samuel Tucker reckoned that starving to death might not be an altogether unpleasant sensation. Of course, the warm light-headedness he was feeling might also have something to do with the last of the rotgut gargle he'd been nursing since he woke up.

He regarded the nearly empty bottle in his hand and shrugged. "No matter. Finally get to see you again, Rita, and little Sammy. My sweet girls . . ."

Even the horse on which he rode, Gracie, no longer perked her ears when he spoke. At one time a fine mount, she was now more bone than horse. The sorrel mare plodded along the lush valley floor, headed northward along the east bank of a river that, if Tucker had cared any longer about such things, he would know as Oregon's Rogue River. All he knew was that he'd wandered far north. And he didn't care.

His clothes had all but fallen off him; his fawn-colored, tall-crowned hat, a fine gift from Rita, had disappeared one night in an alley beside a gambling parlor in New Mexico. The top half of his once-red long-handles, now pinked with age and begrimed with Lord knows what, and more hole than cloth, served as a shirt of sorts. Ragged rough-weave trousers bearing rents that far south had invited welcoming breezes now ushered in the frigid chill of a coming winter in high country. And on his feet, the split, puckered remnants of boots. These were the clothes Tucker had been wearing the day his Rita and little Samantha had . . .

At one time, though, Samuel Tucker had cut a fine figure around Tascosa, Texas. With his small but solid ranch, and with a wife and baby daughter, he'd been the envy of many. But that was in the past, before the sickness. . . . *Mercy,* thought Tucker, *two years and I can't think of it without my throat tightening.*

"At least I don't have to worry about being robbed," he said aloud. His laugh came out as a forced, thin sound that shamed him for a flicker of a moment. Then once again he no longer cared.

The land arched up before him in a gentle rise away from the river. Here and there, trees close by the river for the past half mile had been logged off some years before, leaving a stump field along the banks. Ragged branches long since cleaved from the vanished timber bristled upward among still-green undergrowth seeming to creep toward him. He traveled along the river, and the gradually thickening forest soon gave way to an upsloping greensward just beginning to tinge brown at the tip.

He was about to pitch the now-empty bottle in the rushing brown flowage off to his left when the crack of a gunshot halted him. It came from somewhere ahead. Even Gracie looked up. Two more shots followed.

Curiosity overrode his drunken lethargy and the pair, man and horse, roused themselves out of their stupor and loped up the last of the rise. They found themselves fifty yards from an unexpected sight: two men circling one. The man in the center, a wide-shouldered brute wearing a sheepskin coat, sat tall astride a big buckskin. He held in one hand what looked to be a substantial gun, maybe a Colt Navy, but appeared to have trouble bringing it to bear on the two men, who took care to keep their own horses dancing in a circle around the big man. He tried to do the same, tugging feebly at his reins.

What was wrong with the man? Tucker wondered. Was he drunk? He acted as much. And then Tucker got his answer. The man jigged his horse again, and the big horse tossed its head and stepped hard. Then Tucker saw the red pucker, blackened at the edges. The man had been shot in the back.

One of the other men shouted, then shot the big man's hand. It convulsed and the pistol dropped. The shooter's companion, thin and sporting a dragoon mustache and a flat-crowned black hat with what looked like silver conchos ringing the band, laughed, looking skyward. As he brought his head back down, his laughter clipped short. He leveled his pistol on the big man in the sheepskin coat.

One shot to the gut and the victim hunched as if he were upheaving the last of a long night's binge. He wavered in the saddle. The man looked so fragile to Tucker. It did not seem possible that this was happening right there before him.

The first shooter howled this time. Then he rode up close, reached out with his pistol barrel like a poking finger, and pushed the man's shoulder. That was all it took. The big man dropped like a sack of stones to the grass. The buckskin bolted and the black-hatted man leveled his pistol at it, but the other shouted something, wagged his pistol in a calming motion, and they let the beast run. It thundered off, tail raised and galloping, toward where Tucker had intended to ride. How far was the man's home place? Was he even from around here?

With a bloodied hand planted in the grass, the big man

forced himself up on one knee. He gripped his gut, his sheepskin coat open, puckered about his gripping hand. From beneath the clawed fingers oozed thick blood that drizzled to the grass. Where did the man get his strength? Didn't he know that he was as good as dead, but just didn't yet realize it?

The man had lost his hat in his fall, and a breeze from the north tumbled it a few strides away. His head was topped with a thick thatch of white hair trimmed close on the sides, but the face beneath was a weathered mask, harder than leather, as if carved from wood. And it was the big man's face that froze Tucker. The man had been back-shot, gut-shot, and more, but his expression bore unvarnished rage. Bloody spittle stringed from his bottom lip, his eyes squinted up at his attackers, both a-horseback a few feet away, staring down at him.

Tucker was too far to hear their words, but he heard the jabs and harsh cut of their voices. These were angry men, all three. But a gut feeling told Tucker that the man on the ground had been wronged somehow.

Surely I should do something, say something, thought Tucker. Then he realized that if he did, he too would die. Gracie was a feeble rack of skin and bone, as was he. His only possession, clutched in his hand, was a green glass whiskey bottle. Empty. He didn't dare move. Felt sure that if they saw him, he'd be a dead man in short order.

Isn't that what you want? he asked himself. *Isn't that what you've been doing for more than two years now? Tapering off your days until there is so little left of you that you'll eventually dry up, become a husk rattling in a winter breeze.*

And yet, as he watched this big man struggle to live, to fight these attackers, darting in and yipping at him, like wild dogs prodding a downed deer, Tucker knew he had to help this man. But how?

His decision was made for him when the thicker, shorter of the two men leveled his pistol across his other forearm at the big man swaying on his knees. He squinted down the barrel, and touched the trigger. The pistol bucked and the big man jounced again, flopped partly onto his left side, and lay in the grass, hands clutched tight beneath him.

The Last Outlaws

The Lives and Legends of Butch Cassidy and the Sundance Kid

by Thom Hatch

Butch Cassidy and the Sundance Kid are two of the most celebrated figures of American lore. As leaders of the Wild Bunch, also known as the Hole-in-the-Wall Gang, they planned and executed the most daring bank and train robberies of the day, with an uprecedented professionalism.

The Last Outlaws brilliantly brings to life these thrilling, larger-than-life personalities like never before, placing the legend of Butch and Sundance in the context of a changing—and shrinking—American West, as the rise of 20th century technology brought an end to a remarkable era. Drawing on a wealth of fresh research, Thom Hatch pushes aside the myth and offers up a compelling, fresh look at these icons of the Wild West.

Available wherever books are sold or at penguin.com